Still

Still

Dr. L. Jan Eira

Copyright © 2012 by Dr. L. Jan Eira.

Library of Congress Control Number:		2012921389
ISBN:	Hardcover	978-1-4797-4937-9
	Softcover	978-1-4797-4936-2
	Ebook	978-1-4797-4938-6

This book was printed in the United States of America.

To order additional copies of this book, contact:
Xlibris Corporation
1-888-795-4274
www.Xlibris.com
Orders@Xlibris.com
122012

Dedication

To Jane - thank you for your never-ending love and support.

To Ellie - thank you for being the awesome daughter you are.

To Adam - thank you for your strength.

Prologue

"Low to the ground in the southern Brazilian savanna, the striped cobra beholds her prey," said the lecturer. The medical students and interns sat on the edge of their seats, mesmerized, their eyes glued to the screen. The large room was dark, its only illumination pouring out of the projector.

"The *Bothrops jararaca* finds a small pond to cool off and soothe her dryness." Another slide, this time showing a close-up of the enormous snake, a small body of water surrounded by tall wildflowers and weeds seen in the background, slightly out of focus. She was pale tan with brown stripes and bits of light green here and there. With the touch of a button, the still picture came alive.

"She slithers slowly, with her head a few inches off the ground, hiding among the blades of grass. Her gaze is on the rodent." Nearby, a small rat scurried about. Clueless.

"She is capable of a superfast assault, but if she fails, she knows only too well that her quarry's speed far exceeds her own. The first strike has to count. There are no second chances. A few more slithers and the reptile will be within striking distance," whispered the teacher. The room became enshrouded in silence. Suddenly, the students jumped, straightening up in their chairs, their breaths on hold as the viper's head lunged forward, its fangs fully deployed. Realizing it was about to be assaulted from behind, the rodent tried to move out of the way of its assailant at the same instant enormous teeth prepared to pierce its little body.

"The rat is fast and is able to escape with minimal scrapes." The audience gasped again. Some turned their heads and closed their eyes.

"The victim is able to distance himself from the *Bothrops jararaca*." The professor looked around the room. "But is he home free?"

The answer became obvious as the next few moments of film unfolded. The rat suddenly slowed down, staggered for a few more feet, and slumped over. "How does she do it? What powers does she possess?" The lecturer sauntered in the front of the large hall, his figure encompassed by the still head of the larger-than-life snake, now prominently displayed by the projector. The lights slowly ramped up, dumping brighter and brighter illumination into the room.

"The strike produced two small puncture wounds but not enough to lethally injure the animal. Yet the rat tumbled over, incapacitated, a few feet from the *Bothrops jararaca*. Why?" The instructor looked around the audience.

"She injected venom?" said a woman from the front row.

"Precisely!" said the teacher. He intertwined the fingers of his hands, both indexes in front of his lips. "How many of you here are wondering why I showed a presentation on snakes when I'm supposed to be talking to you about cardiac pharmacology and research?" He looked around the hall, all eyes fixated on his. He walked about in the front of the classroom. "The venom injected into the rodent by the *Bothrops jararaca* is a crude form of an angiotensin-converting enzyme inhibitor or ACE inhibitor," he said. "The prey sheds some blood from the puncture wounds, but its internal organism releases potent chemicals that stop the bleeding and maintain blood pressure until the injuries heal. These inherent chemicals are lifesaving, but the snake's venom blocks their effects. The end result is that even a relatively small injury will cause the rat's blood pressure to plummet and incapacitate the animal. And this is why today the *Bothrops* lives, whereas the rat . . ."

A young doctor in green scrubs sitting in the back row looked up at the ceiling, then around the room. A wave of nausea began to invade his body. He brought his right hand to his nose and covertly took a slight whiff; then again, as stealthily as he could, he smelled his white lab coat. Daniel, the only other person sitting in the same row, three seats away, looked at him briefly, then back to the front of the lecture hall.

"But, Dr. Gavin, this *venom* is prescribed every day for patients with heart disease and high blood pressure. ACE inhibitors are a good thing, aren't they?" said a young woman in the front row.

"That's right. We have learned that some patients develop an inappropriate and harmful revving up of these chemicals. Using ACE inhibitors in their management is beneficial and even life-prolonging. We have taken a deadly poison and transformed it into a healing therapy, with excellent clinical results," said the professor.

"Hey, Will," whispered Daniel, "are you okay, man?"

"Yeah," he whispered back, drying his sweaty palms on his scrub pants.

"Do you smell something?" asked Daniel. "You keep smelling your clothes."

"I thought I did," he whispered. "But it's all in my mind. I'm okay now."

"There have to be many other examples of so-called poisons or venoms that can be transformed into miracle cures, aren't there?" said a young man from the middle of the large classroom, his right hand still in the air.

"That's exactly right," said Dr. Gavin. "There is a lot of ongoing research in this area, and much more is needed."

Will stirred nervously again in his seat and looked at Daniel. "I'm fine. Quit staring at me. Pay attention to the lecture."

"You don't look fine, man," whispered Daniel. "You broke out in a sweat, and you're as pale as a ghost."

"I'm okay," he said. "Pay attention. Don't worry about me."

Three rows up from them, a young woman with blonde hair in a ponytail bit her lower lip and squinted her eyes as she furtively glanced at Will.

"By the way," said Dr. Gavin, "see me if you are interested in doing a rotation here with us, and I'll tell you more about it and sign you up."

"You look like shit, man," said Daniel. "Want to step outside? I'll help—"

"What are you, my mother? I'm fine, damn it. Leave me the hell alone."

"Okay, man. Whatever." Daniel sat up straight and turned to the front of the classroom.

"Any other questions about today's presentation or research opportunities in general?" The lecturer looked around the room. "Okay then, class is dismissed."

The young doctors stood and began a slow procession out of the lecture hall and out into the open air. It was a sunny but cold morning, the sun peeking through the clouds, proclaiming it was time to begin the work of caring for the sick.

"Wait up," yelled a young woman, walking briskly to catch up, her white lab coat flaring in the breeze. Her ponytail flopped side to side as she hurried, dodging between classmates. "Great lecture, huh?"

"Yeah," said Will, briefly looking over his shoulder at her. He removed a tissue from his pocket and wiped his forehead. The coolness of the outdoor air provided some relief.

"I love research," she said. "I may go into research. As a career, I mean. After our residency, which will go forever." She rolled her eyes, then looked back at him.

"Great," he said, a wan smile forming on his face.

"I know, I know. Four months down, three years minus four months to go," she said, a twinge of nervousness in her smile. They walked in silence, herded by the masses. "What rotation are you doing this month? ER, isn't it?"

"Yeah."

"I'm in ICU." She looked at the ground. "Busy place, that ICU."

He nodded.

"Do you like research?" she asked. "It's the only rotation they allow two residents at a time. I thought maybe you and I could . . ." She kicked a small rock, sending it toward the grass by the walkway. Then she looked up at his face.

"No, thanks," he said. "Lilly, I'd like to be alone. I'm not feeling—"

"Have you ever done research?" she said. "I tried to in premed, but couldn't. I applied but didn't get accepted."

"I was involved with research once," he said. "A long, long time ago."

1

The conversation Sarah had earlier with Chuck was still distressing her to no end. But the events of the next hour would make her concerns trivial and completely meaningless.

Sarah walked into the bedroom, her kitten cradled in her arms. The cat's buff-colored coat complemented perfectly her kelly-green nightgown.

She entered the bathroom. "Why can't you be more like Merlin?"

"Useless?" said Chuck. "That's the cat's new name."

"Merlin is the most beautiful cat ever," said Sarah. "Can you forget I told you anything at all?"

"You can't un-ring the bell, Sarah," said Chuck stepping out of the shower. He wrapped a towel around his body. "Now that I know, I have to tell him."

"She's my friend. She confided in me." Sarah slowly lowered the cat onto the tiled floor. "Please don't say anything."

"He's one of my best friends, Sarah. I'm going to tell him about Marie and what's-his-name."

"His name is Mike, but please don't. It'll ruin their marriage."

"She ruined their marriage, not me." He dried his hair with a towel. "Goddamn it, Sarah, I'm done discussing this with you. I'm telling him today at lunch." Chuck hurried out of the bathroom.

"You're such a hardheaded son of a bitch, Chuck," she shouted. "I could just strangle the life out of you." She brushed her teeth then turned on the water in the shower. "Chuck, wait up." She walked out of the bathroom and entered the bedroom. She looked side to side. Merlin was poised in full comfort on the bed. "Where are you?" She proceeded briskly to the kitchen. "Can we talk about it tonight? Rethink the whole thing?" He wasn't in the kitchen. She opened the door leading to the garage. "Chuck," she yelled out. The garage door was sliding closed. She ran to the front door. "Chuck, wait." She waived at him. He was backing up the car out of the driveway. "I didn't get my goodbye kiss this morning," she whispered to no one. Once it reached the street, Chuck's car sped away. Sarah noticed a vehicle parked on the street a few yards up from her driveway. The car was partially obscured by the bushes. She looked at her watch and rushed back to the bathroom.

In the shower, Sarah thought she heard a noise. The sound of a door opening and closing in the distance. Maybe the kitchen door.

"Chuck, is that you?" All she heard was the sound of the shower water falling at her feet. "Did you come back?" No answer. She turned off the water. "Chuck, is that you?" She stepped out of the shower stall and covered up with a robe. "Did you change your mind?" She walked to the bedroom but no Chuck. "Merlin, is that you making all this ruckus?" The extended tip of the cat's tail stuck up from behind the bed, like the tip of a submarine's periscope. "You scared the shit out of me, you silly cat." Sarah returned to the bathroom. She turned on her hairdryer and bent down, letting her long brown strands fall in front of her. Staring at her feet, she pointed the dryer at her wet hair. It was then she noticed a pair of boots, a man walking slowly toward her. He stopped a few feet away.

"You came back. Are those new boots?" she yelled over the noisy appliance. "Give me a second." It was then her heart stopped. Merlin's dead body was thrown at her feet, blood trickling from its mouth. She stood up, the hairdryer still in her hand.

The man grabbed her neck and overpowered her with ease. He placed a rag over her mouth and nose. The dryer fell on the tile, whirring noisily. Sarah struggled to free herself from his strong grip. She clawed at him, but her will to fight and scream for help soon vanished, and she slipped into darkness.

When she regained consciousness, she realized she was lying prone on her bed. For a second, she contemplated the thought that the whole thing might have been just a horrible nightmare. Sluggishly, she looked around the room, side to side. Behind her, to her left, Sarah got a glimpse of the monster. He was holding up a syringe, tapping its side. She tried to get up and flee, but he held her down with a chokehold and placed a knee on her chest. He jammed the needle deep into her neck and pushed down the plunger. She felt a sharp sensation and winced. She tried to scream loudly, but only produced an inconsequential whimper. Within seconds, Sarah felt her muscles become heavy, as if she was being held down to the bed by thousands of pounds of an invisible force field.

"Would you like me to dress you up, Sarah?" he said, his voice raspy. "You can't go outside the house wearing only your robe. What will the neighbors say?"

The man disappeared into the closet and returned in a few seconds with three dresses. Sarah tried with all her might to escape, but her profound weakness turned to clumsiness, and she managed only to fall out of bed.

"Where are you going, Sarah?" he said. He dropped the dresses on the carpet, picked her up effortlessly and dumped her back on the bed. "Which one would you like to wear today?" He held up the three outfits. She just stared, her eye muscles responding to her wishes not at all. "The brown and yellow?" he asked. No response. "The blue one?" Nothing. "The red?" She tried again to scream, but her efforts resulted only in a soft grunt. "The red one it is." He disrobed her and put the dress on her. When he was finished, he sat on the bed at her side.

"I need your phone." He picked her cell up from its bedside charger. He looked through its functions and, finally, pushed a speed-dial button. "Chuck," he said into the phone a moment later, "this is your worst nightmare."

2

The Cessna punched into a bank of clouds, the blue sky suddenly becoming obscured from the passengers. Ben scrutinized the panel of instruments, his mind diverted back to the troubled world from which he was escaping.

"Let it go, already," said Amy. "I can see the worry lines deepening on your face."

"I'm trying," said Ben. "These thoughts don't come with an on/off switch."

"It's not your fault when bad people do bad things."

"I know, Amy. If only I had listened to her words. Really listened." He briefly looked at Amy, then his gaze returned to the instrument panel. "She might still be alive today."

"At that point, it was only a marital dispute," said Amy.

The airplane emerged from the massive cloud, the sunlight's sudden brightness stinging their eyes. Amy placed her right hand in front of her eyes. Ben swung the sun visor down.

"We're going to get a bit of turbulence in a few," said Ben. "It shouldn't be too bad." He pointed to the weather radar display, bits of yellows amid the greens in their flight path. "We'll be past all this stuff in a few minutes."

Amy turned to the backseat. "Billy's still asleep," she said. "The iPod thing's still in his ears."

Ben flashed a forced smile.

"I can see this case is really bugging the heck out of you. It has changed you so much." She put her hand on his shoulder. "I want my old Ben back. The one who's funny and smart and attentive to my every need. Make the Ben who doesn't smile and worries and thinks about his case continuously go away."

"Amy, she literally begged me to protect her from him. I should have known he'd—"

"You couldn't have known he would get drunk and kill her. There was no way for you to know that at the time."

"I know," he said with a deep breath. "I know."

"How are you holding up in court?" asked Amy. "I know it's opening up old, unhealed wounds."

"It's been tough."

"And this from a man who takes on every challenge with a smile."

"Court appearances to testify are always rough on me."

"Not for my Ben."

"Even for your Ben," he said. "I don't like lawyers." He scanned the panel of instruments. "Well, I don't like other people's lawyers." Both smiled.

"It's almost over. And soon the bastard will be in jail where he belongs and where he'll rot for the rest of his miserable life."

"I hope," said Ben. "For now, let's enjoy this little vacation."

"Great. Can't wait to—"

"November-Three-Bravo—Sierra, descend and maintain three-thousand feet," commanded a voice from inside the headphones.

Ben keyed the transmitter button and acknowledged the air traffic controller's instructions, then lowered the nose of the airplane. The aircraft began its slow descent.

"Are we almost there?" said Billy. He had replaced his iPod earbuds with his aviation headset. "I'd be there already if I went with the team." He looked at his watch. "The bus was scheduled to arrive ten minutes ago. They're probably already warming up."

"Don't start the bus thing again," said Ben. "We should be on the ground in another few minutes."

"Did you get a good rest, honey?" said Amy. "You'll need all the rest you can get for the game today. I hear these guys are pretty good."

"So are *we*, Mom. Have no fear. We'll *crush* them to death."

"Billy, I don't want to hear you talk like that. You're a soccer player, not a gladiator."

"Don't call me Billy. I'm not a baby anymore."

"You are too my baby," said Amy. "You'll always be my baby."

"I told you. I don't like to be called Billy."

"Okay, the two of you," said Ben. "Settle down. I need some peace and quiet if I'm going to land this thing safely." The three looked outside the airplane, a gorgeous blue sky all around. With an Australian drawl, Ben said, "Thank you for flying Ben Sinclair Airlines. We hope you slept like a baby for the whole flight since you were up until God knows what time last night watching TV. Place your backrests and tables in the upright position and make sure your seat belt is secured about you comfortably. We'll be landing in a—"

"November-Three-Bravo-Sierra, cleared to land runway two-one," declared the air traffic controller.

Ben made final preparation for landing at Vermillion Regional Airport.

"There's the runway at our twelve o'clock," Ben said. "We'll be touching down shortly."

"Can we see the soccer fields from here?" asked Billy.

"I'm not sure. Look around, and tell me if you see them. I bet you that's the hospital over there," said Ben, indicating to the right of the airplane's nose. "See those large buildings with the huge parking lots around them?"

"It's a big place," said Amy. "I'm excited to visit their research department. It's top-notch."

"I'm just excited to have a few days off," said Ben. "I can use the R and R."

"Soccer fields to your left. I bet you that's where we'll be playing," said Billy.

"Bet you're right," said Ben.

Like a feather floating smoothly through the air, the single-engine Cessna 182 Skylane drifted steadily down the glide slope until the wheels felt ground. With an almost imperceptible bump, the plane was no longer airborne. Ben taxied to the parking area as the passengers began to gather their belongings. The door opened and Amy emerged first. Right behind her was Billy, a soccer ball and an iPod in his hands. Stepping onto the wing, he took in a deep breath.

"You guys are from Zionsville, Indiana, right?" asked a young man approaching the aircraft.

"Yes, we are," said Billy.

"Well, welcome to Danville, Illinois. I'm Wayne," he said. "You a soccer player? What team?"

"Zionsville Crush."

"What age group?"

"Sixteen."

"Hey, are you here to play in that soccer game at the high sschool?" he asked.

"Yup," said Billy.

"Beautiful day for it, although we're supposed to get heavy thunderstorms and showers later this evening and all night."

"Top off all tanks," said Ben, exiting the cockpit.

"Yes, sir. I got your message—keep the plane in the hangar for the weekend. I'll take care of everything," he said. "Do you need ground transportation?"

"No, we have somebody picking us up. They should be arriving soon, if they're not here already," said Ben.

The Sinclairs walked to the welcome center. Amy entered the building, Ben and Billy right behind her.

"He's not here yet. I'll give him a call and tell him we've arrived," said Amy, dialing on her cell phone and walking off a few feet.

"Want to watch a little TV? On a big TV?" said Ben, smiling and pointing to a large screen mounted on the wall. Ben and Billy sat down on a couch.

Amy's mobile connected with a computer voice announcing that the number dialed was not in service.

"That's strange," she murmured. Amy looked at her cell phone as she walked toward Ben and Billy. "The number Pat gave me to call isn't in service," she said.

"Do you think you wrote it down wrong?" said Ben.

"Honey, this is the twenty-first century. Who writes down numbers anymore? This is the number in the caller ID."

"I thought you said this guy was pretty detail-oriented and efficient," said Ben. "Not making sure you had the right number to call seems like the sort of thing he wouldn't miss on."

"I agree. This is highly unlikely. What time is it?"

"Nine thirty-nine," said Ben.

Amy reread the previously e-mailed message from the man who had organized this jaunt:

> *Okay, everything is all set. Dr. Hughes and I are looking forward to your visit. I'll be at the airport at 9 AM, sharp. I'll take you and your family to the hotel first, then you to Heartland Regional and your family to the soccer field. Your talk is at 11 AM and Billy's soccer game is at 1 PM. Don't worry, I'll make sure you get to the game on time. Pat Tetrodo.*

Amy used her smartphone to search for information about the hospital and soon was on the phone with Dr. Timothy Hughes's secretary.

"How may I help you?" answered a woman.

"My name is Dr. Amy Sinclair from Zionsville, Indiana. I'm scheduled to give a talk this morning at Heartland Regional Hospital. Dr. Hughes's personal assistant, Mr. Pat Tetrodo, was supposed to pick me up at—"

"I'm sorry, Mr. Pat who?"

"Mr. Pat Tetrodo," said Amy. "He invited me to deliver today's conference on Dr. Hughes's behalf. He was supposed to pick me up at the airport at nine, but he's not here."

"I'm sorry, doctor. I'm Dr. Hughes's secretary and assistant. We don't have anybody here by that name," said the woman. "But you say you're supposed to give today's conference here at Heartland?"

"Yes." Amy clenched her jaw. "I'm the guest speaker for today's conference."

"I'm sorry, but our guest speaker today is Dr. James Dill. I set up his itinerary myself."

"This is all very confusing. I was invited by Mr. Pat Tetrodo to come deliver today's talk." Amy massaged the back of her neck. Ben looked on, bewilderment covering his face.

"May I suggest you come over and discuss this with Dr. Hughes?"

"I'll be there soon."

3

"Get over your fears, Jim," he said to himself. "You can do this in your sleep. Public speaking is our friend." A smirk. He drained the last bit in his coffee cup and, for a second, contemplated pouring himself another. "Better not. You're a nervous mess already," he mumbled. He took a gulp of orange juice and placed a luscious strawberry in his mouth and, for a long moment, savored its flavor. Someone knocked on the door. Softly.

"Who is it?" he said. "It's way too early. Not supposed to leave to the hospital until ten o'clock."

The knock again, this time a little less timidly.

"Who is it?" he said louder. No answer. "Who is it?" he repeated at full volume, approaching the door. He peeked through the peephole. A man. Definitely a man. A man with a cap. "What is it?" Jim said.

"Hotel maintenance, sir. There's a drip from the ceiling in the room below you. I'd like to check for leaks in your bathroom," said the man.

"For crying out loud," Jim said. "I need to get dressed and be out of here in thirty minutes." He placed the hotel robe around him and cinched the cloth belt about his waist. "Can't this wait a few minutes?"

"Unfortunately, this can't wait."

Jim grabbed the door's top lock.

"Can you come back in a few minutes?"

"It'll only take a moment."

The second lock unlatched. The doorknob began turning. A strong shoulder forced the door open, smashing it hard against Jim's body. He fell backward and hit the carpeted floor heavily, the blow to his chest and the surprise of it all temporarily stealing his breath away.

"What do you want from me?" Jim gasped.

"Do you still have a gallbladder?" asked the man, placing a heavy knee on Jim's chest.

"I have money. Do you want my money?"

"I want your gallbladder."

The man pushed harder with his knee. Jim struggled in vain to breathe and escape. He tried to roll side to side, his hands clawing for a piece of the assaulter. The man's gloved fist struck Jim's temple, the whack leaving the doctor stunned. The man pulled out a syringe from his breast pocket, removed the needle cap, and squirted out a few drops.

"I can't breathe. Let go of me. I'll give you all my money."

"I don't want your money," said the man. "But you'll be making a wonderful donation shortly."

A needle punctured Jim's neck, and its liquid contents emptied in the vicinity of his jugular vein.

"Help," he yelled frailly, his lungs half deflated. "Somebody help me, please."

Profound weakness overcame Dr. James Raymond Dill, and his cries became nothing more than the feeble gurgles of a man about to die.

4

The Sinclairs left their luggage at the airport and got into the taxi.

"This is a weird puzzle," said Amy.

"I happen to be really good with puzzles," said Ben. "I just finished a puzzle. It took me only two weeks. The box said *three to five years*."

"Pur ump bump," said Billy, playing air drums. "Good one, Dad."

"Don't encourage him," said Amy, her eyes rolled up, her head shaking. "We'll get this whole thing straightened out. Once we do, we'll figure out what our next step is." She looked outside the car as bits of the quaint town of Danville passed by. There were mom-and-pop shops everywhere. Small groups of people conversed here and there. An older man walked a small dog past a barber shop, the round red-and-white-striped pole rotating.

"I say we get a couple of hotel rooms, with a Jacuzzi," said Ben.

"And a swimming pool," said Billy. "Like, indoor and out."

"With several pools," said Ben. "And massage parlors." Ben and Billy nodded and winked at each another. "We watch Billy's game, kick back and enjoy the time off. Come Monday, I'm back in the war zone." Ben gave a deep sigh. "I have to be back in court with that murder case."

"Dad, isn't that like the only real murder in Zionsville, like *ever*?"

"The first for me. I think there was a murder in town about twenty-five years ago," said Ben.

"Normally, I'd just think the right hand isn't talking to the left," said Amy.

"Mom's not paying any attention to what we're saying," whispered Billy. Ben nodded.

"But that Mr. Pat Tetrodo's cell number is disconnected and Dr. Hughes's secretary never heard of him at the hospital just isn't adding up. Why would he lie to me about being Dr. Hughes's assistant? And why would anyone trick us into coming here by creating some concoction about me giving today's lecture at Heartland Regional Medical Center? What do you make of it, Ben?" said Amy.

A police car with emergency lights and sirens blaring sped by their taxi and disappeared onto a side street.

"We'll get to the bottom of it," said Ben.

Another emergency vehicle rushed by, then another. Both had approached from different directions but turned onto the same street; and soon, like the first cop car, they too were out of sight, the siren sounds still lingering.

"Do you think it's a murder case?" asked Billy.

"Of course not," said Amy. "Danville is a peaceful small city, like back home."

"Actually," interjected the driver, "there have been a couple of murders here in town, and a whole bunch of people have gone missing recently. They're probably dead too. The police are still trying to catch the killer."

"Oh my," said Amy. She looked at Ben then back at the driver. "When was this? Recently?"

"Oh yeah," said the man. "I don't know, maybe a week or two ago."

"Were the victims all related?" said Ben.

"I don't know," said the driver.

"Cool," said Billy. "A real killer, just like on TV."

"No, not like on TV," said Amy. "This is real life. Murder is not cool, it's serious stuff."

The cab ride continued wordlessly for a long moment.

"They'll solve the case and apprehend the murderer," said Ben, craning his neck to see another patrol vehicle speed by. "As for our situation, I'm sure this isn't a big detective mystery. Somebody got their dates mixed up. I'm sure there's a great explanation for it all. We'll laugh when we realize what happened. Then we'll get into our Jacuzzi and swimming pools."

"Don't forget the massages, Dad," said Billy.

Amy bit her lower lip. "He told me he was Dr. Hughes's assistant and that he was inviting me on his behalf to deliver this talk. Today's date." She looked at her watch. "This hospital." She let out a loud snort and looked out the window.

We are delighted that you have agreed to talk at our Grand Rounds Conference, Dr. Sinclair. By the way, you told me last week when we first spoke that your son is a soccer player. You wanted to check his pre-season schedule before committing to us. Well, we are very proud of our Danville Rockets. They're a soccer club here in town that has done quite well. I took the liberty of arranging a game between the Danville Rockets and the Zionsville Crush. Both coaches agreed and the field is booked. So now you'll have two reasons to visit our fair city.

The car drove on and soon entered Heartland Regional's main campus. The hospital was modern and its massive dimensions almost out of place, given the small size of the town. The building had a fresh, modern look to its façade, its three enormous wings providing symmetry and sophistication. The structures were surrounded and adorned by a mote of shrubbery and beautifully designed and well-kept gardens.

Ben paid the cab fare. The group got out of the taxi and walked into the main lobby, Billy still holding onto his soccer ball. Elegant marble columns gave the entrance a majestic appeal.

"Pretty nice," said Ben, looking around. A concierge-type kiosk was to one side of the palatial atrium, attracting newcomers. Many people walked about. A sign indicated the direction of the research and pathology wing. "This place reminds me of an airport terminal or a hotel lobby."

"Where are we going?" said Billy. "I gotta get out to the soccer field with my team. Are we going to be here long?"

Amy shrugged her shoulders. "I'll be as brief as I can."

"This way," said Ben, pointing to the ornate placard. "Research is obviously a big deal here at Heartland, isn't it?"

"I think it's by far its main function. It really is a first-class operation," said Amy.

The family walked down a marble hall. Pictures of old buildings and distinguished-looking doctors symmetrically ornamented the walls and told the rich history of Heartland Regional Medical Center. The first part of this large wing was comprised of the Department of Pathology, with multiple office entrances. The second portion of the wing consisted of a research facility that seemed to go forever.

"National Bioresearch Institute is well-known in the field of research," said Amy. "They're our competitors in the sense that we both compete for grants from the government. I'm hoping to be able to tour the facility while we're here."

The family stopped in front of a door labeled *Dr. Timothy Hughes, Chief of Department of Pathology and Research.* They entered a small waiting area with elegant and comfortable chairs and couches. There was no one around. Billy was immediately drawn to an enormous aquarium in the back of the room.

"Wow, cool. Look at all these fish," he said, taking a seat next to the glass tank. In it, bright-colored elegant creatures swam gracefully, some green, others yellow or blue, each decorated by colorful designs more flamboyant than a rainbow. The water was perfectly clear. A castle was perched atop a hill covered with a dark green coat of sea moss. Shells with exotic shapes and architecture, here and there, added brilliantly to the peaceful motif in the aquarium.

Ben sat next to Billy, all eyes fixated on the fixtures and the movement inside the tank.

"How many fish do you think there are in there?" asked Billy, his eyes moving side to side, taking it all in.

"I don't know. Why don't you count them?" said Ben. "That'll keep you busy for—"

"There are one hundred and ninety-seven at last count," said an older woman approaching from behind. "Eleven different species of angelfish. You can only see a small portion of the aquarium. The other part, behind that castle over there, is even bigger. The back portion faces the lab, so the researchers can enjoy the beautiful fish as well."

"I believe we spoke earlier on the phone," said Amy.

"I've been expecting you." The woman walked to her desk, Amy behind her. Ben and Billy remained, in full fascination of the aquarium. "Dr. Hughes will be with you momentarily." She sat down behind her desk and gestured for Amy to sit. A sign read: *Patricia Cotter, Administration Secretary.*

"I'm trying to figure out this big mess," said Amy.

"I'm sorry for all the confusion, but I'm sure Dr. Hughes can help you figure things out. He's on the phone right now. He'll see you as soon as he's done," she said, still smiling. "He's looking forward to meeting you. He's heard a lot about you and your research work in Indiana."

Billy placed his soccer ball on the empty chair next to him, his gaze still mesmerized by the aquatic scenery. The ball fell off the seat and rolled toward the secretary's desk.

"Another soccer player, huh?" Patricia asked. Billy nodded. "My grandson is about your age. He plays too. He can't get enough of it."

"Me neither," said Billy.

"I bet you're playing the Danville Rockets today," said Pat. "My grandson did say he was playing a team from Indiana."

"Yup, that's us," Billy said.

"Today's game is all Josh has talked about for the last two weeks. He says your team is pretty good. Probably the best team they've played in a while. I've taken time off work. I'm planning on being there to watch. Where's the rest of your team?"

"They're already at the fields, I'm sure," said Billy. "They came in by bus. We flew in."

"Well, we'll have to get you out to the fields as soon as possible," she said. "How are you getting—"

"Hi, Dr. Sinclair. It is a pleasure to meet you," said a man. "I have heard a lot about you and your research endeavors." Amy stood up and the two shook hands. The older man was wearing a blue suit and a red tie, looking quite professorial. Despite an attempt to disguise it, Dr. Hughes's face was heavy with sadness, his shoulders hunched. "Let's step into my office," he said to Amy. The two disappeared deeper into the building.

"This is all very strange, Dr. Sinclair," started Dr. Hughes.

"Please call me Amy."

"I prefer Tim, myself. Here's what I know. We had invited Jim Dill from Barnes Hospital in St. Louis to give us today's conference. He flew in yesterday and stayed at a hotel in town, a few blocks away. I sent a limo to get him at ten o'clock today." Tim picked up a glass from his desk, his hand shaking creating tiny ripples through the water. "I just got off the phone with the driver. Dr. Dill was murdered this morning in his hotel room. Meanwhile, you showed up saying somebody we don't know here invited you on my behalf to give this talk." He removed a tissue from a box and blew his nose, the tremor in his hands more obvious now.

"What are the police saying?" said Amy.

"The police are there now starting their investigation."

"Did you know Dr. Dill?" asked Amy.

"Yes, but not really well. We had met a few times at conferences." He sipped from his glass of water. "I'll cancel today's symposium."

"Do you mind if my husband comes in here with us? I'd like to get his thoughts on all this. He is a police detective," said Amy.

"I'll ask Patty to bring him in."

Ben arrived in the office and sat down. Tim and Amy summarized their previous short conversation.

"We need to let the police know what we know," said Ben, getting up from his chair. "We've been tricked here, and I'm sure that's connected to the murder somehow. Who is the target here? Amy? Me?" He looked right at Amy, his gaze on hers.

She shrugged her shoulders, "We can't know that yet," she said. "But I'm afraid we are very much in the middle of this whole thing. Somehow. What could this beast want with us?"

"The target could be the hospital," said Tim. "Or the research department."

"Someone wants me to come to Heartland Regional. And he or she went through a lot of trouble, including murder, to get me here. So this whole thing has to be about this hospital and me. Both." Amy looked at Tim, then Ben.

"Can you think of anything that would connect both research facilities?" said Ben.

"We should see if there are any research projects we're working on that may somehow tie us in together," Tim said. He punched some keys rapidly on the keyboard of his desktop computer then got up from his chair. "These are all our ongoing research protocols. See if anything here seems likely to be a common denominator." She sat down and examined the screen. Amy felt a growing chill crawling up her spine.

"I don't see anything suspicious," said Amy after several moments.

"What about personnel?" said Ben. "Anyone recently fired from either research facility that might have held a grudge?"

"We've hired and fired people over the years, but someone capable of murder? I don't think so," said Tim.

"There was a man we recently fired," said Amy. "Remember, Ben? He ended up in jail. What was his name?"

"I don't recall his name. I think that guy was disturbed but pretty harmless," said Ben. "But I'll look into it." He squinted his eyes. "What about the soccer game? What about Billy?"

"What about Billy?" said Amy.

"Can he be the target?" said Ben. "The man who arranged this trip also organized Billy's soccer game."

Amy got up quickly and dashed to the door. She flung it open, Ben right behind her. They ran out toward the secretary. Toward the magnificent aquarium with the beautiful fish.

The chair where Billy was previously sitting on was now empty. Amy ran to the left side of the room. Ben to the right.

"Billy," Ben and Amy called out at the same time.

"He left," said the secretary, a smile on her face.

"What do you mean 'he left?'" said Ben.

"I assumed you knew," said Pat. "Someone came and picked him up. They went to the soccer field at the Danville High School, so your son could meet up with his teammates. I didn't want to bother you. I knew you had something important to discuss."

"Does he have a cell phone?" said Tim.

"No," said Ben.

"You let a man you didn't know take this couple's son without their permission?" bellowed Tim. "How could you, Patty?"

"I imagined it had all been planned that way."

"Call us a cab?" said Ben.

"We'll get you there," said Tim. "Patty, call security right away and tell them we need transportation stat. Have them bring a vehicle to the main entrance."

"Call the police and have them meet us there," said Ben. The secretary nodded and picked up her phone.

"Hurry! There's no time to waste," said Amy.

Ben and Amy ran out to the main lobby, Tim right behind them. A few moments later, an SUV marked "Security, Heartland Regional Medical Center" arrived, and the couple got in. The vehicle sped away, leaving Tim standing alone by the hospital entrance.

5

"Morning, Carol," said Miranda, passing by the secretary.

"Good morning, Dr. Phillips."

"What's going on? There was nothing on the schedule for this morning as of last night. Any unexpected new cases?"

"No, things are quiet," said Carol, knocking three times on the top of her desk.

"What's happening to this place? Usually they're dying to see me."

"They are, aren't they?" she smiled. "Well, they ain't dying to see you right now." Carol gave an extended smile. "Enjoy the quiet while it lasts. It won't stay quiet for long. Especially with that killer still out there."

"You're right." Miranda flashed a smile. "Is Sarah here yet? I need to talk to her."

"She should be here shortly," said the secretary. "I'll check."

"Any of the lab work back on the murder cases?" said Miranda.

"I called the lab in Chicago yesterday late afternoon. They said it usually takes this long and then some to get those results back. Sorry," said Carol.

"I've got charts to finish and sign off on. I'll be at my desk if you need me. Have Sarah come see me when she arrives." The secretary nodded. Miranda entered her office. On the door a sign proclaimed: Miranda Phillips, M.D., Department of Pathology. She placed her Starbucks on her desk and looked at the piles of charts. She sat down, picked up a chart and began reading through it. She signed in three places and threw the chart in the Done pile. She picked up another and leafed through, studying it.

"Sarah's not in yet," said Carol, knocking on her door. Miranda gestured for her to enter.

"She's always one of the first ones in," said Miranda.

"I'll try her cell phone," said Carol. "Don't you wish you only had these to do?" She pointed to one of the two stacks. A sign declared it to be the Heartland Regional Pathology pile.

"Sure, these are easy; quick review, a couple of signatures on each, and it's done. On to the next case," said Miranda, signing a page, closing the chart, then throwing the paperwork in the Done basket.

"But the other pile is quite a bit more complicated, isn't it?"

"Sometimes I wish we weren't the county medical examiner," said Miranda. "But we are." Carol left the office.

"Have they caught the bastard yet?" asked a man, pushing open the door into Miranda's office.

"Hey, the great Jack Stevenson has arrived," said Miranda. "Wheel that hot-rod wheelchair in here and talk to me."

"Are the detectives coming in today?" Jack said. "I think they've been here just about every day this week. Don't they know we're too busy to babysit their asses? We got work to do." He navigated the wheelchair skillfully into the room.

"I expect they'll come in or, at least, call. They're all excited with a mass murderer on the loose. Go figure." Miranda signed another chart and closed it, then threw it onto the Done pile. "The labs we sent to Chicago are still cooking. Any good news from you? Have you analyzed the samples I gave you yesterday?"

"It takes time, my love," said Jack. "I may have some preliminary results by this afternoon. What about that nanosequencer you and Hughes keep promising? That would speed up the quest several-hundred fold."

"We've been over this, Jack. We've applied for a nanosequencer, but those things are regulated and cost a trillion bucks."

"It was a gazillion bucks just a few days ago. There must be a special going on. Quick, order two today," said Jack.

"Yeah, I wish." Miranda took a sip of coffee. "I'm told we might get one by the end of the year, if we're lucky."

"That's what Hughes keeps saying. You know the National Research Laboratory in Zionsville, Indiana has one, right? How are we supposed to compete with them for grants without a—"

"They're a whole bunch of rich brats in Indiana. Besides, it's all political. And luck." Miranda smirked. "We'll get you one in due time."

"And for now, my dear, progress will be at a snail's pace," said Jack. "More people will die as we take our time analyzing the samples the old-fashioned way, with sticks and stones and rubber bands."

"Hopefully, Chicago will give us results soon."

"You know how busy those bozos are up there?" said Jack. "We'd be better off walking the samples over to the rich folk across the border and asking them to analyze our stuff."

"I know. But you can't walk, can you?"

Jack raised his right middle finger at her. "You need to quit with this wheelchair envy. Besides, what I lack with no working legs, I make up aplenty with another appendage."

"Yeah, yeah, yeah."

"Do the police have any theories yet?" said Jack.

"I don't think so," said Miranda. "He's got to be looking for something unique in the gallbladders. I want a complete tox analysis."

"Then get me a nanosequencer or grow old waiting for results, my dearest." Jack smirked, pushing off on his wheelchair, slowly gliding away from Miranda.

"Wheel your sorry ass to the research lab and get back to work. Give me results I can use. I can give you a few technicians. Would it help you to have more hands in the lab on this project?"

"You know I work alone, Miranda. So thanks but no thanks," said Jack.

"Okay, back to work. Let me know as soon as you get something," said Miranda. "I'm going upstairs to say good morning to Mama Mia."

"How are Terri's spirits these days?"

"Better than mine, that's for sure. She's hanging in there."

"Tell her to come down to the lab and visit, if she's bored." Jack left the small office, leaving the door ajar.

"Dr. Phillips, Sarah's not answering her cell or her home phone. Her husband isn't answering his phone either."

"Did she tell anyone she was going to be late or away?"

"She would have told me," said Carol. "You know the victim profile the police were discussing?" Miranda nodded. "Sarah and her husband fit it perfectly."

6

The SUV raced to the soccer fields. As the Danville High School buildings came into view, Ben and Amy sat up close to the edge of their seats, their gaze probing the distance. Their eyes scanned the school buildings, the open spaces, the playing fields. There was a baseball diamond, a football field, and several soccer pitches, only one of them occupied by many people. The farthest one. The one they couldn't see very well, partially hidden by one of the buildings.

Their ride came to a sudden halt, and the couple exited the SUV. They slammed the doors shut, already dashing toward the fields. They skirted the building, their eyes on the farthest soccer field, the typical ground markings appearing particularly fresh. On either side of this field, there were bleachers, but these were empty. As they reached behind the obstructing structure, in the distance, by one of the soccer goals, a group of teenagers sat down on the grass. One older man walked slowly, side to side, near the boys, apparently giving instructions.

"It's our team. Is he there?" said Amy, out of breath from sprinting.

"Not sure yet," said Ben, running at her side.

They continued to dart toward the sidelines, the people on the field gradually coming into focus.

In the distance, Ben and Amy saw familiar faces.

"There he is," said Amy, breathing deeply. "Number nine."

The team got up as a man wearing a dark blue warm-up jogging outfit approached. He was carrying a large cooler labeled *Gatorade* which he placed on the ground heavily. The man opened up the container and began dishing out bottles.

Billy received a bottle. "This one's for you," they barely heard the man say.

"Thank you," said Billy. The boy drained a large amount of Gatorade and walked toward his teammates who were now gathered together forming a circle.

"Go Crush!" came the collective yell, as the group scattered, each player walking to their designated post on the field.

"They're having a scrimmage," said Ben, sitting down on the bleachers. Billy noticed them and waved. Both parents stood up and waved back. Billy and Ben exchanged thumbs up.

"My heart's still pounding," said Amy, sitting back down.

"Mine too," said Ben. "So what do you make of—"

"Sir," they heard a man say from behind them. "Ma'am." Ben looked toward the parking lot. A cop car was parked haphazardly, its driver's door ajar. "Did you call the police?" A well-built man in uniform was standing by the cop car, a holstered revolver on his hip.

"I'll go talk to him," whispered Ben.

"Want me to come with you?" said Amy.

"No, you relax and watch the scrimmage. I'll be right back."

"Someone called the police dispatch and asked that a patrol car meet the Sinclairs here. Is that you?"

"I'm Ben Sinclair. I'm a police detective in Zionsville, Indiana. There have been some strange things happening today. In the midst of it all, some man took our son without our permission from where we were at the hospital."

"Heartland Regional?" interrupted the cop.

"Yes." The officer took notes on a small pad. "My wife is a doctor. She was asked to be the guest speaker at a conference today," Ben resumed the description of the previous events. "The doctor who was murdered this morning was also scheduled to give the conference—"

"How do you know about the murdered doctor?" The officer's eyes moved up from his notepad and looked at Ben over the dark sunglasses.

"We were told at the hospital," said Ben. "My wife was there to—"

"Let me stop you a second. I'll need to have you talk to the primary detective on that case," the cop said. "The lieutenant will want to talk to you and will contact you within twelve hours. If not, give us a call at the station." The officer handed Ben a business card.

Ben continued to give the cop details when, out of the corner of his eye, he suddenly noticed Billy on the field stumble a few steps and fall to the ground.

"Shit!" said Ben. "My son just collapsed." He began to run toward the soccer field toward his fallen son. He yelled, "Gotta go!"

7

Detective Lieutenant Lela Rose pulled into the Hilton lot and parked her unmarked car, her cell phone to her ear. As she got out of her ride, she placed her mobile in her pocket. She opened up the trunk and removed a pair of gloves and shoe-covers and stuffed them in her jacket side pocket. She walked to the entrance of the building.

"Morning, Lieutenant," said a uniformed police officer, lifting up the yellow tape surrounding the entrance into the building.

"Is it still morning?" she said, ducking underneath the tape.

"Yes, ma'am. Quarter to twelve," he said, smiling, looking at his wristwatch.

"You make a wonderful timekeeper. I knew you were good for something, Jensen," she said, continuing her walk into the hotel lobby. She sported a dark gray pantsuit, an off-white shirt under her jacket. Her hair was short and well-kept. Behind the tough appearance lay some elements of a plain but beautiful black woman, her cheeks prominent, her dark brown eyes sharp.

"Morning, Lieutenant Rose," said one of the detectives, as they made eye contact. She had just entered the hotel's main foyer.

"You that newbie from Evansville, Indiana?"

"Yes, Lieutenant." He wore dark blue pants and jacket but no tie. His shoes were polished to perfection. "Austin Rube," he said, extending his right hand.

"You just made detective, huh?" she said, ignoring his gesture.

He looked at his own hand then placed it in his pant pocket. "Yes, ma'am."

"Okay, now we know you can pass exams. We'll see how well you do out here in the real world solving murders?" He nodded. "So tell me, Ruby. What do we have here?"

"Rube, ma'am, not Ruby," he said.

"Rube," she whispered, nodding her head slowly. She shook her head. "No, to me, you're Ruby." She took a deep breath. "Where's the crime scene?"

"Doctor James Raymond Dill is the victim," he said, following her. "He was here at the invitation of the med center to give a conference scheduled for eleven o'clock this morning. He arrived last night. The body was found when the driver came to take him to the hospital. They were supposed to meet in the lobby at ten o'clock. The front desk called his room, but he didn't answer the phone. Security opened the door and found him. They say they didn't touch anything."

"Is it the—"

"Yes, ma'am, the same MO."

"Where's the DB?"

"The what, please?" he asked.

"The dead body," she said. "FNA" she whispered, loud enough to be heard.

"I'll take you there," he said, touching the Up elevator button. "Third floor."

"We're walking," she said, already halfway to the staircase. "The killer most likely went up and down this way. We'll do the same and look for clues. We'll check the elevators on the way down."

"Yes, ma'am." Austin looked at one of the two uniformed officers who stood idly guarding the elevators. The cop had a mischievous smirk on his face. "FNA?" Austin said.

"Fucking newbie asshole," said the cop, grinning.

Austin shrugged his shoulders and raised his eyes, then followed Lela into the stairway without a word.

"The murder scene is a stage," the lieutenant had said to the large group of *new police recruits. "Everything is important. The killer is sending you a message, all of it a clue, sometimes deliberately. Other times, not so much. But it is always crucial that the scene be inspected and scrutinized for the message. It's there for you to find."*

"Talk to the main desk clerk," said Lela. "Find out how the perp knew which room the doctor was in."

Austin nodded. "Down the hall. Room 334."

"I don't believe this was a random kill," said Lela. "None of these other rooms seem to have been disturbed. Nonetheless, just in case, have all these doorknobs checked for fingerprints."

Two cops and "Police—Crime Scene" yellow tape guarded the entrance.

"Morning, LT," said one of them.

"Is it still morning, Bailey?" she said examining the entrance to the room. She pointed to the lock. "Not forced," she said putting on shoe-covers and tight rubber gloves. Austin followed suit. "He let the perp in willingly. May have known him or, more likely since the victim is from out of town, the perp wore some sort of disguise. Maybe hotel attire." She faced Austin. "Any security cameras around?"

"None up here, Lieutenant. The hotel has cameras in place down in the main lobby. I've told management to make those available to us."

The two detectives entered the room placing menthol camphor ointment under their noses. "Got to love it when the stench of spilled blood and shit mixed in with piss inundates the senses." They stood silent for a moment, looking into the room. "Did anybody hear anything? Have you canvassed the rooms on this floor?"

"There were only three other rooms occupied at the time. Most rooms had vacated by then."

"Check the list of all the guests," said Lela. "The killer might have stayed here last night." Austin nodded. "Time of death?"

"Preliminarily, I put time of death between nine-thirty and ten this morning. We know the deceased ordered room service which arrived a little bit after nine o'clock. He ate his breakfast before the killer arrived." Austin removed a notepad from his jacket pocket and began to leaf through it. "Of the hotel guests I talked to, one man thinks he was in the shower and didn't hear a thing. Another one had arrived here around four in the morning and was still sound asleep. He heard nothing. The third room was occupied by a couple, both in their eighties, who also arrived *very late* last night. Ten o'clock in the evening, they said." He smirked. Lela remained serious. Austin continued. "They were both sleeping in and had taken out their hearing aids."

Rose walked further into the room.

"Very little blood, relatively speaking," she said, approaching the body. She crouched down. "Here's a puncture mark." She pointed to the dead man's neck. With her pen, she pushed the edge of the white hotel robe aside to expose the right upper chest and shoulder. A slightly reddened swollen area was barely noticeable.

"What's that?" asked Austin.

"This area was bumped forcibly right before death. I suspect the doctor opened the door and the unsub, uh—the unknown subject, the bad guy, pushed hard on the door which hit right here," said Lela, pointing with her pen in a circular fashion, "and knocked him down.

This probably took his breath away and gave the unsub the element of surprise." She stood up. "He also hit the doctor on the head. See the temple bruise?" Austin nodded. "This would have incapacitated and dazed the vic." Lela pointed a few steps away from the body. "The unsub dragged the vic from there to here and at some point injected him in the neck."

"The unsub must have knowledge of the human body," said Austin. "What is he injecting?"

"I'm good, Ruby, but not that good," she said. "Make sure you request a full drug analysis. The previous cases were injected with some chemical, but the lab people still don't know exactly what it is. I'm sure it's the same thing they'll find in this guy." The pen in her right hand pointed at the dead man. "This is definitely the work of our mass murderer." As she spoke, Lela had again taken a knee next to the body and opened up the doctor's robe. Now prominently displayed was a ten-inch deep gash in the right upper quadrant of the abdominal area. "He makes this incision post-mortem," she said, now looking at Austin.

"Could it possibly be a copycat?"

"Nah. The details are identical to the previous murders, including things we never released to the media." Lela walked around the corpse. "No, this is the real McCoy."

"I already put in a request for a full drug analysis," he said. "Do you think he took the gallbladder this time too?"

"I bet my reputation on it," said Lela.

"Do you have any idea as to why he takes the gallbladder?"

"I'll be damned if I know why the hell he takes them. A heck of a souvenir, huh, Ruby?"

"Lieutenant, when I was in Evansville, we had several incidents at the hospital there. Newton Memorial Hospital," Austin said.

"The Rat Poison Murders," said Lela. "We have newspapers and TVs in Danville, Illinois. The news was national. Hell, probably international." She looked up from the dead body and right at Austin. "So what?"

"We ended up solving the case with the help of a doctor. A young guy named Dr. Norris. He's pretty good at figuring out the medical stuff."

"You think we don't have capable doctors here in podunk Danville, Illinois?"

"Oh, no. Nothing like that. I just thought—"

"It's okay, Ruby, you're trying to help. And that's a good thing. Anyhow, we have a great research lab here in town, and they're helping us with the case. The FBI lab in Chicago is also investigating some of the chemicals. We'll get a hit soon."

"How many murders has he committed so far?" asked Austin.

"This is number three that we know of. The first one was eight days ago. There's been a slew of missing people, going back five weeks, and many missing pets over the last two months. I'm betting they're all dead and missing a gallbladder." She looked around the room. "He's ramping up fast and getting more efficient at it. He's getting more bold and sure of himself and taking on more risk. He'll make a mistake. They always do."

They heard footsteps right outside the room.

"The gatherers are here," she said.

"Want us to wait some, Lieutenant?" asked an older man from the door, *CSI* stamped on his jacket's left breast pocket.

"No, come in. We're just finishing up."

The hotel room flooded with people wearing blue booties and rubber gloves.

"What should we tell the media, Lieutenant?" said Austin as the two walked toward the elevators.

"Let's wait on that for as long as we can. No sense panicking the masses, huh?"

"Where do we go from here?"

"We have to wait until he makes a mistake," said Lela, "but so far, he's committed perfect murders."

Lela's cell phone chimed.

"This is Miranda Phillips from Heartland. One of our employees, Sarah Pickens, is missing. Her husband too. I believe they were kidnapped by the gallbladder collector."

"Why do you say that?"

"This you have to see for yourself, Lela. Meet me at her house. I'm texting you the address."

8

"I'm fine, Dad," said Billy, getting up. Ben and Amy were at his side, breathless from the sprint, looking him over.

"Are you feeling okay now?" said Amy.

"I'm fine," said Billy.

Billy's teammates and coaches began to walk away from the area. "You're embarrassing me," whispered Billy. Will you please get off the field? We're trying to get ready for this game."

Ben and Amy retreated back to the bleachers and sat down. A gentle breeze wafted over the soccer field, carrying the fresh scent of trees and grass. The cooling effect of the light wind felt good, the heat of early spring threatening to dehydrate even the most enduring of athletes.

"Come on, ladies," yelled Coach Lewis. "Let's get on with the warm-up routines. I want to have another quick scrimmage."

The boys quickly drained their beverages and threw their towels and warm-up suits onto a pile. Soccer balls began to bounce here and there, filling the empty pitch with activity.

"Thornton, McBride, Blanco, Sinclair, and Cunningham, let's see some shots on goal," shouted Coach Lewis.

"He seems okay," said Ben. "But I have a really bad feeling about this."

"Me too," said Amy. "Do you think we're just paranoid?"

"Probably." Ben waved at Billy who had looked in his direction, their eyes connecting briefly.

"This whole thing may have been planned by the coaching staff," said Amy. "I bet you Billy forgot to tell us somebody was going to swing by the hospital to get him. You know how Coach Lewis is all about practices and being on time."

Ben nodded. "You'd think his coach would let us know." Ben bit his lower lip. "He may have forgotten too."

Amy fished out a stick of gum from her purse. Then her digital camera.

Lela and Austin arrived at the house. There was a car in the driveway. Miranda walked briskly toward their vehicle from behind the house and signaled for the cops to approach. The three walked into the backyard.

"When Sarah didn't show up at work, I decided to come by the house," said Miranda.

"What makes you think Sarah was abducted?" said Lela.

"When I arrived, there was no answer to my knocking," said Miranda. "I looked around the house and discovered that the kitchen door was unlocked. That seemed unusual. Anyhow, I got in. And this is what I found." Miranda gestured for the cops to enter the house. She closed the kitchen door behind them.

"What's that noise?" said Lela.

"It's coming from in there," said Austin.

"I'll show you," said Miranda. "It's coming from the master bathroom."

"Ruby, call for a CSI team to come out here," said Lela, inspecting the breakfast nook space right off the main kitchen area. Austin nodded and sauntered off, cell phone in hand. "Miranda, we'll need your fingerprints." Lela walked further into the domicile. "Did you disturb anything in the home?"

"It's all as I found it," said Miranda. "The only thing I touched was the kitchen doorknob."

The two women walked into the master bedroom, the detective in front, her hand on her holstered revolver at the hip. Lela noticed the strange noise getting louder. It was clearly coming from the next room. The bed was unmade, a blue and a brown dress, still in their hangers, were strewn on the floor.

"Sarah is a neat freak at work," said Miranda. "These dresses on the carpet like this and the unmade bed are very unusual, knowing her."

Lela nodded and walked into the bathroom, the hairdryer still whirring noisily on the tile. Next to it, lying in a small pool of blood, was a dead cat.

The boys had separated into small groups, each with an assistant soccer coach, each concentrating on a certain task. Billy's group was gathered around one of the goals performing short passes to each other and then kicking the ball at the goalkeeper. Amy began taking pictures with her new camera.

"I love this thing. It has a great zoom," said Amy, her right eye peering through the Canon EOS 7D. *Click, click.* "This is a great picture." She showed Ben the digital screen.

"He looks good, but the background's too blurry," said Ben. Amy again peeked into the camera, focused the lens, and continued clicking.

"What do *you* know?" *Click, click.* "Another poster-worthy picture," she said, showing him.

"I knew I'd create a monster when I bought you that camera."

"You're just jealous I can take such beautiful close-ups and action pictures," said Amy, still clicking away.

Almost ten minutes passed as the boys practiced this and that soccer move, once in a while taking a few seconds for a slug of Gatorade. Amy and Ben noticed Billy had turned to one of his teammates. It looked like Billy was showing him his tongue. After a short exchange, Billy began to walk away when he suddenly fell to the ground. Instantly, Amy and Ben got up on their feet and, once more, ran to their son.

"I'm all right," said Billy, trying to sit up. "My legs gave way. They became weak, and I fell."

By now, the whole team surrounded Billy.

"Sinclair, what happened to you?" asked Coach Lewis. "Can you get up on your own?"

Billy attempted to stand. "Give me a minute."

Amy got on her knees next to Billy and examined his legs. "Push with your feet against my hands," she asked. Billy complied. "There's definitely some degree of muscle weakness."

"I'm okay, Mom. It's not a big deal," said Billy, looking into countless staring eyes. "Can I get back to playing?"

"I'm calling for an ambulance," said Amy, dialing 911.

9

Sarah was aware she was being carried by a big man from a vehicle into a cold, dark, dilapidated building. She willed her muscles to move to no avail. She wanted to struggle. To scream. To run away. But all she was able to do was lay there. Still. She was powerless even to wipe her own tears. Her unmoving eyes permitted her only to stare at red blotches on the passing graying ceiling tiles. Leading out from the crimson splotches, there were multiple streaks of arterial spurts of different lengths and widths. Sarah's peripheral vision allowed her to see a small portion of the drop ceiling surrounding the bloodstained tiles, several square panels missing. She could see a bit of the inside of the aluminum roof. She was delivered onto a cold, hard, metal table. A meat slab.

The man approached her and came into her field of vision. Then disappeared. Her head rotated to her right, and Sarah could now feel the cold steel against her check. She wished she could move. But she could not. Tears dripped from her face and nose and splashed onto the frigid slab. From her new vantage point, Sarah could now appreciate more of her surroundings. She spied a large counter containing multiple types of lab equipment. There was a centrifuge, islands of white matter with congealed blood partially covering its walls. A wooden rack propped up several glass test tubes, one half-filled with a dark reddish liquid, another with jagged surfaces, pieces of yellowish tissue hanging onto the edges. A Bunsen burner sat on the counter, flameless, its rubber hose attachment partially disrupted by a sharp knife's cut. There was a neatly half-folded green surgical towel. On it rested three scalpels, blood blotches on one of the blades. There were five clamps and two tweezers, bits of decaying tissue still attached to their tips.

"Comfy?" he said, straightening up her head. Her unmoving eyes now again faced the bloodied ceiling tiles. He placed some sort of headrest under her skull, balancing and steadying it. He disappeared again from her sight.

Sarah's breathing was difficult. She had the perception of insufficient air entering her lungs. She willed her breathing muscles to work faster and harder, but nothing changed. She again tried desperately to move her eyes, to scan the room, to see where she had been carried. She needed to have this information to devise a way to escape this madman. But she couldn't. None of her muscles obeyed her commands. Stubbornly, Sarah vowed to keep the faith alive. The faith that Chuck would come for her. That Chuck would bring the police into this room of death and misery and disentangle her from the clutches of this maniac. That Chuck would save her.

The man carried a cup of hot tea, sipped from it, and placed it on the cold slab, next to her head.

"I wish you could taste this tea, Sarah," he said. The man took another sip of his tea, letting the warmth pierce his nasal passages. Sarah heard the passing wind ricocheting off the walls and roof and smelled the Earl Grey. The man placed a cashew in his mouth.

"I've known I'm special since," his gaze glimpsed into the dimly illuminated portion of the large room, "probably middle school." He sipped his hot tea then placed two raw cashews into his mouth. "In the beginning, I knew I had unique desires that others didn't. In fact, desires others seemed to avoid at all costs. Oh, like torturing your cat or killing dogs. It gives me goose bumps even now, just thinking about it." He extended his naked right arm, his left index finger pointing to the small bumps, hairs on end. "See?" He waited, his gaze fixed on Sarah, who lay there impassively, her only outward sign of emotion being the intense fear in her unmoving, wide-open eyes and the cascading tears. "For instance, I love to see fish out of water—the gills flapping, begging for water. Dying fish look a little bit like you right now, Sarah." He slapped his own right knee, laughter in his words. "Okay, okay. I know what you're thinking, Sarah. Why is he telling me these things? Why now? Why here? I understand your frustration." He came close to Sarah and looked down at her. "But this you should know, Sarah." Another cashew in his mouth. "Your contribution is not in vain," he said, still chewing. A swallow. "You'll help the human race. With your aid, we will save millions of lives, you and me. And the others. The world will thank us for our efforts and accomplishments. We will be famous. There will be news stories telling the world about us and what we've accomplished. We'll be rich and—" A timer chimed in the distant portion of the large laboratory. "Please excuse me for a second, Sarah."

The man walked away from the table. Sarah remained silent and still, her breaths even slower and shallower now.

"You're starting to get a bluish hue spreading through your face, Sarah," he said, returning. Her flaccid body ached against the hard metal surface she was on. Tiny splashes of tears bounced off the metal table and sprayed her neck.

"So imagine my surprise when she told me no," he said, now facing her. "She refused to let me work in her lab. The greatest research mind of all time's about to make a great discovery, and she turns me down." Another chime sounded. "Please excuse me once again. I'm almost done and ready for you, Sarah. Are you almost ready for me?"

He got up then vanished again from Sarah's peripheral vision. She took a frail breath, gurgling noises in her mouth from saliva yet to be swallowed.

"You can't believe how much help you've been," he said from a distance. "I couldn't do this without you." Reemerging, he smiled. "Sarah, are you still with me, honey?" No response. He looked deep into her eyes assessing her condition, his face only a few inches from hers.

"There's a trickle of life still peeking out from your gaze," he said. "But not much. You're almost ready for me." He had a long sip of tea. Then another. He placed the teacup next to Sarah's head. "You remind me of my Christine," he whispered.

*   *   *

The alarm clock buzzed.

"You first," he mumbled.

"I think it's your turn to get in the shower first. I get twenty more minutes," she said. "I was having the weirdest dream."

"Shower first. Wake me up when you're done."

"Listen. I dreamt that I died."

"I thought you never dream," he said.

"I almost never dream. But I did last night. Today. I had a dream that I died." She sat up in bed. "It scared the hell out of me."

"Okay, Christine. That's very interesting." He turned over, his back now to her. "Wake me up when you get out of the shower."

She slid out of bed and sat on the edge, her arms reaching to the heavens. She walked over and spread the curtains open. Sunshine poured in with the promise of a beautiful, bright, and warm early summer day ahead. He uttered something incomprehensible.

"You're a hopeless case," she said. "Incorrigible." She walked into the bathroom and turned on the shower. The door remained ajar.

"Who's incorreeeggiii? Whatever you said?" he slurred. "And hopeless?"

"You are, mister," she said walking back into the bedroom. His head was under the pillow. She rubbed the covers over him. "I want to talk to you about my dream. I dreamt I died." He moved his head slightly from beneath the pillow and allowed the sun rays to torment his eyes.

"Aghhh," he said, his eyelids now more apart. "Christine, please close the curtains until you're done in the shower. I get thirty more minutes."

"I have to talk to you about this dream," she said walking back into the bathroom. An electric toothbrush came on.

"Christine," he said. "You haven't heard a thing I said, have you?" He approached her and kissed the back of her head. He stood next to his wife, stretching his body. He began to walk away when he heard a loud thud.

"Christine." He looked back to see her lying on the tile floor, lifeless. Her eyes had no focus, and her color had rapidly faded from her face. "Christine." He ran to her. "Christine," he shouted over the toothbrush still vibrating. "Christine, wake up, honey," he cried. "Don't leave me, baby. I can't make it without you." He held on to her, his embrace so tight. "Christine."

His right hand shaking, he reached for her neck to feel her pulse. His own heart hammered fast. She gave no signs of life.

He reached for two towels on the counter and used them as pillows under her head. He ran back to the bedroom. Christine's cell was perched on a charger at her bedside. It took three tries to correctly enter 9-1-1.

"Come one, come on. Answer the damn pho—" he yelled into the receiver. "My wife just collapsed. She's in cardiac arrest. I need an ambulance stat. She has Brugada syndrome and is prone to cardiac arrhythmias. I'm starting CPR. Come quickly, please. Help us, please."

*   *   *

He wiped a tear. He picked up the teacup and drank from it. He bent down to look into Sarah's eyes once more.

"Do you have any more breaths in you?" he whispered softly. "No?" In her eyes, he saw nothing as life had vanished from them. "Okay, Sarah, you *are* ready for me." He grabbed a scalpel from a nearby table and admired it for a long moment. And then he went to work.

10

Miranda entered the hospital room and sat down near the bed. Her mother was in the bathroom.

*   *   *

An eleven-year-old girl knocked on a door. A sign indicated: *Dr. Terri Phillips, Director, National Bioresearch Institute.*

"Hi, Mom," the girl said entering the large office. "Look at my grades. I got all As."

"Great job, Miranda. I'm so proud of you. Let me see this report card of yours."

"When I grow up, I want to be a doctor just like you, Mom. I want to discover new medicines and help people, just like you." Miranda ran to her mother, who kissed her forehead and took the paper from her hand.

"All As. You keep it up and you can be anything you choose."

"Mom, have you ever saved someone's life?"

"I guess so," Terri said. "I invent drugs that other doctors use to save people's lives. Does that count?"

"I don't know." The girl contemplated the question, her eyes in a squint. "Sure, it counts. But you never saved the life of someone you know? A friend? One of your patients?"

"No, not really. Maybe one day, I will, Miranda." The girl sat on her mother's lap and looked deeply into her eyes.

"I love you, Mommy."

"I love you too, Miranda." The two hugged.

*   *   *

"Miranda," she heard. "Miranda, you seem to be deep in thought. Are you okay?" It was her mother returning from the bathroom.

"I'm fine. I was just thinking about the time I came to visit you in the lab when I was in fifth grade."

"I wish I could go back and relive the time when you were a little girl. You were then and are now a most wonderful daughter." She smiled. "I just finished my lunch. Feel like a little walk?"

Terri placed her hospital robe over her pajamas, and the two walked out into the hall. They turned left, away from the nurses' station.

"My neighbor, Mrs. Houston, is in with nausea and vomiting. She has colon cancer," said Terri. "I think they overmedicated her with narcotics. She sleeps all the time." As they walked by, Miranda peeked into room 733.

"It's early afternoon," said Miranda. "Is she still or already asleep?"

"Actually, both." They continued to walk. "She's been asleep for the last two days. They wake her up to bathe her. When they do, she's barely aware of it. The rest of the time, she slumbers away. They feed her intravenously."

"That can't be good."

"The nursing staff loves it," said Terri. "She's low-maintenance that way." She smiled. Both women continued to walk down the hall to the elevators then back to Terri's room.

As they entered, Terri said, "So tell me more about these cases you're working on. Any luck identifying the poison?"

"Still waiting on a definitive identification, but I've narrowed it down to a type of sodium-channel blocker. A nerve blocker of sorts. That goes along with the police's theory that the murderer paralyzes the victims."

"And why does he take the gallbladders? Any ideas yet?"

"I took your advice and tested the blood and liver cells for organophosphates, but it turned out that they were all negative. I'm testing now for succinyl-choline type agents. We may have some results later today."

"What about the bad guy? Do the police have any new leads?" Terri grimaced in pain. She took a deep breath.

"Do you need more meds?" asked Miranda. She got up and moved closer to the bed.

"Just need to stop a second." Another deep, soothing breath, in then out.

"I'm sorry to see you in this much pain. Let me grab your nurse and get you some morphine."

"Thanks," Terri said, her right hand flat on her chest.

Miranda left the room and looked for the nurse. Her beeper went off.

"Ruthie, she's in a lot of pain. Can you give her some morphine?"

"Of course, Dr. Phillips. I'll do it right now."

She followed the nurse into her mother's room, while she read the message on her pager.

"Another victim," said Miranda to Terri, once Ruthie had left them alone. "This time the bastard killed one of ours. He murdered a doctor."

11

Chuck Pickens could hardly believe what he had just done for the man. Man? No, monster. If not for his love for Sarah, he would have fought back, no matter the consequences. But the man, the savage, took Sarah from him with the promise that he would kill her if Chuck didn't follow his instructions precisely. The villain did assure him that both would be rewarded, if Chuck did exactly as commanded. And he had.

"Go to the airport and watch for the airplane's arrival," the man had said. "The tail number on the plane is N3BS. Follow them when they leave the airport, but don't let them see you. They'll probably take a taxi, and they'll probably go to the hotel or hospital. Find a way to isolate the boy, pick him up and drive him to the Danville High School's soccer field. Tell him you're a soccer coach."

Chuck had complied, and all had gone well. The boy had suspected nothing, so innocent and naïve. He had waited until the team was about to begin warm-ups on the field, then had brought them the cooler provided by the monster.

"Distribute the Gatorade to all the kids, but make sure that the boy gets the bottle labeled *Sinclair*."

That went well too. Then he witnessed Billy collapse to the ground. Twice. Chuck realized he had been transformed into an instrument of destruction. He had become a puppet controlled by a creep so immensely evil inside that he would harm an innocent young man.

Alone, Chuck walked briskly in the woods that separated the high school soccer fields from the nearby neighborhood. There were trees surrounding the small path. This small forest would normally be a serene place to be. But not today. Chuck now ran alone with his thoughts. Thoughts of doom.

"Meet me at the corner of Honeywell and Timberline at precisely twelve-thirty," the man had said. "Don't make me wait. And come alone, if you want to see your lovely wife again."

He arrived at the designated spot with seven minutes to spare. Chuck stood at the corner with sweat on his brow, his chest rapidly heaving in and out, his heart thumping.

"Where's Sarah?" said Chuck when the van came to a halt.

"She's waiting for you," said the man. He was wearing a cap. "Get in. I'll take you to her. Where's the disposable cell phone I gave you?"

Chuck got in the vehicle. "Here," he said. He handed over the small device. "What was in the Gatorade?"

"Did he drink it?"

"Yes. Everything went smooth. He drank a whole bunch from it," said Chuck. "What was in the Gatorade? Is Billy going to get real sick?"

"Never you mind. That's for me to know and for you *not* to know." A forced smile.

"And Sarah? Where is she? Did you harm her? I swear, if you touched a hair on her body, I'll—"

"Relax, bro. We made a deal, didn't we? Sarah's waiting at my place. We'll be there in a few minutes."

They drove in silence until they arrived at a large abandoned warehouse in the middle of nowhere. Tall tress surrounded the old warehouse, the white paint adhering to its walls only in patches. There were few windows, the glass panes missing in most of them. Some type of translucent, dark covering—wood, maybe cloth—prevented peering inside. The roof appeared to be aluminum, some portions missing at one end. The van stopped next to the main entrance and both men got out.

"She's in here," said the man. "After you." He gestured for Chuck to enter as he unlocked the door to his lair. Chuck stepped into the poorly illuminated building with the man right behind him. The door closed.

It took a few seconds for Chuck's eyes to adjust to the low lighting. He stood straight for a moment, feeling his heart thump hard inside his chest. Chuck turned to look at the man. A sudden hard blow to his skull came out of nowhere. Chuck fell on the cement like a rag doll, briefly mindful of the sharp pain in his right temple and the smell of the dirty concrete. Then it all went black.

"And now it's time for you and your lovely Sarah to be together again and for both of you to get your rewards," he said. "Just as I promised."

He uncapped the needle and stared at the syringe with the clear fluid for a moment.

12

The ambulance arrived at the emergency room. The back doors opened, and a paramedic jumped out, followed by Ben. The driver and Amy soon were at their side. Billy's stretcher was slid out of the vehicle and onto the apron, then wheeled into the ER.

"Room eight," a nurse said. In moments, Billy was sitting comfortably on the bed in the small cubicle, Ben and Amy at his side.

"How are you doing, champ?" asked Ben.

"I feel fine. Do I have to stay here long? Our game starts in—"

"Hello, I'm Nellie," said a nurse. "How are you feeling, young man?"

"I'm okay," said Billy. "I fell playing soccer."

"What hurts?"

"Nothing hurts. I wish I could go back. My soccer game starts in—"

"You didn't just fall on the soccer field," said Ben. "Your legs suddenly got too weak, and you collapsed."

"Let me get your vitals, and I'll have one of the ER docs look you over. Maybe you can still get back in time for your game," the nurse said, looking at the young man who was now beaming.

"Yes, score," whispered Billy.

The nurse wrapped a cuff around Billy's upper arm and felt his pulse at the wrist. "One ten over sixty-two. Eighteen and fifty-two," she said out loud as she wrote numbers down on her report sheet. She stuck a thermometer in Billy's mouth. "Under the tongue." Billy complied. The nurse clicked a button on the gadget, then looked at its display. "That wasn't so bad, now, was it?" she said, writing a number down on her report. "One of the doctors will be here soon." She left the room. Ben and Amy looked at one another, unsure of how to feel or what to say.

Several long minutes later, an older man in scrubs entered the room.

"I'm Dr. Roy Sanders," he said, his eyes on the chart he carried. "Soccer, huh? What's hurting? How did you hurt yourself?"

"Nothing hurts," said Billy. "I feel fine."

"So what brings you to my emergency room? And don't say the ambulance."

"I fell down during warm ups. But I didn't hurt myself. I was wondering if I could go back and play. We have our first game of the preseason this afternoon."

Amy took a step forward. "Billy collapsed. He has muscular weakness involving both legs."

"Did you pass out?" asked Sanders.

"No, nothing like that," said Billy.

"Tell me again, in your own words, what happened exactly. Take me back to the first moment you realized something was wrong."

"We took a break for Gatorade. We sprinted out to the field and started our warm-up routine. A few minutes later, my arms and legs began to feel strange."

"Strange how?"

"I don't know. Like my legs were tired. Heavy. Like there was an invisible weight attached to them."

"Okay, go on," said Sanders.

"I fell once, but that time I was able to get up on my own. But the second time, my legs were so weak that I needed help to get up on my feet."

"Are you feeling better now?" asked Sanders.

"Yeah, I'm fine now."

"Any other symptoms?"

"My tongue and lips got tingly. They felt to me like they became thick. More or less like at the dentist, when he gives you that needle thing. You know?" The doctor nodded. "I asked one of the guys on the team to look at my lips and tongue. He told me everything seemed fine to him."

"Let me take a look." The ER doctor looked toward the parents. "Will you step outside for a few minutes? I'll be with you soon."

After what seemed to be an eternity, Sanders emerged.

"He seems okay right now," he said. "I can't find anything wrong with your son. He's as healthy as the proverbial horse."

"What about muscle weakness?" said Amy. "Did you appreciate any at all? I thought he—"

"You're worried about nothing. Your son is as fit as a fiddle, and I'm discharging him. I told him he could go back to playing soccer right now." The doctor turned and walked away. He handed the paperwork he was carrying to a nurse, who, in turn, passed him another five charts.

Ben and Amy looked at one another. They reentered Billy's room.

"He said I was fine and ready to go back to playing soccer right now," said Billy. "I feel fine too. Can we get going? If we hurry, I can still make the game with time to spare."

"I'm not comfortable with this," said Amy. "You collapsed, and we still don't know why."

"I'm fine, Mom. You worry too much. Even the ER doctor said so."

"Well, let's go then," said Ben. He helped Billy out of the bed and onto his feet.

"See, I'm fine." He got dressed and the three walked into the hall. Restless ER personnel came and went.

Ben and Amy looked at Billy. "Your stance, your body language seem odd," said Ben. "Are you sure you're okay?" Billy stood alone, his parents' gaze scrutinizing his posture and movements. It was then that Billy collapsed backward onto the floor, his skull hitting the tile hard. A trickle of blood emerged, a small pool of crimson now shadowing his head.

Amy screamed.

Emergency room personnel swarmed to the young man.

"Billy," said Ben. "Can you hear me?"

"He's out. Let's get him back into the room and on the heart monitor," said one of the nurses. "Get Dr. Sanders back here, stat."

13

Chuck tried with all his might to escape, but his body would not obey his wishes. His muscles were heavy and weak. He willed his voice to scream, his legs to flee, his fists to strike. But to no avail. All he could do was lay there.

The man pulled him by the shirt's collar, Chuck's feet dragging on the floor. Chuck had the sensation of losing one shoe, then the other. Pain from scraping his heels on the hard cement shot up his legs agonizingly. The man let out a loud grunt as Chuck felt his own torso heaved onto a cold metal surface. The feet were hoisted up next. Chuck faintly appreciated Sarah's shampoo and perfume and knew she was nearby. He tried to yell out her name but no words came out. *Where is Sarah? I know she's here, but where?*

Chuck desperately craved for hope but could find none. He knew by then he was going to die. The question was more when and how. Given his predicament, Chuck wished he could at least turn off his hearing and close his eyes, lest he bear witness to the final blow, the blow that would put his misery to a welcomed end. But he could not. All Chuck could do was listen to the lunatic in the room and stare at the ceiling, his peripheral vision allowing for very little else, his eyes unmoving, his eyelids unblinking and wide open. The gash on his temple and his heels still smarted. Chuck could feel the cold sweat beads rolling down his forehead.

"You can call me the inventor," the man said, placing a pillow underneath Chuck's head. "Comfortable?"

He was again out of Chuck's view for a moment.

"I don't want to bore you with the delicate details, but this is really important stuff," said the man as he returned by Chuck. "Ingenious, really. Scientists won't touch the stuff because it's poison." He raised a small test tube with a clear liquid inside to Chuck's eye level. He swirled it around gently.

The room was cold and dimly lit. Chuck was now able to appreciate a faint fishy chemical scent hovering over him. Chuck surmised he was in some kind of laboratory inside the abandoned warehouse. A laboratory where evil plots were devised and carried out.

The man put the container down in a test tube rack. "A deadly poison without an antidote. So everybody's afraid of it. It took a great mind to delve into the unknown. Find out more. Somebody to dare ask the right questions: 'What happens to the poison after it gets into the body? How does the body handle it? What secrets does the metabolized compound hold?' The bottom line is this, Chuck: How can we turn a poison into a miracle cure?" He stopped as the teapot whistled. "Excuse me, Chuck. I'll be right back. I really need a cup of tea right about now."

The man got up and walked away from Chuck's field of vision.

"I get the poison from these beautiful fish called *Pomacanthus paru.* Angelfish." He placed a cashew in his mouth and sipped from the teacup. "But I can make a miracle cure out of it. Our livers metabolize it into methyl-alanyl—" he smirked. "I'm sorry. You don't really care about the technical stuff and the names of these compounds, do you, Chuck? It's complicated. Too complicated for you." He tossed a smile. "I get it. You're more of a gist kind of a guy. Okay." He positioned the cup under his own nose and allowed the steam to permeate his nasal passages for a long moment, then took a sip. He ate another cashew. "So the poison gets into the system, and in less than ten minutes after ingestion, it concentrates in the liver where it is metabolized to this other compound. But get this, Chuck, the metabolite is no longer poisonous. It's a drug that, with minor modifications, becomes a perfect cure." The man got up from his chair and looked deeply into Chuck's eyes. "I see you're a bit confused. The man got up and sniffled. "Did I tell you about my Christine?" He held a picture of a woman to Chuck's unmoving eyes. "She was the love of my life. But she died." He wiped his eyes with a tissue. "She died in my arms, Chuck, from a genetic disorder that causes life-threatening rapid heartbeats. It's called Brugada syndrome." He sipped from his teacup. Another sniffle; another cashew. "Interestingly, Chuck, when you inject it into an animal, you don't get the miracle cure. Nonhumans metabolize it differently. They add the alanyl group but not the methyl. You wouldn't think that little detail would make that much difference, but it does. The compound is useless without the methylation process. Go figure." The man placed a cashew in his mouth. "I love these things. Want one?" No reply would ever come. "No? Okay." The man swallowed down the cashews and drank from his teacup. "By the way, you must thank Sarah for me. When you see her. It won't be long now, so don't forget. She gave me a lot of information about her coworkers and friends. All very important stuff. The two of you lovebirds will be together really soon. Together in the park, by the lake. Very romantic. I owe you two that much. Please don't forget to thank her for me; will you, Chuck? I'd really appreciate it."

Chuck's breathing was becoming shallow and puny. The man continued, "A blue-grayish discoloration is already covering most of your skin." He disappeared from Chuck's view again. Chuck heard the clinking of instruments for a long moment. Then the man was nearby again.

"Chuck, I gotta tell you something else. When I picked up Sarah today, she was in the bathroom. That's where I lost my Christine. I lost her in the bathroom, just like you, Chuck." He took a tissue and blew his nose. "I learned in medical school during my psychiatry classes that special people like me don't have emotions. No feelings. By the way, isn't it interesting that I got to diagnose myself? I learned about myself from books. And school. This one time, my condition was a pop quiz. What do you think about that, Chuck? I aced that exam, of course." A sip of hot tea. "I always knew I was special, but I didn't understand why. Hell, I thought everybody was like me until I learned about me in forensic psychiatry. The study of the criminal mind. I loved that class. I learned so much. I learned that special folks like me don't have feelings. *They can't display emotions,*' they taught us. Well, Chuck, I'm here to tell you that's total bullshit. I had plenty of real feelings for Christine. She was my life." He wiped a tear. "The love of my life."

The man threw his tissue on the floor, stood up, and walked over to a blackboard where complex chemical formulae were on display, just on the edge of Chuck's peripheral field of vision. Picking up a piece of chalk, the man frantically began making lines from one group of symbols to another, yelling, "If only I had the right equipment and reagents. If I was allowed to do my research, I could have developed the perfect heart drug and save my Christine." More lines, each inscribed with greater rancor. "I can save so many lives if only I had the proper equipment. Why would anybody refuse me the equipment I need? I can save so many people's lives if only . . ." He suddenly stopped, dropped the chalk at his feet, and slowly turned back to his guest. "Chuck," he said, "are you wondering if I'll save *your* life?"

14

"Welcome to our unit." The nurse helped Billy transfer from the stretcher to the hospital bed. She held a hospital chart bearing the name *William M. Sinclair* on the cover.

"The back of my head hurts," said Billy, feeling the bandage.

"You got a doozy of a laceration and a contusion from when you hit the floor," said the nurse. "Do you remember any of it?"

"I remember pieces, but not all."

"Not remembering is part of the concussion," said Amy.

"Dr. Jenner will be seeing you shortly. I spoke with her a few minutes ago, and she's on her way here."

"So how long must I stay here?" asked Billy. "I'm guessing I'm not going to make the game."

"That's right," said Amy. "You have to be observed overnight due to the concussion. And we still need to figure out why you developed the sudden muscle weakness."

"Are you a doctor, Amy?" asked the nurse.

"Yes. Well, more of an administrator now."

"How so?"

"I started out with an MD," said Amy. "Cardiology. Then Billy came along, and I became a mom for eight wonderful years. By then, cardiology had changed so much, I didn't feel in the loop any longer. I got an MBA and a PhD in business administration and eventually became the head of a research unit back home in Indiana."

A woman wearing a white coat and a bright smile entered the room. A name tag read: *Natalie Jenner MD, Chief of Neurology.* Ben and

Amy stepped outside Billy's room while she performed her bedside evaluation. After several minutes, she walked toward mom and dad. "There's definite diffuse, symmetric muscle weakness. There are also minor sensory abnormalities on his lips and tongue. Does he have a history of asthma?"

"No history of asthma," said Amy.

"What do you mean by sensory abnormalities?" asked Ben.

"His ability to feel around his lips and tongue are diminished," she said.

"Dr. Jenner, why did you ask about asthma?" said Amy.

"Call me Natalie." She smiled. "He has a mild wheeze when I listened to his lungs. It may be nothing."

"Where do we go from here?" said Amy.

"I'm going to order a brain MRI to be done today and an EEG for the morning. For now he seems stable." The doctor walked off.

"How are you feeling, Billy?" said Amy as they arrived at Billy's bedside.

"I'm a little bit sick to my stomach. May I have a glass of water?"

"Sure," said Amy, pouring.

"Knock, knock," said a man from the doorway.

"Hi, Coach Hanks," said Billy, forcing a grin.

"How are you doing, sport?" said Hanks, nodding at Ben and Amy and then looking back at Billy. "Your whole team and coaching staff, we're all worried about you, little man."

"Did you cancel the game?" said Billy.

"No, they're playing right now. Some of the boys wanted to cancel and come see you. Most felt you would want the game to be played. There are a lot of people watching. Still scoreless, last I heard." He walked closer to the bed. "I was designated to come check on you. So give me some good news to bring back. The boys need some encouragement from you. They need to know you're okay."

"Oh, yeah. I'm okay. Just a little weak. And pukey. I'll be out of here in no time," said Billy.

"Did you get enough to drink?" said the coach. "Did you get dehydrated? I tell you kids, you can't get enough water and Gatorade to drink on a day like today. I never want to see you dehydrate out there."

"Yeah. That man brought us Gatorade. I was drinking a whole bunch of it the whole time. Every chance I got, I—"

"What did you say?" asked Ben.

"I drank a whole bunch of Gatorade every chance I got," said Billy.

"No, before that. You said 'that man'? Wasn't he one of your coaches?"

"He's from here in town," said the coach. "His name is Chuck. He said the high school provides Gatorade for the boys to—"

"Can you call your people and have someone find Billy's bottle?" said Amy. "Have them bring it here right now. Tell them not to drink from it. It may contain a poison. Billy, where did you leave the bottle?"

"I dropped it off on the sidelines. The bottle had my name on it."

"What did it say?" said Ben.

"It said 'Sinclair' in big letters right on the bottle," Billy said.

"I'll make the call," said Coach, cell phone in his hand. He walked outside the room.

Ben followed him. "We need the police to collect it. There may be fingerprint evidence on the bottle. Go ahead and call, but tell everybody not to touch it. Just keep it where it is and safe. Got that? Nobody touches it." Coach nodded and proceeded with his call. Ben looked at his wife, who had accompanied the men into the area outside Billy's hospital room. "Amy, let me see your camera. There may be a picture of the Gatorade man."

"Ben, I'm scared," said Amy, handing the camera to Ben.

"Here he is," said Ben. He reentered the room. The others followed him. "Son, take a look at this picture. Is this the man who gave you the Gatorade?"

"Yes," said Billy.

"Is he also the guy who got you at the hospital and drove you out to the soccer field?" said Ben.

"Yes," answered Billy. "The same man. Chuck."

"Goddamn bastard," he said, dialing on his cell phone. "This son of a bitch poisoned you."

15

The jog through the park had been grueling, and the cross-country team members were feeling praiseworthy. There was a lake with calm, clear water on which ducks swam. Despite the inviting weather, the park had remained practically unvisited at this time of day. Near the lake's edge, there were thick woods, providing ample shade and serenity to several park benches. A couple was sitting on one of the seats. The lady gazed lovingly into the man's eyes.

"Nice job, guys. I think we shaved off almost a minute this time," said Kevin.

"Are we running tomorrow?" asked Kyle.

"Yeah, let's meet by the lake at noon tomorrow."

"Hey guys, look at those two lovebirds over there," said Mitch.

"Get a room," said Kyle.

"This lake smells awful today," said Mitch.

"Is it coming from over there?" said Kyle. "Where those two are sitting?"

"Have you guys noticed how those people haven't moved an inch since we've been here?" said Kevin. "What's that dripping underneath the bench?" Kevin ran toward the couple, cautiously at first, but at full force later. The other boys followed him.

"Sir, ma'am, are you okay?" said Kevin, now a few feet from the bench. He suddenly stopped cold as the dripping crimson had the definite stench of congealed blood. "Call 911 right now. Anybody have a cell phone?"

"I do," said Mitch. "I'm dialing."

As a premed student and a volunteer first-responder, Kevin knew what to do. He reached for a pulse on the man's neck. The couple was positioned in a mock embrace. As he pulled on the man, both bodies fell off the bench and thumped against the grass heavily. She was wearing a red dress and he a dark blue warm-up jogging outfit. The clothes had been torn, exposing portions of their abdomens. Kevin tugged on the garments. Large gashes were surrounded by bloodstains in the right upper portion of the victims' bellies. The boys were arriving at the bench, one by one. Two averted their eyes. Several others began to dry heave and walked over to the lake's shore.

"No pulse here," Kevin said, quickly moving on to the woman. "Any of you know CPR? The man is still a little warm. He may have been stabbed recently. The woman is long gone. She's cold and very dead." Kevin knelt down near the man and began to compress the breastbone rhythmically.

One of the boys retreated to throw up near the lake. Four others followed him and did the same. Then another. The other boys looked away into the woods, retching.

"Were these two stabbed by the killer we've been hearing about on TV?" said Mitch once he stopped dry heaving.

"Probably," said Kyle.

"Where's that damn ambulance? And the police?" yelled Kevin.

"They're coming," said Mitch. "The dispatcher said they'd be here in a few minutes."

"Look at these drag marks coming from the woods back here," said Kyle. "Looks like the killer dragged these two onto this bench and staged them like this."

"What a sick mind," said Mitch. He got on his knees and began throwing up again. "I can't believe this sick bastard would—"

"Where's that ambulance?" yelled Kevin again, continuing to rhythmically press down on the victim's breastbone.

An approaching siren could be heard in the distance. Then another. And another.

"One-one-thousand, two-one-thousand, three-one-thousand . . ."

16

"Let's review what we already know," said Lela to the newly convened task force. Behind her, there was a corkboard where multiple pictures were hung, stuck in place by pins. "We have three homicides now, all over the last eight days. There are also eleven people missing, starting approximately two months ago." She pointed to the photos behind her. "Before people went missing, there were multiple pets that mysteriously disappeared from here in town and surrounding areas, including dogs, cats, pigs, parrots, guinea pigs, and ferrets. These animal abductions began about three months ago." She walked around in the front of the large room and looked outside one of the two windows. "I believe these abductions of pets and humans are all from one doer. One goddamn mass murderer. I further believe all the missing are dead and missing a gallbladder. It looks like this killer injects his victims with some paralyzing chemical, kills them, then cuts their abdomen open with a scalpel. He obviously has had surgical training of sorts. He may be a surgeon, a veterinarian, a nurse or surgical tech. He knows anatomy and has good surgical skills. He removes the gallbladder, which he then takes with him."

"Do we know why he takes the gallbladder?" asked one of the officers, his hand still in the air.

"The usually theory in these circumstances is that the killer does it to keep a souvenir. A keepsake. Something to remember his act by. Personally, I believe the bastard has a special goal in mind with the gallbladders. Some research project, maybe. Some experiment."

"Maybe he likes his coffee with toast and gallbladder," someone said, sending the room into laughter. All except Lela.

"Do you think this is funny, Sergeant?" she scolded. "Get the fuck out of my sight. You're off this case. You're on desk duty for the next two weeks. Let's see if you think that's funny." She slowly scanned the room, which was now hushed. "Any more funny guys?" The man exited the room with a backward glance and noiselessly closed the door behind him. Silence continued to reign.

"I have put all of my soul into solving these murders," continued Lela. "I have not been able to sleep, eat, shit, or screw normally since it all started. And I'm getting pretty tired and cranky. This is real serious, people." Her double-barrel gaze scanned the room, side to side. "We don't really know why he removes the gallbladders or what he does with them afterward. We do know he removes the gallbladder postmortem. As you can see in the pictures on the board behind me, he leaves the gash open for all to see. He doesn't take the time to suture the wound. That tells me he feels no remorse. This is just his way of telling us he's in control. That says he's narcissistic. We know he uses surgical-grade gloves, and his surgical tools appear to be professional-grade as well. Not concocted at home."

"Where does he get the surgical instruments?" asked one of the cops. "Have we looked into that? There can't be that many places that sell those things."

"With the Internet, you can get anything, from anywhere in the world. That said, the most probable place for him to have gotten surgical instruments is the hospital here in town. I checked with the Heartland's surgery department. Unfortunately, they don't keep close track of their instruments, so if a few things went missing, they wouldn't necessarily detect it. And they haven't missed anything, but it doesn't mean he's not getting his stuff from there." Several cops nodded, some took notes. "We know he's precise and organized. He's escalating, which is really bad news for us. This morning, he killed a doctor in a hotel room. The hotel itself was crowded, which tells me he is getting more daring. More systematized. The doctor was in town to deliver a lecture at the med center." Lela paced in front of the conference room. "He's highly intelligent. He's quick and strong. He overpowers his victims rapidly and easily. There have been no defensive marks and no tissue recovered from fingernails on any of the vics. He's not interested in rape. None of the vics have been violated. All his kills and presumed abductions have been within thirty miles of the city. So he lives here. Probably works here at either a medical or veterinary facility. My money is on Heartland

Regional, specifically their surgical department. I have three female FBI agents posing as surgical nurses stationed there, but so far this has not produced any leads."

"Does he work alone? Could there be more than one bad guy here?" Austin said.

"All the signs at all the crime scenes and the profile indicate a single assassin. I also profile the unsub to be a man in his thirties or forties and with a lot of psychopathology. He's grandiose, delusional, and on a mission. These features are a really bad combo. He probably believes, deep down, that he's doing humanity a great favor. He sees his victims as useful tools for his endeavors."

"Do we know why the incidents started three months ago? Any precipitating factors? For that matter, why is he escalating?" said one of the officers.

"No ideas about that yet. But there definitely would have been some precipitating factor that led him to derail and begin the killing spree. He may have lost someone special, someone that anchored him to reality before. This person may have left him, moved away, or died. The FBI is pursuing the strong possibility that there was an event that threw him over the edge. So far, zilch. He may have moved to this area when the murders began, which will make finding out these things near impossible. There have been no murders with this MO reported in the state, national, or international databases. So he appears to be homegrown. We're hoping he'll make a mistake soon, but so far he's been very careful. No evidence at all left behind in any of the crime scenes has been helpful. He appears well-informed about criminology and may have worked in the law enforcement field or forensic pathology before or even now."

"Any idea as to how long it'll take to ID the presumed poison?" Austin asked.

"No. We have the local lab at Heartland Regional working on this as well as the FBI lab in Chicago. We think the agent incapacitates or paralyzes the—"

A woman opened the door in the front of the room, stuck her head in, and said, "Lieutenant, there's an urgent message for you." She handed a piece of paper to Lela. She read it, crumpled up the note, and threw it into the trash bin. "Goddamn it!" she yelled. "The son of a bitch just killed two more."

17

Billy watched TV, a pale, unhealthy appearance slowly spreading all over his face.

"We have to let the police know what we know," said Ben looking at Amy. "We need to let them know we have his picture."

"Ben, we're not getting involved with the investigation. Let the local police do that."

"Yes, yes. I know. I'm trying to get the local police to pick up the Gatorade bottle and analyze it. There may be fingerprint evidence on it. When the lead detective calls me back, I'll just let him know what we know. I'll e-mail him the picture. But I'm having difficulty connecting with him. I'll call the station again." Ben left the room as one of the nurse walked in.

"How are you doing, young man?" the nurse said.

"Okay, I guess."

"We'll be taking you for the MRI in a few minutes. They're coming up to take you downstairs. After the scan, they'll bring you right back here."

"I hope this test will give you some clues to figure out what's wrong with me," said Billy.

"How's that nausea? Did that medicine I gave you start to work?"

"The nausea is a little bit better, but my breathing is getting worse."

"You didn't tell me that before," Amy said.

"I need to take deep breaths a lot. I feel like I'm running and have to breathe deep and fast," said Billy.

"Let me listen to your lungs," said the nurse, placing the stethoscope on his back. "Deep breaths, in and out." She listened. "There is more wheezing in there. I'll see if your doctor wants to give you a breathing treatment to open up your airways."

"Thanks," said Billy.

"I'll page Dr. Jenner," said the nurse. She may want to order a pulmonary consultation. I'll be right back."

"Will you tell her I'm also spitting up a lot of spit. It's getting harder for me to swallow."

"Sure, I'll let her know. I want to resolve these issues before you go down for your MRI test." The nurse left the room briskly.

"You can't swallow at all now? When did that get worse?" said Amy, looking at Billy.

"Just a few minutes ago. I've been making a lot of spit for a few minutes for some reason. My mouth fills up. I can swallow a little, but it's hard, and I can't swallow fast enough. Can I get a cup to spit into?" Amy brought a plastic cup near Billy, and he began to expel a large amount of saliva.

Ben walked in. "What's going on?" he said.

"Billy is having difficulty swallowing, and he's more short of breath. The nurse is paging Dr. Jenner."

"How's the nausea?" asked Ben.

"It's still there. Maybe a little bit better," said Billy.

"We're going to transfer you to ICU, and I'll get a pulmonologist and an intensivist to see you on consult," said Dr. Jenner approaching Billy's bedside.

"What do they do? Those other doctors?" said Billy.

"The pulmonologist is a lung specialist. The intensivist is an ICU specialist," said Dr. Jenner.

"That means I'm very sick?" asked Billy.

"We don't really know why you got sick yet. And new symptoms are appearing at a fast rate. So I want to get as many doctors on your case as I can. The more heads we can put together, the better, don't you think?"

Billy nodded, a combination of concern and disgust engulfing his face.

"All of us will work hard and as fast as we can to help you get better soon. I promise. Now, these people are going to transfer you to a stretcher and wheel you downstairs to the intensive care unit." She looked at the nurses. "And no wheelies on the way there." Billy smiled. "I'll see you there in a few minutes."

"What about the MRI?" said Amy.

"We'll wait on that for right now. I want to stabilize him first."

The nurse came in with several of her cohorts. A mask with oxygen was placed on Billy's face. In no time, he was on his way toward the elevator. Ben and Amy conversed with Dr. Jenner and two newly arrived physicians, Dr. Claude Messing, an intensivist, and Dr. Marlene Mathis, a pulmonologist. Quick introductions were made.

"Dr. Jenner filled us in on the details of your son's case. I understand Billy's been very healthy until today. Is that right?" asked Dr. Mathis. Amy nodded in agreement.

"Does your son use drugs?" said Dr. Messing.

"No, never," said Amy. Ben shook his head.

"Sometimes the parents are the last to find out about these things," said Natalie.

"Soccer is his life, and he would never jeopardize that," said Ben.

"This whole situation sounds like acute poisoning," said Amy, trying to sound professional but all along fighting a feeling of doom.

"I agree. Organophosphates are the strongest of all possibilities," said Dr. Messing. "I'm going to give him a trial dose of pralidoxime. We'll see if he improves with that."

"Improves with what?" asked Ben.

"We're all in agreement that Billy was most likely poisoned," said Dr. Messing. "Of the strongest possibilities are a group of agents known as organophosphates. These are used for many purposes, mostly as pesticides. We're going to administer a drug intravenously to see if Billy gets better. It's a trial. A test dose. If he improves, we'll know we're on the right track."

"We'll send out tests and keep at this until we see results," said Dr. Mathis. "I have a son Billy's age. I know how you must be feeling, Dr. and Mr. Sinclair. We'll do everything in our power to help Billy. You can count on that." The doctors stepped away from the group.

Ben and Amy entered Billy's ICU cubicle.

"Mom, Dad, I don't feel so good," said Billy.

The monitor overhead began chirping loudly.

"His BP is dropping," said a nurse. "Page Dr. Mathis, Dr. Messing, or Dr. Jenner stat. Something bad is going on, and we need them here right now."

"I'm on it," said another nurse disappearing from sight.

The damn bastard who poisoned you will pay, thought Ben. *He will pay dearly.* The couple was escorted out to the waiting room by a nurse.

More nursing staff entered the ICU, pagers yelling in unison. The longer the alarms persisted, the greater the activity entering the small room.

"The BP is dropping fast," Ben and Amy heard the nurse yell out. "Where the hell are those doctors? We need to do something, and we need to do it now!"

18

Miranda and a pathology tech were working on Dr. Dill's postmortem when Lela walked into the autopsy suite.

"You have to see this, Lela," said Miranda.

"I can't wait," said Lela. "What did the son of a bitch do now?"

"Look in here," said Miranda shining a flashlight into the right upper quadrant gash, its edges fully retracted.

"What am I looking at?" said Lela, putting on a gown and rubber gloves. "What are those? Numbers?" She got close enough to peer into the cavernous abdominal wound. "No, looks like letters."

"They're numbers and letters," said Miranda.

"What does this say?" said Lela, gazing deeply into the cavity. "A-M-V-S-I-M or N. N, I think. Then C-I-A-I, no, C-L-A-I-P? What's all that mean?"

"It says: AMY SINCLAIR," said Miranda.

"Then there's a series of numbers underneath the letters?" she said. Lela looked up at Miranda. "Now, you're gonna tell me you have that figured out too, right?"

"You know it."

"I'm telling you, the shit I see in this job. I have gotten messages from perps, but never engraved on a liver. That is the liver, isn't it?"

"Yes."

"I guess this is a livergram," said Lela. "Never got one of those before."

"The letters and numbers were seared in postmortem with a cautery pen. The numbers are a phone number. I looked up the number. It belongs to a researcher named Dr. Amy Sinclair from Zionsville, Indiana."

Lela took out her pen and copied the name and phone number on her notebook. She started to walk toward the door. "Oh, doc, there are a couple of dead bodies coming your way. They'll be here soon. We're working on identifying them now. I'd like you to help us first with the ID."

"Let me guess, they are gallbladderless."

"You guessed it. Let me know if there are any other messages for me inside these bodies." Shaking her head in disbelief, Lela stepped out of the autopsy room, leaving Miranda and the tech to return to the business of gathering clues from the dead body on their table.

Four floors up, Billy had stabilized with IV medications to augment the dropping blood pressure. Ben and Amy were again at his bedside. Ben stepped out of Billy's ICU room, his cell phone to his ear.

"If I could just speak to a detective, this is a very important—"

"Sir, all the detectives are extremely busy right now," said the police operator. "I'll have an officer speak with you as soon as possible, and he'll fill out a report. It may be later today or even tomorrow until I can get someone to follow up on this."

"I called earlier today, and I'm still waiting on someone to get back to me from that call. I want to make sure you understand this is important, and it can't wait," said Ben.

"We're doing the best we can. It's been very busy around here."

Amy stepped out of Billy's room looking at her cell phone. She showed him the display, the caller ID box showing *Blocked ID*. He wrinkled his forehead as she walked away.

"Look, goddamn it," said Ben. "This is all bullshit. There's a grave situation here, and I need—"

He suddenly looked at the cell phone screen. "Goddamn it! The bitch hung up on me."

"This is Lieutenant Lela Rose of the Danville Police Department. That's Danville, Illinois," said the woman's voice in Amy's ear. "I am a detective. I need to talk to you, immediately."

"You need to talk to *me*? Aren't you looking for my husband? Ben Sinclair?" Ben approached her with squinting eyes. "My husband has been trying to get a hold of you for a while, but what could you possibly need to talk to me about? Is this about my husband's report?"

"What kind of report?" said Lela.

"My husband called your headquarters about two hours ago and again a few minutes ago. In fact, he was on the phone with your dispatcher when your call came in."

"He needs to talk to a detective in Danville, Illinois? Aren't you in Zionsville, Indiana? That's your hometown, right?"

"We're visiting Danville. I—"

"Where are you now?" said Lela.

"At Heartland Regional Hospital. In ICU."

"I'll be right there."

19

They were sitting in a corner of the ICU waiting room. There were other small groups of people in the large area but none close enough to overhear their conversation.

"Dr. and Detective Sinclair, I didn't call you in response to your previous report." Amy looked at Ben. Lela continued, "Dr. Sinclair, your name and phone number were gathered in connection with the ongoing investigation of a series of murders here in town. Let's just say that your contact info was left on the last victim, who was murdered earlier today."

"Well, I hope you can rule us both out pretty quickly," said Ben. "We've never been to Danville, Illinois, until today. We arrived around nine this morning. You have to believe that if I or my wife were the murderer, we wouldn't leave her name and phone number on the body."

"I'm sure you can appreciate my obligation to decide for myself who is and is not a suspect in my own investigation," said Lela. "But for now, Dr. Sinclair, I am intrigued as to how you fit into this whole scheme. There must be some connection between you and the killer. Any ideas?"

"Ben, tell her about what has happened to us since we've arrived," said Amy.

Ben began. Amy felt herself pulled into what was becoming a horrible ordeal, like the sensation you'd get from the strong pull into the path of a rushing train. She felt her heart thumping hard. *Why us?* she thought. Ben's words seemed surreal, like someone telling of a nightmare.

"Did you know Dr. James Dill?" said Lela.

"Never heard of him until today," said Amy. She looked at Ben, who was shaking his head.

"You don't seem so sure," said Lela.

"I'm sure."

"This is crazy," said Ben. "The hesitancy you hear in my wife's words is due to the tremendous stress she's under. We're all under. Our son was poisoned today by some madman and may be on his deathbed."

"Okay," said Lela. "I understand."

"The man who arranged our visit to Danville gave the name Pat Tetrodo, but no one at Heartland has ever heard of him," said Ben. "We've learned his name is Chuck somebody—Pickens or Perkins. He's the one who poisoned our son by having him drink from a Gatorade bottle." Ben produced a picture he had printed off the digital camera from his pocket and handed it to Lela. "Here's his picture."

"Where's the bottle now?" said Lela, her eyes examining the picture.

"It's still on the soccer field at the high school. It needs to be bagged for evidence and its contents analyzed," said Ben.

"I'm on it," Lela said, fishing her cell phone from her pocket. The detective walked off a few feet and began issuing orders on her phone. Ben looked at Amy and tried to force a smile. When Lela hung up her cell, she returned to them.

"Any thoughts as to why or how the murderer would have your personal cell phone number, Dr. Sinclair?" asked Lela.

"I don't know. But I do give it out freely," said Amy.

"Somehow, the killer wanted you two and me to connect," said Lela. "But why?"

"I don't know," said Amy.

"I think our meeting, in a way, was inevitable," said Ben. "You're the lead detective on the murders, and we're one of the latest victims."

"That's true, but then he's forcing the timing of our meeting on us." Lela sat down and crossed her legs. "Do you have any enemies, Dr. Sinclair?"

"Not that I know of."

"I'm thinking the mysterious Mr. Tetrodo is this Chuck character. I think he was the one who arranged our trip here and the man who poisoned our son," said Ben. "And he's got to be your murderer."

"Nothing's that easy," said Lela. "But I now know the identity of one of the dead bodies on the way to the morgue."

"You think the man who poisoned Billy is dead?" asked Amy.

"Yes, I had an unidentified dead male body found in the park a few hours ago. That man is the man in your picture. There was a woman with him that remains unidentified, but I bet I know who she is now." Lela touched her chin. "By the way, how did you find out the man's name?"

"He told Billy and the Zionsville soccer team coaching staff," said Ben.

"That's something I will look into. He may have lied about his name, but—"

"Dr. and Mr. Sinclair," a woman said from the doorway.

Ben and Amy immediately got up on their feet and gazed at Billy's nurse.

"Billy's condition has deteriorated. His doctors need to talk to you right away."

"Take my card," said Lela handing it to Ben. "Keep me in the loop."

20

"We've administered pralidoxime, but it had no effect at all," said Dr. Messing. "Billy continues to display progressive worsening of his symptoms of nausea, increased salivation, difficulty swallowing, numbness, sweating, and shortness of breath. His diffuse muscle weakness has also progressed, and we've begun to worry about his breathing efficiency."

"What does all that mean?" asked Ben.

"It doesn't look like organophosphate poisoning is the problem," said Amy enveloping Ben's trembling hands in hers. "What's the next step?"

"We'll get the brain MRI now, then an EEG," said Dr. Jenner. "We've ordered more blood work. When these tests are completed, we'd like to perform a lumbar puncture. This will allow us to analyze the fluid around Billy's brain for clues."

"Meanwhile, we'll keep a close eye on him," said Dr. Mathis. "It's not looking good."

Billy looked puny. His color was ashen, and he appeared as frail as they had ever seen him.

"How are you feeling?" said Amy.

"Not too good, Mom," said Billy, holding both an empty emesis basin and a box of tissues. "Thank heavens for this puke bucket. I never again will leave home without it."

"Well, your sense of humor still works," said Amy.

"The doctors are doing a whole bunch of tests to figure out what's wrong with you and make you feel better, okay?" said Ben. "I need you to stay strong."

"Okay, Dad. I will."

"We'll get to the bottom of all this," said Amy, squeezing his arm. She smiled.

"How come you and the other doctors can't figure out what's wrong with me?" said Billy.

Amy swallowed hard and looked at her trembling hands as she grabbed the bedrails.

"Sometimes, people have unusual and rare symptoms that aren't so easy to figure out," said Ben. Amy nodded, trying not to break down and cry.

"I understand," said Billy.

"We'll figure you out, Billy," said Amy, her words tremulous.

"I know."

"I'm going to find the man who poisoned you and make him pay for what he did to you, Billy. To us." Ben forced a smile.

"What will you do to him when you find him, Dad?"

"I'll make him drink the poison and see how he likes it."

"Okay," whispered Billy.

"We'll be right back," said Amy. "We'll just step out a minute." The couple left the cubicle.

The couple arrived in the waiting room.

"I'm going down to the research laboratory and organize a research team to work to find an antidote to save Billy," said Amy.

"Oh no you're not," said Ben. "The crazy son of a bitch who poisoned Billy is unlikely to have known him. I'm betting that he probably did it to get back at either me or you. Maybe both. I'm going to get the police to guard this room, and you're staying with Billy. I need to know both of you are safe and protected."

"Ben, I'm the head of a research laboratory. I need to be doing something to save our son."

"I understand how you feel, Amy, but absolutely not. I'll be damned if I lose my son and wife in this godforsaken ordeal." He put his arms around Amy, who began sobbing.

"I have to, Ben," said Amy. "I have to . . ." Her words trailed off into a sob, tears now running down her face.

Ben wiped her tears. "Billy has a hospital full of doctors and researchers, but only one mom." He looked deeply into her eyes and smiled. "He's lucky to have you as a mom. And I'm lucky to have you as a wife and life companion." Amy continued to cry. "I'll go organize the researchers and get them working on an antidote. You, do not leave Billy's side."

"Go, then," said Amy. "Go assemble a research team right now."

"I'll call Dr. Hughes," said Ben.

"They'll have to start from scratch and work fast. I'm not sure Billy will survive the night."

"How long do you think we have?" said Ben.

Amy swallowed and took a deep breath, her eyes swollen and red. "I think Billy has less than ten hours to live." Amy began to cry again. The two hugged. "And find the bastard responsible for poisoning our boy?" Ben nodded. "Go, Ben. Go find a cure for Billy."

21

Amy and Ben reentered the cubicle and stood there a moment looking at Billy. He looked depleted of any energy, his eyes closed.

Ben broke the silence, "I'll go now. Call me right away if anything changes."

Ben walked by the nurse's station.

"Detective Sinclair," said Billy's nurse. "I can fix it so that you can access Billy's room on your smartphone and see his progress any time you'd like." She pointed to the video feeds displayed on the computer screen in front of her. "Here's Billy in ICU-3." With her pen, she pointed to the third square from the top. "There are cameras mounted high on the wall in front of each ICU bed. We use this Internet-based system to keep an eye on our patients when we're not in the room. I can set you up to get real-time visual feeds from Billy's room, if you'd like."

"That would be so tremendously helpful," said Ben.

"It'll only take a sec," she said taking his mobile. She pressed a series of buttons and gave him a smile while waiting. "All done." She handed the phone back to him.

Ben looked at the display. He saw Billy's bed, his monitors and Amy sitting by his side.

Ben entered the staircase. He took another glimpse at Billy and Amy displayed on his iPhone. Billy's eyes were still shut. He had an oxygen mask around his face. Several IV bottles peeked down on the bed. Amy sat patiently holding on to Billy's hand. Above his bed, a series of monitors enunciated the rest of the growing heartbreaking drama: blood pressure, 78 over 42; heart rate, 98; oxygen saturation, 91 percent.

Ben could plainly see that the blood pressure and oxygen levels were trending downward, while the heart rate, upward. He turned off the Internet function and continued down the stairs.

"I will find you," whispered Ben to himself. "And when I do, you will tell me the exact identity of the poison, and you will give me the antidote. And you will pay for this. Make no mistake about that."

Ben dialed a number on his cell phone.

"Dr. Hughes, this is Ben Sinclair," he said into the phone. "I don't know if you are aware of it, but my son, Billy, is in ICU here at Heartland. He's been poisoned. Amy and I desperately need your help. We need for you and your people to find the identity of the poison and its antidote. Billy is going downhill fast."

"Let me arrange a meeting in thirty minutes in the research laboratory conference room," said Tim. "I'll gather my main laboratory researchers. We need to coordinate our efforts and plan our strategy."

Ben called Lela and told her about the upcoming meeting.

"I'll be there," said Lela.

"Also, Lela," said Ben. "I need a favor. Will you have your guys guard my son and wife in ICU? I have a strange feeling the bastard will try to get at them."

"I already dispatched several men up there for round-the-clock surveillance."

As Ben was being introduced to the team sitting around the table, a wave of hope came upon him. This hope was the first positive thing that he had experienced in several hours. It was a feeling he desperately craved. At the table were Lieutenant Lela Rose, Dr. Tim Hughes, and Jack Stevenson, a man in a wheelchair, the main tech at National Bioresearch Institute.

As Ben looked around the table, the door to the conference room suddenly opened. All eyes turned to the entrance.

"Terri, are you well enough to be here?" said Tim when he saw the woman.

"Nothing wrong with my brain, Tim." She was being wheeled in by a younger woman wearing a white lab coat who sat down at the table next to the newly arrived older lady once she was situated at the table.

"Ben, this is Dr. Miranda Phillips," said Tim. "She is the main pathologist here at Heartland and the county's medical examiner." Miranda and Ben exchanged a handshake and a smile.

"Thanks for being here," said Ben.

"And this is Dr. Terri Phillips, who happens to be Miranda's mother," continued Tim. "Terri is my predecessor. She created and ran the research facility here for decades until she retired about nine months ago when I took over."

"Miranda told me about you and your son," said Terri. "I know Amy from research meetings. I'll speak for everyone here when I say that we'll do everything in our power to help Billy." Ben nodded. "You're wondering about the hospital pajamas. I've developed pneumonia and dehydration. I'm all better and going home in a couple of more days."

"We have theorized that the mass murderer we've been looking for and the man who poisoned Billy are one and the same," said Lela.

"The first step is to definitively identify the poison," said Miranda.

"I've been talking to Dr. Amy Sinclair," said Tim. "She's been at her son's bedside and regrets not being able to be here working the problem with us. She and I did a computer search for every database possible for the type of poison that could be producing Billy's symptoms. She and I believe that the tetrodotoxin family fits the best given the clinical symptomatology."

"I hope that's not the case," said Terri. "Tetrodotoxins have no known antidotes."

"It just dawned on me," said Ben. "The man who tricked us into coming to Danville gave the name of Pat Tetrodo. I just made the connection with tetrodotoxin."

"Unfortunately, I am in full agreement with your impressions," said Jack. "I discovered this morning that the poison is in fact a sodium channel blocker of the tetrodotoxin family."

"There are no simple tests available to make the diagnosis," said Terri. "Perhaps a good first step might be to develop a quick test to verify tetrodotoxin exposure."

"I'll work on that," said Miranda.

"The killer seems to be paralyzing the victims rapidly," said Lela.

"Billy seems to be suffering from similar symptoms but not as acutely," noted Tim.

"We believe that the poison has been injected into the murdered victims by the killer, which explains why it acts so quickly," said Miranda. "Beginning within seconds. In Billy's case, the poison was administered orally mixed in a large bottle of Gatorade, therefore the slower onset of action."

"Is it expected to have milder consequences?" asked Ben.

"Unfortunately, no," said Terri. "I'm afraid tetrodotoxin is as dangerous when administered orally. It'll just be slower in taking its effects."

"Jack, what do you need to come up with an antidote quickly?" said Tim.

"A nanosequencer and a lot of prayers," said Jack.

"I think I can provide both, said Ben. "My wife's research facility in Zionsville, Indiana has a nanosequencer. It's the size of a large suitcase with wheels. I'll get it here for your use within a couple of hours."

"Bring it," said Jack. "The nanosequencer will speed things up a thousandfold."

Ben removed his cell phone from his pocket.

"Is Dr. David Robertson still in Zionsville?" said Jack.

"He's one of the main researchers there," said Ben.

"I'm sure he could be helpful, and he's probably proficient with the NanoTech unit. Do you think you might be able to persuade him to come along and help us?"

"I know he would, if Amy asks him." Ben moved away from the group, cell phone in hand.

"Jack, I'd like you to give me some tetrodotoxin," said Terri.

"You want the actual poison?" said Jack "Why?"

"Watching from the sidelines just isn't my style," said Terri. "I'd like to do some of my own experimentation and see if I can devise an antidote."

"I'm surprised you like to get your hands dirty, Terri," said Tim. "As a lab director for many years, I love the thinking and organizational part, but I have long forgotten the actual day-to-day laboratory work."

"I love to research and experiment—get my hands dirty, as you say. You can't do that at board meetings. You have to get out the test tubes and beakers, the Bunsen burners, the centrifuges, and the microscopes," she said, smiling. "I won't get in your way, Jack. I can work in the microbiology lab, in the next wing over, if it's okay with you, Tim. That lab should have all the equipment I need, and it'll be deserted after six tonight." Tim nodded.

"I'll get you tetrodotoxin," said Jack. "Let me know if you come up with something. The more heads we have working on the antidote, the better."

"Speaking of heads," said Tim, "our lab technicians, secretaries, and other supporting staff are about to go home for the evening. Do we need anybody to stay longer?"

"I work alone," said Jack. "I don't mind Dr. Robertson. He brings a lot to the table, and I need that. As far as doing the benchwork, I prefer to work alone."

"I may need some muscle in the morgue to help with moving bodies and the physical work," said Miranda. "Can a couple of the morgue techs stay and—"

"If all you need is muscle power," said Lela, "my officers can provide that. I'd like to have as few people working in research and pathology as possible." Miranda nodded.

"Tim," said Lela. "I need to interview each of your lab workers before they leave the premises."

"I'll arrange that," said Tim. "But why?"

"Police business," she said.

Ben opened the door and spoke, "It's all done. A pilot buddy of mine will fly Dr. Robertson and the NanoTech here from Zionsville. They'll be here in a couple of hours."

"I'll have one of my men provide ground transportation from the airport to the hospital," said Lela.

"I need to get ready for the NanoTech interface with our equipment," said Jack, pushing off from the table, his wheelchair rolling back. "Let's get this show on the road! We don't have any time to waste."

22

"His breathing just seems so rough," whispered Ben to Amy. On the ICU bed in front of them, Billy lay exhausted, sleeping. "It seems like he's struggling with every breath."

"He is," she said. "It's gotten worse, little by little." The couple held hands. "Billy's loud wheezing with every exhalation is a really bad sign. It indicates that his airways are constricting due to the persistent effects of the poison." She looked from Billy to Ben then back at Billy. "The benefits of the inhaled medications are meager now, at best." The monitor above pronounced his blood oxygenation to be steadily declining, the minute-by-minute trend showing a downhill slope.

"What will happen?"

"It won't be long now that a tube will have to be placed into Billy's windpipe to help with his breathing. He'll be put on a respirator. His diaphragmatic muscles are weakening. Despite supplemental oxygen, Billy's saturation monitor now reads 87 percent. It should well over 90."

Billy opened his eyes.

"How are you feeling, son?" said Ben.

"Okay, Dad," came a fragile, croaky reply. "My mouth is numb, and my breathing is very short. It's like I'm running at a hundred miles per minute."

"The doctors have found the poison in your system, and they're working hard to find an antidote." said Ben.

"An antidote would be great." Billy attempted a smile. "An antidote and a Coke."

"Coming right up," said Ben.

"I feel sick to my stomach again," said Billy. He began to retch feebly. His nurse rushed in.

"Let me suction that stuff out of your mouth for you," said the nurse. She placed the catheter in Billy's mouth and pressed a button. Immediately, saliva entered the vacuum tube on its way to a large container at the bedside.

"Sorry. I'm too weak to do it now," said Billy. "My arm muscles can't lift that catheter anymore."

"Don't be sorry," said the nurse. She listened to his lungs. "I'm going to give you a medicine in your IV that will help dry up those secretions and reduce your nausea."

"Thank you," said Billy.

She felt his skin and examined the urine bag hanging on the side of the bed, recording all her findings on a handheld computer tablet.

"You'll feel better in no time," she said. "I'm also going to bump up the IV fluids and dopamine drip rate. BP is dropping again." She pointed to the monitor. The numbers read 82 over 36 on the blood pressure. The heart rate was 108. "We have all the results back for all the tests—head MRI, cerebrospinal fluid analysis, all routine blood and urine tests—everything completely normal."

"Great news," said Amy. The nurse left the cubicle, leaving the Sinclairs once again alone.

"What's going to happen to me, Mom?"

"Your muscles are being attacked by the poison," said Amy, her tender eyes soothing his. "The toxin makes all the muscles in your body weaker and weaker. That's why you can't breathe well, from your breathing muscles getting affected."

"Is that also the reason I can't swallow so well?" asked Billy.

She nodded. "Yes." Amy pointed to a number on the screen overhead presently at 82 percent. "You may require a respirator to help you breathe. If you do, the doctors will have to insert a tube into your breathing pipe and hook it up to this machine right here." She pointed to a bedside contraption the size of a microwave unit. "It's right here next to you on standby for now, in case you need it."

"I understand." With these words, Billy began to settle in and, within moments, fell asleep.

Ben abruptly got up and left the ICU. He walked briskly to the staircase. Witnessing his boy in this feeble condition made his blood boil, and he was starving for revenge. He needed to do something to help his son.

Please, God, help Billy pull through. Take me instead. His cell phone chimed.

"The officer just returned from the airport with Dr. David Robertson and the NanoTech unit," said Lela. "They're setting up the device in the research lab right now."

"Let's do this," said Ben. "We probably have less than eight hours now."

23

Ben entered the laboratory just in time to observe the finishing touches. The NanoTech was ready to work. And so were Jack and David.

Entering the lab, Ben spied something familiar and smiled. He saw the back part of the aquarium with countless strikingly colorful angelfish. From this vantage point, he couldn't see the beautiful underwater scenery he had observed earlier in the administrative office's waiting room with Billy, but a myriad of beautiful fish swam around the large tank peacefully.

"David, thanks for coming and bringing the NanoTech," he said. They shook hands.

"No problem, Ben," said David. "Tim, Miranda and Jack filled me in on everything, and I'm ready to go."

"We now have definitive confirmation that the poison Billy ingested orally is the same as the toxin injected by the murderer on the loose, which is a tetrodotoxins," said Miranda.

"Any ideas as to why the killer removes the gallbladders?" said David.

"My mother thinks . . ." Miranda smirked. "My mom is now retired from research, but—"

"Dr. Terri Phillips," said David. "You look a lot like her. I've attended many of her lectures over the years. I'm quite a fan, actually."

"Well, she thinks tetrodotoxin is metabolized by the liver. After hepatic processing, the metabolite exits the liver and concentrates in the gallbladder," said Miranda.

"In English," said Lela.

Miranda continued, "When the poison is injected, the liver breaks it down in a matter of a few minutes into a different compound. What this new chemical is or what it does is unknown, but that's what we have to find out first. That newly formed compound is probably maximally concentrated in the gallbladder. Our thinking is that the killer is collecting this material. For what reason, we have no clue."

"That explains why the killer waits for the victims to die before removing the gallbladder," said Lela. "Once they are incapacitated, which should happen quickly with injected poisoning, he would be free to extract the gallbladder right away. But it would be best to wait longer so the stuff accumulates in the gallbladder to the maximum."

"I agree," said Miranda.

"What if the drug is ingested orally?" asked Ben.

"The same things will happen, but at a much slower pace," said Miranda. "Over several hours, instead of minutes."

"If tetrodotoxin is quickly metabolized by the liver, why does it paralyze the victims and kill them?" asked Lela.

"We just don't really know yet," said Miranda. "This is a deadly poison with no antidote. There's not much research . . ." Her words trailed off into deep silence, her gaze now on Ben.

"When it paralyzes muscles, does it affect the heart muscle too?" said Ben.

"Eventually, yes," said David.

"We must understand the interaction of tetrodotoxin and the liver enzymes," said Tim. "That's our first order of business."

"I can do that," said Miranda. "In fact, I began doing so over an hour ago."

"I'll work with David to continue to analyze the samples we've collected from Billy and the murdered victims. Now that we have the nanosequencer, the process will be much quicker," said Jack, already wheeling himself away from the table.

"Let's go," said David.

"I'll make some calls and see if anyone in the research field has any interest in tetrodotoxin metabolism that might help us," said Tim. "I'll be in my office."

"We'll leave you to do your thing," said Ben. "Lela, will you walk out with me?"

The two pushed through the door and entered the hospital proper.

"What's on your mind?" asked Lela.

"I think the killer is in this hospital right now," said Ben. "Make sure this laboratory is guarded by your best men armed to the hilt."

"Let me remind you, Ben, you are not a detective in Danville, Illinois. Here you are just a civilian."

"No, I'm a victim. And I can help you."

"No way," said Lela. "You stay out of my way. This is my investigation, not yours." She looked Ben in the eye. "I know how you feel. But you let me do my job. I have your number. I'll call you if I need you. Go be with your family. They need you."

"You need cops in here," said Ben. "You need guns walking the halls, searching each room. Why won't you let me help you?"

"I don't need *your* help, Ben. I need you out of my fucking way."

"Like hell, I will," said Ben. "That's my son in that bed upstairs. Dying. I'm not just going to go hold his hand until you call."

"I better not have two god damn criminals to search for later today, Ben," said Lela. "So help me, I will put your ass in my jail faster than you can say *'Boo!'* Count on it." She walked away. "Don't get in my way."

24

Upstairs in her hospital room, Terri was already hard at work.

*   *   *

"Billy is deteriorating at a fast pace," said Miranda.

"How's your progress down in the research lab?" said Terri.

"Jack and David are working as fast as they can to come up with a solution to this whole ordeal. With nano technology, the process will be much faster, and we're all hoping and praying they'll come up with something positive and soon."

*   *   *

Armed with a calculator, a computer, and a notepad, Terri was determined to contribute. Countless numbers of scrap papers were strewn around her bed. She wrote complex chemical formulae on her papers as she progressed with her calculations.

"Assuming normal liver function and no other outside influences, the most probable hepatic transformation of the tetrodotoxin molecule is either," she spoke as she scribbled, "if the molecule is methylated, or this if it is acetylated first." She squinted her eyes briefly, wet her lips with her tongue, and then continued.

"Dr. Phillips," said Ruthie from the door. "You have been at this for an hour now. Can't you stop and rest a few minutes? I can see this whole thing is taking a toll on you."

"No time," said Terri. "I have to get downstairs to the lab to test out some of my theoretical work, but first I have to get it all down on paper."

"I know this is important to you, but—"

"It's extremely important to a great young man who needs my help right now. I'll take a break in a few minutes." Teri smiled.

"Dr. Phillips," said Ruthie. "You need your rest."

"My daughter asked me once, many years ago, if I'd ever saved someone's life," said Terri putting her pen on her paperwork. "She wondered if I'd ever myself saved a life. Do you know what I told her?" The nurse shook her head. "I told her I invent drugs that others use to save lives. But really, I never have. This is my chance. Once, before I die, I want to save a person's life. Is that too much to ask?"

Ruthie left the room and Terri picked up her pen once more. She analyzed the formulae she had inscribed on her papers, and began writing again.

Downstairs in the research lab, David and Jack were mixing reagents and chemicals and writing scientific observations and conclusions on a blackboard as they went.

"We're getting in the groove here," said David. "We need to learn all the facts about tetrodotoxin metabolism. That has to be the quickest way to develop a safe antidote."

"We'll be the first ones in the history of mankind to develop an antidote to tetrodotoxin," said Jack. Multiple vials of reagents were perched on the counter, numerous pieces of equipment, large and small, within reach.

"I wouldn't be surprised if the antidote won't have important clinical implications," said David. "It's very possible it can be used to treat different conditions."

"It's likely it'll have sodium-channel blocking properties, so I think you're right." Jack added the contents of a small bottle into a beaker and began to stir it.

"I'm amazed how much you can do," said David. "You know, given your disability and all." He put a drop of a green liquid onto a slide and placed it under a microscope."

"Due to the constraints imposed by a life confined to a wheelchair," said Jack, "when I was hired, the hospital's maintenance department manufactured these special table counters to allow me to perform my lab duties from a lower position. This way, I don't have to get in and out of a regular chair. I just wheel myself right to the table, like this," Jack smiled, demonstrating, "and I'm at work. I can reach these reagents and get to my microscope when I need to."

"They must like you around here."

"No, I'm just their token disabled research lab guy," said Jack.

Back in her room, Terri worked away diligently but alone, putting pencil to paper.

We must not allow the murderer to win this battle, she mused, her thoughts providing much needed energy to persevere. *Billy Sinclair will not die from this poison. Not while there's life in my body.*

Ruthie entered Terri's room and put her hands on her hips, her gaze on her patient. "Dr. Phillips," she said. "Really? Do I need to go get restraints? You said you'd take a break twenty minutes ago."

"I'm almost done with this theoretical analysis," said Terri. "I'll take a short nap and rest in a few minutes. Then I plan to go downstairs to the microbiology laboratory, where I need to verify a couple of the reaction steps in vitro. It's necessary to see if the theoretically likely is, in fact, reality."

"I don't think you have the strength to continue at this, Dr. Philips," said Ruthie. "I can read it in your eyes, in your face. You're exhausted!"

"Billy Sinclair will not die today. Not on my watch," Terri said. "I will not rest until I find a way to save his life."

"Speaking of saving lives," said Ruthie. "I spoke with your doctor earlier, and he agrees you shouldn't leave your room. I'll leave orders to not allow you to leave the unit even if restraints are needed to prevent it. When my shift is over, I'm placing an orderly with you all night to make sure you rest and quit this nonsense."

"Nonsense?" said Terri. "Are you kidding me? This isn't nonsense. I'm fighting to save a boy's life. Don't you understand that?"

"My responsibility, Dr. Phillips, is *your* life," said Ruthie. "Dr. Terri Phillips will not die on *my* watch."

25

"Captain Magee, I realize it's very late in the evening, but I need you to give me the dirt on your Detective Ben Sinclair," said Lela.

"Ben's my best detective," said Magee. "He and his family left to go to Danville earlier today for a soccer game and a medical conference. What's going on?"

"I'm investigating a series of murders. Ben and his family are part of my investigation. What can you tell me about Detective Sinclair and his wife?"

"Ben and Amy Sinclair are good people. He's a good cop. Good man."

"When was the last time he's been out of Zionsville before today, that you know of?"

"I've seen Ben every weekday and most weekends for the last six years, at least," said Magee. "Look, lieutenant, Ben's a caring, intelligent guy with over ten years on the force. I trust him with my life. You'd be a fool not to let him help you with your investigation, let alone suspect him of foul play."

Austin knocked on the door to the conference room adjacent to the Research Laboratory. Lela was sitting by the table reviewing papers inside folders labeled *Danville Police Department—Confidential.*

"Ruby, we're using this conference room as our command center here at the hospital," said Lela. "What did you find out?"

"The Boone County Sheriff's Department and the Indiana State Police both spoke highly of Sinclair as a person and as a cop," said

Austin. "They endorse him fully. Given his work schedule and weekend activities, it seems unlikely Detective Sinclair has been out of Zionsville, Indiana for the last three months."

"I spoke with two of his superiors at the Zionsville PD, and both say the same thing," said Lela.

"Are you going to ask him to help us?" said Austin.

"Hell no," said Lela, getting up. "This investigation is our job." She removed her holstered Glock and examined the clip. She reloaded the clip forcibly. "I want all entrances into this facility guarded. Nobody gets in or out without our okay."

"Yes, ma'am."

"Call the FBI, county and state police and have them send us as many bodies with guns as they can spare. I will speak to the hospital security chief."

Austin left the room and Lela fished her cell phone from her pocket.

There was a knock on the door.

"I looked you up," said Ben. Lela got up, squinted her eyes, and placed her hands on her hips, her gaze on Ben's. "Well, you're the primary investigator on a series of murders by a man that may very well turn out to be my son's killer. You're an impressive woman, Detective Lieutenant Lela May Rose. You have a PhD in criminology and behavioral sciences. Someday you'll have to tell me what you're doing in Danville, Illinois, instead of Washington or New York. But another day." He smiled at her. "I got a call from my superiors back home in Indiana, and I know you've been asking about me. Now that you know a lot more about me, I hope you've changed your mind about letting me help you with the investigation. What can I do?"

"Ben," said Lela, "I thought I had made that crystal clear. You are a cop in Indiana, but we are not in Indiana. As you yourself put it, you and your family are victims. Would you let a victim help you with a mass murder investigation?"

"Lela, you need all the help you—"

"I don't know how to make myself any clearer. The answer is no. Go upstairs. Be with your family. I'll let you know if anything interesting—"

"Are you fucking kidding me?" said Ben, looking her in the eye. "I can't believe this is happening." He paced around, like a lion behind bars. "I am not—"

"Joe," yelled Lela. In seconds, two police officers opened the door.

"Yes, Lieutenant," said one of them, both men carrying Heckler & Koch MP-5 semiautomatic rifles in their hands.

"Escort Detective Sinclair up to ICU," said Lela sitting back down, her eyes already on the paperwork on the table.

"Yes, Lieutenant," said one of the cops, his hand on Ben's arm.

"Lela, you're making a big mistake," said Ben. "I can—"

"He won't be needing the handgun strapped to his left ankle while he's in my town." The cop that wasn't holding Ben's arm frisked Ben's lower left leg, then lifted up his pant leg. He undid the strap and confiscated the small pistol, which he handed to Lela. She briefly analyzed the weapon, removed the clip, then placed both in her pocket.

"I'm a cop just like you," said Ben. "I can't believe—"

"I'll let you slide this time, Ben," said Lela, calmly. "Call it professional courtesy."

"Why won't you let me help?" said Ben. "This doesn't make any sense."

"You might not have known, but it's illegal to carry a gun in Illinois without a proper permit issued by the State of Illinois. I'm willing to bet you don't have one of those, do you?"

"Lela, you are making a huge mistake."

"You can have your peashooter back when you leave town."

"Lela, I'm a police detective," said Ben. "I can help you with this murder investigation."

"Really," said Lela. "How many murder investigations have you been on?" She smirked. Ben looked down at his feet. "You forgot? Well, let me remind you. One. One, you created." She pointed right at Ben's chest, her index a few inches from him. "A woman was killed by her drunk husband because you didn't pick up on the signs."

"That's a cheap shot," said Ben, moving side to side. The two cops held his arms tighter.

"You were investigating the abuse for weeks, and the signs were all there. You missed them. Now, she's dead."

"I can't believe you'd—"

"Do I need your help?" said Lela, her head shaking slowly. "Men, take him up to ICU. Make sure he stays up there in his son's ICU room. He can't leave there without my permission."

"You're making a big mistake, Lela," yelled Ben.

"If he gives you any trouble, cuff him and place him under arrest for obstruction."

"Yes, Lieutenant," said both men. They walked out the door.

"This is a free country," said Ben, his words barely audible now. "You can't detain me without cause. And you need me down here to help . . ."

A few minutes later, Austin arrived. Lela took a seat, placed the files she was reviewing on the table, and gestured for him to sit down.

"The killer has to be a medical person, someone with a strong research and surgical aptitude," said Austin. "We can't trust anyone working in that lab or anywhere in this hospital."

"Yes, I agree," said Lela. "I think the killer is in this facility, right now, and he won't get out alive. We'll find him."

"The facility is huge, and there are a lot of places to hide," said Austin. "The hospital's security department is bringing in as many men as can shoot a gun decent. We're getting help from the county and state police and the FBI. With the cops, we can recruit ourselves in a pinch from Danville PD, altogether, I'm counting on getting twenty-two officers in here within the hour. Beyond that, we'll get another twenty, maybe twenty-five, but not for at least three or four hours."

"Hell, it'll be all over by then," said Lela.

"I've placed teams made up of police and security officers at all the exits. They all know what to do. Visiting hours were over at eight o'clock. It's now almost nine-twenty. It's hospital policy to lock most of the outside-leading doors at this time. Few people are expected to enter or depart the hospital from this time on."

"I want this son of a bitch killer in handcuffs and in my jail, pronto," said Lela. "Put extra reinforcements in ICU and in the research lab. I want the researchers to remain undisturbed and protected, and I need the Sinclairs to remain safe. The bastard who poisoned him may try to finish the job on the boy."

"Yes, ma'am," said Austin. "What about security cameras? I've noticed a few throughout this facility."

"I've assigned one of our guys to the security office. He and one of the hospital's security guards are in charge of constantly watching the cameras. They're to report any unusual activities to me right away." Austin nodded.

"I want to go over the basics again, Ruby," said Lela. "We have to make sure we didn't miss anything." Lela got up and paced the floor as she spoke. "The people who have been abducted or murdered to date, what do they have in common?"

"Nothing," said Austin. "All these people had different backgrounds, different socioeconomic strata, different interests, jobs, etc. We haven't yet looked into those found dead today, but we know the woman worked in Pathology here at Heartland."

"Let's look at all of them critically now," said Lela.

Austin began to look through the files on the table. "None of the victims before today ever worked at this hospital. Three of them had been hospitalized patients but all over two years ago. Four of them had visited the emergency room for minor things over the last ten years, the most recent seven months ago."

"You hunt where you live, where you feel comfortable, where you know. Anybody in research protocols?" said Lela.

"Research protocols? Wouldn't they be listed in the hospital records?" said Austin.

"Hang on," said Lela. She fished out her cell phone and dialed. A few seconds later, she looked up another number. "Neither Miranda nor Tim are answering their phone. Probably not getting a signal back in Pathology. That lab is deeper into the building." She pushed another button on her mobile. "Ben, it's Lela. If you've cooled off your head a little bit, I need to talk to Amy. I want to talk to her about research protocols."

"You know you're a son of a bitch, right?" said Ben.

"And damn proud of it," said Lela. "Now, get her on the phone."

"You're on speakerphone, and we're alone in a small conference room," said Ben.

"When you enroll patients in research protocols," said Lela, "do they get listed in the hospital records?"

"No," said Amy. "Record of subjects in research protocols are extremely confidential. They wouldn't be on any hospital database. They are listed by code numbers only."

"I can get a subpoena, but that would take too long," said Lela.

"We need a computer guru from the hospital," said Ben. "Someone we can trust, and someone we can get pronto."

"Thank you, Amy," said Lela. "You too, Ben. Stay with your family. I'll keep you in the loop and let you know if anything interesting happens."

"Wait, Lela," said Ben. "I can help with—" Lela hung up the phone shaking her head. She sat down and turned to Austin, "We have profiled the killer to be a man and that he works alone. He's definitely a strong and agile man. He's also at least six feet tall, or close to it. We know that from the trajectory of the needle stabs in the neck. We need to find a suitable computer geek, but let's look for a petite woman."

"How will we find one?"

"I have an idea," said Lela. She dialed a number on the desk phone in front of her. "This is Detective Rose from the Danville Police Department. What room is Dr. Terri Phillips in?"

26

Lurie Kutrow was in her midsixties and about five foot nothing. She wore a perpetual scowl.

"Thank you for agreeing to help us in such a short notice," said Austin.

"There's nothing I wouldn't do for Dr. Terri Phillips," she said. "But it's a little ridiculous that you bring me in here at this late hour. Can't this wait until the morning?" She sat down in front of the computer and typed something. Soon, she had gained access to its inner workings.

"Unfortunately no, Lurie," said Lela. "This can't wait. We need this information right away." Lurie looked at Lela then back at the screen.

"Let's do this quickly," said Lurie. "I want to go back home. What do you need to know?"

"First, before you begin, what we discuss in here must remain confidential. Is that clear?" said Lela. Lurie nodded. "We think the mass murderer we've been looking for works here at the hospital, probably in the research department. We believe that he has used the computer system to gather information."

"Holy shit," said Lurie. "You need me to help you catch a criminal? And he's in this hospital right now?"

"We believe so," said Lela.

"What if he finds out I'm helping you and comes after me?"

"We'll provide you with maximal protection until we apprehend the killer," said Austin.

"There are two men armed with automatic rifles right outside that door," said Lela. "They'll remain there or with you wherever you go, until we have the bastard behind bars."

"You better catch him, then," said Lurie. "I can't be guarded by cops for the rest of my life."

"We'll catch him," said Lela. "With your help."

Lurie nodded and looked at the computer screen.

"Can you find out how many research projects involving outpatient subjects there are going on right now?" said Austin. She began to type commands on the keyboard. Lela and Austin took a few steps and positioned themselves behind the woman, their gaze on the display.

"Don't rush me, goddamn it," said Lurie. "Even computers need a few seconds to get the information out to you."

Lurie turned her attention to the screen in front of her and resumed typing rapidly. Within moments, every ongoing research endeavor was on display. "Here."

"Will you print that for us?" asked Lela. Lurie hit a key, and within seconds, the small printer, situated in the corner of the room, came alive.

"Can you access the names of the subjects?" asked Lela. "We have a list of the people murdered or abducted. We want to compare names."

Lurie's fingers resumed typing diligently. The printer squealed again and papers spewed out onto the tabletop. Lela took the list of names and a pen.

"Abbey, Brazer, Cochran, Dombroski, Fogerty, Kennedy, Lisbow, Ludlow, Michaels, Penrod, Potter, Shuman, Tauscher, Wilbur—all of the fourteen people abducted or killed before today are on these research lists," said Lela.

"Can you tell which personnel had access into their computer information?" said Austin. "Demographics, research data, test results, and so on?" Lurie nodded, her attention back on the screen.

"None of today's three murders are on here," Lela said.

"Three more today?" Lurie gasped.

"I'm afraid so," said Austin.

"Well, we know why he picked the three from today," said Lela. "Dr. Dill and the Pickens were selected because of the Sinclairs, somehow."

"It wasn't Sarah Pickens was it?" said Lurie, getting up from behind the computer and walking toward to cops. "She's one of my computer workers here in Pathology, and she didn't come to work today, which is totally unlike her."

"Sarah was found dead today," said Lela. "What can you tell us about her?"

"Sarah is my . . ." Lurie paused, tears beginning to cascade down her cheeks. "She *was* my main computer data entry person here in Pathology."

Lela offered her a box of tissues and she took one.

"I'm sorry about the loss of your friend," said Austin.

"Let's catch this madman. Where do we go from here?" said Lurie, wiping her tears then blowing her nose. She sat back in front of the computer, fingers at the ready.

"The murderer has to be from here, just as we thought," said Lela. "How does he pick his vics, exactly?"

"Are all of these on one research protocol or different ones?" said Austin.

"Multiple studies," said Lurie, looking back at the screen, her fingers typing again. "There are four protocols. No," she stared at the screen. "There are six different research protocols."

"Let me see the actual protocols," said Lela. Lurie stood up and motioned for Lela to sit in front of the screen. She did. After a moment, she looked up.

"Each victim was coming in to get blood work done. Some of them have given other specimens such as urine and stool. A few had CT scans or scans of different parts of the body. A couple had skin or muscle biopsies. So they're here physically at the research lab. The killer knows their medical history and address. Probably gets to know them personally." Lela looked up from the computer at Austin.

"Sarah Pickens may have been working with the murderer," said Austin. Lurie began shaking her head. "Maybe unknowingly. Maybe by coercion."

Lurie bit her lip, "Sarah would *never* cooperate with this monster of her own free will," she said. "No way, no how."

"I'd like to see where Sarah worked. Did she have a workstation?" said Lela.

"I'll take you there."

27

Billy was asleep.

"He seems to have a little bit more struggle in his breathing," said Ben.

"He's utterly exhausted," said Amy. "But thank god the monitors show his vital signs have remained stable."

A policeman stuck his head into the small cubicle. "Lieutenant Rose agreed to let you go downstairs to the research area. But I'm to go with you. I'm to place you immediately under arrest if you try anything funny. Are we clear on that?" Ben nodded.

When Ben reached the research laboratory, he noticed four cops with loaded Heckler & Koch MP-5 semiautomatic rifles. The officers and their weapons made him feel safe, sad, anxious, and fearful, all at once.

"You can go right in, Detective Sinclair," said the one in charge. "You got fifteen minutes."

Ben entered the laboratory, his police escort right behind him. "How far did you get?" he asked. "When can we get the antidote?"

"I was able to discover an essay that'll give us a quick way to see if the victims were given tetrodotoxin," said Miranda, who had joined Jack and David in the lab.

"We have found that after administration, tetrodotoxin is rapidly metabolized in the liver first to its methylated form, which is then further oxidized and a silyl group added. Its final state becomes a trimethylsilyl derivative," said David.

"What the hell does all that mean?" said Ben. "My boy is dying upstairs, goddamn it. I don't have time for this mumbo j—" He peered into three pairs of sad, confused eyes and took a deep breath. "How long do these reactions take?"

"The whole thing takes about ten minutes in the body," said David.

Jack nodded. David continued, "For us to duplicate these reactions in the lab, it would take several hours per reaction."

"With the use of nanotechnology, we have been able to gather this information in less than an hour. It would have taken me a couple of days to accomplish the same thing without it," said Jack. "We're making good progress, Ben."

"What are the properties of this trimeth thing compound? Is it an antidote?" asked Ben.

"Working on it now," said Jack.

"How's Billy?" asked Miranda.

"He's struggling to breathe quite a bit more."

"Ben, when you or anybody else come in here to check on our progress, you slow us down," said Jack. "We don't have time to talk or explain what we're doing. We'll let you know as soon as we come up with something."

Ben nodded and left the research laboratory, the cop right behind him. Ben's cell phone rang.

"Come up right away, Ben," said Amy. "The doctors want to talk to both of us."

Waiting for the elevator, Ben looked out a window. The night was dark and foggy; the rain had begun to fall. He pleaded with his exhausted brain not to let him down.

*   *   *

"Dad, do you like being a policeman?" asked a seven year-old boy playing with a toy train.

"Sure do, Billy. I love it," said Ben, putting down the newspaper. "Why do you ask?"

"I want to be a policeman just like you," he said, pushing the train on its tracks. "If Mom or me are hurt by bad guys, will you catch them and kill them?"

"Of course, I would. I would get my guns," he said, getting up from the chair and kneeling next to Billy. Then, pretending his right index finger and hand were a gun, "I would put my revolver on their chest, like this." He placed his index finger on Billy's chest, tickling him in the process, "and I would shoot them like this." He tickled his boy's chest then belly, causing Billy to squirm with delight. "And I would shoot them some more like this." Billy wiggled and laughed, writhing with affection.

"Shoot me some more, Daddy," yelled Billy, when Ben began to ease off.

"Then I would shoot and shoot even more," said Ben, rubbing his hand on Billy's chest.

"The bad guys better not mess with me or Mommy."

"Billy, I want you to understand something very important," said Ben, sitting his son on his lap. "My job is not to kill people. Even bad guys. My job is to figure out who the bad guys are and stop them from doing bad things. When I catch bad guys, I don't shoot them. If I did, I'd be a bad guy too. My job is to put handcuffs on them and bring them to jail. Then a judge and jury decide what to do with the bad guys. That's how it works. Do you understand, Billy?"

"Yes, I do, Daddy. But I like it better when you use your hand as a gun and poke me in my belly. It makes me laugh," said little Billy, a big smile on his face.

"Okay, here comes the gun again," said Ben, smiling.

"You're like a superhero, Dad."

"You are, Billy. Mom too. Do you know why?" said Ben.

"Why?"

"Sometimes I have a really bad day at work, and I feel down and out. I'm sad and tired. When I get home and hug you and Mom, I feel better right away. You two are to me like spinach is to Popeye. You two are *my* superheroes." Ben and Billy smiled.

*   *   *

"Hey! Sir, are you coming in?" asked a woman's raspy voice. "Are you going up?" Ben realized the elevator door had opened and was being held ajar for him.

"Yes," said Ben. He and the policeman got in.

"Are you Billy's dad?" asked the woman. Ben nodded. "He's pretty sick, ain't he?"

Ben nodded again. "I wish I could do something about it."

"It would kill me," she said. "If my boy was dying, and all I could do was sit and wait."

"Well, tell this police officer right here," said Ben. "He doesn't seem to understand that concept." The cop stood taller and tossed a smirk at Ben, then the woman.

Amy stood up slowly when Ben entered the ICU cubicle. Without a word, they held hands then both sat down. Billy struggled in his sleep, a loud wheezing escaping with every breath. Oxygen saturation was now 86 percent.

The nurse walked in with Natalie and Drs. Mathis and Messing.

"We've been discussing how long to wait until we intubate Billy," said Dr. Mathis. "At some point we'll need to put a tube into his airway to assist with his breathing. His respiratory muscles are now pretty weak, and he's struggling hard to get enough air in and out of his lungs." Amy and Ben nodded slowly.

"His color is beginning to get dusky. The O2 sats have been hovering low around the mideighties. He's getting pretty tired, I'd go ahead with it now," said Dr. Messing.

"We've been trying to avoid it, but we all realize it's inevitable," said Natalie.

Amy's eyes inundated with new sparkly tears.

"He'll get too tired, and the oxygen saturation will soon drop very fast. The whole thing will turn into an emergency," said Dr. Mathis. "He's sleeping now. I can give him an anesthetic and intubate him now, if we are all in agreement."

"Go ahead," said Amy. Ben nodded.

"We'll wait outside." Ben kissed Billy on the forehead, then stepped aside so Amy could do the same.

"Billy," said Amy, her hand on his forehead, his eyes now open. "Do you remember we've been talking about putting a tube into your mouth, then into your windpipe, and into your lungs to help you breathe?"

"Yes," he whispered, his words croaky.

"The doctors are going to do that now. You'll go to sleep for a while and when you wake up, you'll have the tube in already. Remember that, and try not to fight it. The nurses will keep you sedated while the tube is in."

"Okay, Mom. I'm ready," said Billy. "I love you and Dad." His voice was feeble and hoarse.

"We love you so much," said Ben. "We'll be right outside the room while this is done." He gently guided Amy out to the waiting room.

The second hand on the large clock in the waiting room seemed to have slowed down, the tick-tock now unhurried. Ben and Amy paced the floor.

"What's taking so long?" said Amy. Ben shrugged his shoulders and looked out the window. Outside, lightning strikes and thundering in the distance accentuated the gloomy feeling in the room. The rain was now steady, wind gusts occasionally spraying the glass panes.

The nurse peeked into the large waiting room, then escorted Ben and Amy back into Billy's cubicle.

"Everything went well," said the nurse. "Billy is resting more comfortably now. He's sleeping like a baby."

Ben and Amy first noticed that Billy's wheezing was gone, replaced by peaceful air exchange via the ventilator. A clear plastic tube connected Billy's lungs and the ventilator. *Swish, swish*—oxygen in, carbon dioxide out. Billy's face was now much more serene. Amy and Ben couldn't help looking up at the monitor: oxygen saturation, 98 percent. "Much better," Amy said. Blood pressure, 94 over 62 and the pulse was 98. "Much, much better." Ben sighed and smiled.

The couple stood there, wordless, peering down on Billy, his eyes closed, his body exhausted.

Amy held Ben's hands and said, "Billy's condition is much more stable now."

"I need to get out of here and find the son of a bitch who did this to our son. And get Billy the antidote."

"The cops won't let you. You know that."

"I have to find a way to get past these damned cops," said Ben. He looked outside the cubicle. Two officers conversed with two nurses by the nurse's station a few yards away. A man wearing white pants and shirt walked by pushing a large container full of clean bed linens. This gave Ben an idea. Noticing the cops were both looking away, he shushed the man and got into the hopper.

"Please don't tell the cops," he whispered from within, placing a white sheet over his body. "Wheel me out. I'll pay you. Please."

The man looked right then left. "You'll get me in a heap of trouble."

"Please," said Ben. "I'll give you fifty dollars."

"I have a few more pickups," said the man.

"Hurry up, then," said Ben. "Just get me out of here. Quickly."

The man pushed the container to the other side of the unit and made his deliveries. In approximately ten minutes, he walked toward the exit. He smiled at the two officers who smirked back. Suddenly, a loud cell phone chimed from inside the hopper.

"What's that noise?" said one of the cops.

"It's coming from in there," said the other. He walked toward the noise and lifted up the white linens, uncovering Ben. "Where do you think you're going?"

28

The cops escorted Ben into Billy's room.

"Ben, you won't believe this," said Amy. "I just forwarded an e-mail to you that I received from someone calling himself Angelfish." He removed his cell phone from his pocket. The message simply read: *Want to play a game?*

"I'm scared, Ben," said Amy.

"I know, sweetheart," said Ben. "Do not, under any circumstance, step a foot out of this unit where the police is able to protect you. You leave this to me."

Ben called Lela. "Amy just received an e-mail from our friendly neighborhood mass murderer. He's calling himself Angelfish," he said.

"How can you be so sure?" said Lela.

"Tetrodotoxin comes from angelfish."

"This guy is a cocky, confident bastard," said Lela. "Overconfidence leads to mistakes. Bring the cell phone down here to the command center. Let's see if my computer expert can figure out where the message came from."

Lela looked at the mobile device, then handed it to Officer Woodruff, who was sitting in front of a computer. "I'll have an answer for you in about ten minutes, Lieutenant."

Ben and Lela walked away a few feet, toward a window.

"How's the investigation going?" said Ben.

"It's going just fine," said Lela. "I'm not at liberty to discuss details with you, Ben. You understand."

Ben shook his head and rolled up his eyes. "What do you make of the e-mail?"

"I'm sure it's a trap for your wife," said Lela.

"My thoughts exactly," said Ben.

"If that's the case, it's Amy the bastard has a beef with," said Lela. "But why?"

"I don't know." Ben looked at his cell phone. "How do we turn this in our favor?"

Lela thought for a second. "Answer the e-mail."

Ben typed: *First of all, you leave my wife out of this. From now on, you deal with me. And no, I don't play games. All I want to do is save my son.* Before pushing the send button, he looked at Lela, who was reading the words. She gave a shrug then a nod of approval. The message was transmitted.

A few moments later, the iPhone chimed, interrupting the anticipation in the room. Ben looked at Lela.

Okay, Officer. I'll deal with you from here on. But I want your responses much quicker than this. I want your e-mail reply within a minute. This is a fast game, Detective, and time is everything. Now, here's my demand: I want you and all the police and security guards as well as all the Research and Pathology personnel to leave the hospital. I want everybody out of the research/pathology wing stat. Pronto. I want all the exits unlocked and no guards. Are we clear on that? Until you do, I will kill somebody every hour on the hour starting at midnight. It is now 11:48 PM. But I will let you decide who the victims are. The game will increase to more people getting killed per hour, if I see any more police or security enter the hospital. Are the rules clear?

Ben: *Why are you doing this?*

Lela looked on over his shoulder.

Angelfish: *Who will die first? Press 1 for a sixteen-year-old drug abuser, or 2 for a seventy-year-old healthy grandma with a minor attack of gout, with plans to be discharged in the morning.*

Ben: *I told you, I don't play games.*

Angelfish: *Of course you do, Detective. This will be a lot of fun! You'll experience the omnipotent feeling of the mighty Dr. Amy Sinclair. You'll make life and death decisions, just like her. So who is the first to die tonight? If you meet my simple demands, this may be the only casualty of the game. Decide fast.*

Ben looked at Lela. "Do you think this is real?"

"I don't know. This guy is narcissistic enough," said Lela. "Ben, how would he know you're a police detective?"

"I don't know. Whoever is doing this has done a lot of research and knows a lot about Amy. So knowing her husband is a cop is probably not going to help us."

"You're right," said Lela.

"If he was to do this," said Ben, "how could he get it done alone? Does that mean he has accomplices?"

"I profiled him to work alone," said Lela. "But you know profiles aren't always one hundred percent. Can't rule our accomplices."

"Lieutenant," said a man, CSI engraved in large letters on his blazer. "This e-mail was sent from a smartphone here in the hospital. The number is registered to National Bioresearch Institute."

"This lab, huh?" said Ben. "He's not even trying to disguise it."

"This tells me he's not a computer geek," said Lela. "And that he does have big brass ones. Thanks, Woodruff."

"You're right about his big brass ones," said Woodruff. "The signal is straight on. Most computer-savvy perps would ping the signal from elsewhere to make it difficult to find them." He shook his head. "Not this guy."

"But this means two things," said Ben. "One, we now have conclusive proof the killer is in the hospital right now and works out of this lab. Two, his little game probably means we're getting too close to him. Or he's getting ready to do something, and he needs us busy and out of the way, running around the hospital, trying to find the next victim."

"Lieutenant," Lurie yelled out. "The code team was just alerted for two simultaneous code blues. Two people just died, at almost the same time. This almost never happens."

"Billy?" said Ben. Lurie began typing furiously into her computer.

"Rooms 371 and 352," said Lurie. "Not your son. Not this time."

Without a word, Lela ran out of the room, Ben right behind her. The command center door slammed shut.

Room 371 was crowded with people in scrubs and white lab coats, some yelling out instructions, others carrying out orders, others coming and going. All in panic mode.

"Sarge," said Lela to a police officer. "The motherfucker is here in the hospital. I need more manpower in here now. I need bodies and guns. We have to search these halls, rooms, closets, even the goddamn shitters."

Ben's phone rang. It was Amy. "Billy's blood pressure dropped suddenly, and he's having a seizure. Come quickly."

29

"He had several seizures," said Dr. Jenner. "That means his brain wasn't getting enough pressure and oxygen. The good news is that he responded to the medication."

"How are they doing downstairs with the antidote?" asked Amy.

Ben shook his head slowly. "They need more time."

"Ben, I need to be downstairs working in the lab," whispered Amy, her gaze on his. "I need to come up with the antidote to save our son. They won't be able to keep Billy alive for much longer."

"Absolutely not. I don't want you out of this unit. It's not safe. The bastard is looking to hurt you. He poisoned Billy to get at you."

"Ben, the police can protect me downstairs as well as they do here," said Amy. "But in the lab I could be—"

"Amy, no!"

"Ben, think about it," said Amy. "I'm a researcher and I—"

"No more discussion. You are not leaving this area. Period. End of story."

Ben rushed out of the cubicle. The police sentinels nodded.

"You're good to pass, Detective Sinclair," said the one in charge. "Don't worry about the bad guy getting to your son or wife. That'll happen over our dead bodies." He gestured to the other four cops. All nodded.

As Ben walked briskly to the stairway and down the stairs, his thoughts momentarily returned to yesteryear.

*   *   *

"Mom, Dad, I don't like to be called Billy anymore," said the young man. "I just turned sixteen, and Billy makes me sound like a kid. Like a baby."

"But you'll always be our baby," said Amy. "No matter what your age is."

"What would you like us to call you?" asked Ben.

"I don't know. Maybe William or Bill. Maybe Will. Anything but Billy." He thought for a moment. "Not Willy, either."

"Just for the record," said Ben, "I don't personally think Billy makes you sound like a baby at all. I know some grownups that go by Billy. And they're well respected."

"That's true," said Amy. "What makes you a kid or a man isn't your name, but your actions. Your behavior."

"I guess you're right," said Billy. "I just don't like Billy anymore, is all."

"Well, let us know when you decide on what we should call you," said Ben. "But truthfully, we're so used to calling you Billy, don't be surprised if it'll take us a while to catch on. I am an *old* dog, and this is a *new* trick."

"We'll try our best," said Amy.

"Okay," Billy said. "And I'll give you a pass on Billy for the next three months. Is that fair?"

"Any progress?" Ben asked, as he arrived in the research lab. "We're losing the battle upstairs. And quick."

"Yes," said David. "We now understand how to block the effects of tetrodotoxin. We're designing a molecule that'll do that. Almost done. Once we have the new substance, we'll have to do a few bench tests."

"We'll want to make sure the new drug is efficacious and safe," said Jack, rolling his wheelchair nearby.

"We tried to obtain this new molecule by administering tetrodotoxin to a rat hoping to speed things up," said David. "We found out nonhumans metabolize the toxin through a different chemical pathway."

"To get the antidote, we have to start with poisoning a human so as to collect the hepatic metabolite from the gallbladder about ten minutes later," said Jack.

"I don't care about any of that bullshit," yelled Ben. "How long do you need? My son's running out of time."

"We should have something in an hour and a half. Two, at most," said David.

"Two more hours still?" Ben yelled, pacing side to side. "Goddamn it. Billy doesn't have that kind of time."

"Let them do their work, Ben," said Austin, who had entered the room overhearing the yells. "You're delaying the process." He grabbed Ben's arm and escorted him outside the lab. "Just between you and me, Ben, I think Detective Rose made a mistake not including you in the investigation from the beginning. Fortunately, I think she's coming around. We certainly need the manpower. She just went over to talk to Dr. Phillips in Pathology. I'm going there now. Want to come along?" Ben took a deep breath, nodding.

"Both patients died having had no response whatsoever to the resuscitation efforts," said Miranda. "The first patient was indeed a sixteen-year-old boy, an IV drug abuser who was in with endocarditis. That's a heart valve infection, but he had been responding well to IV antibiotics. He was going to be okay. The other victim was, as foretold by the e-mail, a seventy-year-old woman who was admitted with unknown joint pain but turned out to have only a mild case of gout—a type of arthritis. She received treatment and was ready to be discharged this morning."

"Nobody saw anyone unusual around the patients before the code blues were called," said Lela. "The deaths were sudden and unexpected."

"What about surveillance cameras?" said Ben.

"We've reviewed the local feeds starting thirty minutes prior to the cardiac arrests," said Lela. "There were multiple nurses and orderlies walking around the nursing unit before the cardiac arrests. Seven of them were male. Nobody really suspicious-looking by their demeanor or actions. We couldn't get clear images of the faces on any of them. Four of them are tall enough, white, and in their thirties or early forties. I have two of my men canvassing the area and searching for them, but I'm not hopeful it'll lead to anything concrete."

"Both victims died of the same type of tetrodotoxin as all the others," said Miranda. "But this time, we have their gallbladders."

"Get them to Jack and David pronto," said Ben. "They may be useful to them."

"How does the killer get to the patients without being spotted?" said Austin.

"The bastard obviously knows exactly where the cameras are and knows to avoid them and act inconspicuous around them," said Lela.

"There may be passageways we don't know about that he's using in certain high-traffic places. We'll keep looking, but he seems to know how to get around and blend in with the woodwork."

"Have your men looking for tunnels, dumbwaiters, secret passages," said Ben. "Find us construction schematics."

"Are you kidding me?" said Lela. "At this time of night, you really think we should waste time looking for construction schematics?" Lela looked at Ben, then Austin, and back to Ben. She shook her head. "We don't have that kind of time or enough manpower."

"Will intensifying the search lead to more killings inside the hospital?" asked Miranda.

"Probably," said Lela. "His demands were clear."

Lela's cell phone chimed. She read the text message.

"It's Lurie. She's got something for us."

Ben, Austin and Lela walked briskly out of the pathology lab, two officers with AK-47 machine guns right behind them.

"Get back upstairs to your family, Ben," she said.

"Now that I was starting to like you again?" said Ben. "Don't give me that."

"Ben, I'm not fucking around with you," said Lela, stopping. "I'm too busy for that shit, goddammit. Get the hell out of my sight, or I'll have you arrested." The two cops grabbed Ben's arms and pulled him away from Lela, then gave him a push toward the stairwell. Ben struggled to remain on his feet.

"Goddamn it, Lela." Ben turned back to her and tried to force himself through the two guards who resisted his progress. "You need me down here. I can help you." Without looking back, Lela was already inside the command center, the door slamming shut.

30

Lela and Austin closed the door behind them as they entered the command center.

"I have a short list of people who had login access to the computer files of all the victims including Sarah Pickens's personnel file," said Lurie. "There are seven employees who had logged into the computer system to obtain the information." Lurie handed the list to Lela who sat on the edge of the table.

"Of the seven, three are women. Of the four men, one has recently moved to California."

"Have you been able to verify that?" asked Lela.

"Yes, he used his credit card twelve times in California since he left here five weeks ago, including twice earlier today."

"That leaves three men," said Lela.

"Of the three men, I'd start with Brent Weiner. He's a PhD researcher who started working here about three months ago."

"That's about when the animal abductions started," said Lela. "That fits."

Lurie continued, "Weiner has logged on and accessed the files of all those abducted and murdered, including looking up demographic information on Sarah Pickens. Here's his address."

"What about the others?" asked Lela.

"My second choice is Marvin McClellan. He's the head tech for the Department of Pathology here at Heartland. He's had computer access to almost all the victims—all but two. He's supposed to be on vacation in Florida, supposedly deep-sea diving. He supposedly went alone and supposedly left six days ago. But, get this, he's not used his credit cards at all anywhere in the last week. Before that, he used credit cards all the time. Also, he was divorced three and a half months ago. That may have been the precipitating factor you were describing before. Here's his address," said Lurie, handing the detective a piece of paper.

"Who's the third?"

"Randall Dragone worked in the research lab until seven months ago. He was fired after he allegedly stole chemical reagents and equipment from the lab—test tubes, a centrifuge, and a few other miscellaneous items. He refused to leave, and the police were called in. He was arrested and spent a few days in jail here in town. Then he got out but returned to the lab. He had a fistfight with a few of the security officers here at the hospital and was rearrested and put in jail for a few weeks. He was released about four months ago, well before the first animal abduction. Something else interesting about this guy: his login and passwords have been used to get access into a few of the victims over the last couple of weeks, including the demographic employment information on Sarah Pickens. Somehow, he got computer access here at the research lab even though he's been banned from the facility."

"Now we're getting somewhere," said Lela.

"Oh, one more thing about Dragone," said Lurie. "He was arrested in Zionsville, Indiana."

"Zionsville?" said Lela. "Who was the arresting officer?" Lurie's attention returned back to the computer screen as she typed away rapidly.

"Detective Benjamin Sinclair."

"Get the driver's license pictures on these three men," said Lela.

"Already done," said Lurie walking to the printer where three prints lay. She handed them to Lela, who sat down examining each. Suddenly she walked to the door and opened it.

"Get Sinclair down here. Now."

* * *

Ben's unmarked police car was stopped at the Starbucks drive-through window. He received his cappuccino and smiled at the young lady. His cell phone rang.

"Ben, can you come to my office quickly?" said Amy. "There's an incident here, and I need you right now."

In seconds, the Ford's lights all came alive, flashing wildly. He touched his sirens to facilitate his passage out to the street from the parking lot and, within minutes, his car was parked in front of Amy's workplace. Two police vehicles arrived seconds later. Ben and two officers walked briskly to the entrance. A sign read: *The National Research Laboratory.*

"A man by the name of Randy Dragone has been working here for a few weeks," said Amy. She was waiting by the main entrance into the facily.

"What did he do?" asked Ben.

"Disruptive behavior. Anger management issues."

"Where is he?"

"Our security men are trying to calm him down," said Amy turning the corner to the right, then opening up a door. The policemen entered the vast room with multiple long counters, where beakers, microscopes, and vials were perched. In one corner, a man was surrounded by five security guards.

"Hey," yelled Ben. "What's the problem here?" The guards separated, leaving Ben to face the unruly employee. "What's your name?"

"Randy," said the man.

"What's the problem, Randy?"

"No problem," he said. "I'm just trying to go back to work."

"He lied on his application with us about having been in trouble with the law before," said one of the security guards. "When I approached him about it, he—"

"I paid my dues to society," said Randy. "I was in jail. I'd like to go on with my life now. All I want is go to work and be normal again. Is that too much to ask?"

"I can tell you, this isn't the way," said Ben. "Come with us down to the station. We'll straighten this all out."

"This is bullshit, man," said Randy, pacing like a caged animal. "I didn't do anything wrong to deserve this." Ben grabbed Randy's right arm. Randy threw a punch with his left fist, but Ben ducked just in time to avoid the blow. The other cops and security guards rapidly approached Randy and threw him on the tiled floor, subduing his threatening arms.

*   *   *

"Yeah, that's him," said Ben. "Still has a beard. I put him in my jail overnight about six or seven weeks ago. After that, he left town."

Lela fished out her cell phone and walked away. "Ruby," she said into her mobile, "I want you to get an arrest warrant and subpoena to search the house and car of a Dr. Brent Weiner, a Mr. Marvin McClellan, and a Mr. Randall Dragone. I'm going to text you their last known. I want these citizens in my jail as soon as possible."

31

Marie rechecked her patients' medication list to make sure no drugs were due to be administered over the next hour.

"All my babies are sleeping snugly," she said.

"Are you ready for your break?" said Tracey.

"Yes. The only thing to report is room 845. Mr. Westport is here with fever. He's forty-eight. Doctors still evaluating the cause of the fever. So far, nothing. His temp is up a little. I medicated him a few minutes ago, and he seems to be doing better. He's due morphine for pain if he asks for it."

"Between him and my thirty-year-old high-maintenance patient in 832, I may be busy while you're gone."

"Is it okay if I take forty-five minutes today? I need to go home for a few minutes."

"I don't care," said Tracey. "Take an hour. I'll cover for you tonight, you cover for me tomorrow." Tracey finished writing on her chart and closed it. She looked back at Marie. "You know the police are all over the hospital, right? They may not let you leave and come back."

"I'll check with them," said Marie. "I feel safer with the police around, don't you?"

Marie walked toward the elevator and dialed on her cell phone.

"I'm walking down right now," she whispered. "I'm getting in the elevator. See you down there."

When she arrived at the cafeteria, she bought two coffees, two square donuts, and sat down.

"You got me one," said Mike. "Thanks." He sat down at her table then sipped from the coffee. She smiled.

Several minutes later, they grabbed their food and walked out the cafeteria and into the hall. Many people were coming and going.

"Busy place, huh?" said Mike. "What did you tell her upstairs?"

"I told her I needed an hour to go home for a while," said Marie.

The couple walked down the hall toward the dimly illuminated portion of the corridor. Mike opened a door and the two walked in. He locked the door.

It was a small conference room, many seats in a row, a podium and a blackboard in the front. There were two windows through which occasional flashes of light poured in from the lightning storm outside.

"The dim lighting in here adds to the ambiance," said Marie.

"As long as I'm with you, baby, I don't care about the light."

Both placed their food down on one of the chairs. Slowly, Mike approached her and the two embraced. His lips kissed her neck gently, and slowly, his mouth came to hers. Their lips connected, the warmth of each transferring to the other. Marie felt his tongue on her lips, softly, teasing her to open her mouth. She did slightly. He unbuttoned her shirt's top buttons then waited for her to undo his. He caressed her hair, brushing her bangs away from her eyes. Another kiss. Marie felt the warmth of his embrace again and his gentle touch on her face. A few more buttons undone on her, his hands warm and gentle. He tugged on her shirt lifting it out of her skirt. Marie reciprocated, and soon his top was off. She felt his chest muscles with her open palms, caressing, gently brushing his chest hair. She kissed his nipples while he kissed the top of her head. He used his hand to gently tickle her neck and shoulders.

Outside the window, a lightning flash briefly illuminated the small room, each chair projecting a shadow for a brief second. Then the thunder, a low rumble that warned of bad things to come.

She was now undoing his belt. Mike looked up at the ceiling, his hands still on her head. Caressing. Gently brushing, his fingers intertwined with the strands of her long, beautiful hair.

Another lightning strike, another flash of light flooding the room, the furniture in the room again briefly flinging a shadow. But there was a new shadow. Marie stepped back, away from Mike. A big dark figure of a man behind Mike approached the couple rapidly. The loud thunder roared right outside the window, drowning Marie's scream.

32

"David," said Miranda, entering the research lab. "Where's Jack?"

"Bathroom break. His pee bag gets full pretty frequently."

"How's it going in here?"

"We've developed a purified compound that theoretically should produce full tetrodotoxin blockade," said David. "It's a very small amount, but it'll be enough to test to confirm the results. We'll need to determine the proper dose and ascertain if it's safe for administration. If we confirm all these aspects of the drug, we can prepare larger amounts pretty quickly. Hopefully, we'll have something to give Billy in less than an hour."

"That sounds promising," said Miranda.

"How are you progressing with your work in Pathology?" said David.

"Two inpatients were poisoned and killed with tetrodotoxin," said Miranda. "They still have their gallbladders. Do you want them?"

"Yes," said David. "It may be helpful to analyze the contents. Let me text Jack and get his opinion." David began to type on his smartphone.

A few seconds later, they heard a chime.

David read the text response. "Jack says not yet." David looked at Miranda then back at his mobile. He read, "We need to finish the present analysis before we look into that. There may be some ongoing postmortem chemical reactions. Wait on removing the gallbladders until we're ready for them."

"Let me know when you want them," said Miranda.

"We'll keep you informed," said David, his attention already on the test tube in front of him.

Two police officers escorted Ben up to ICU. The group was waiting by the elevators.

"It's eighteen to one," said Ben. "I should be getting—" Ben heard his cell phone chime from inside his pocket. "There it is."

He read the message: *Which one will die? Press 1 for forty-eight-year-old married man with three kids who is having an affair or Press 2 for thirty-year-old unmarried whore with no kids? Ah yes, reminder: Absence of a quick response sends them both to hell.*

"Take me back to Lieutenant Rose," Ben said. "She'll want to see this e-mail."

"We have orders to take you to your son's ICU room and keep you there," said one of the cops.

"Rogers, I don't have time to argue with you," said Ben. "Call her right now. I promise you, she'll want to see this e-mail right away."

"You give us any trouble, I'll handcuff you and throw you in jail," said Rogers. "Lieutenant's orders."

Ben took a step forward, hoping to show the cops the e-mail message.

"Pinto, take him down," said Rogers. He took a step back and drew his Glock. Pinto, a large man of nearly seven-foot stature with gigantic hands and biceps of steel, grabbed Ben's arm, causing the cell phone to go flying from his hand. Ben resisted being subdued, but he was no match for the huge muscleman and soon was in handcuffs.

"Take me to the lieutenant, goddamn it," Ben yelled out.

"We're taking you to jail," said Pinto. "You were warned about this type of behavior."

"You're under arrest," said Rogers placing his weapon back in its holster. "You have the right to—"

"I know my rights, you dumbass. The lieutenant needs to see the e-mail I just received. Two people are about to die because of you. Let me go."

The elevator door opened with a ding.

"What's going on here?" said Austin from inside the elevator.

"Will you get these dumbasses off of me," said Ben. "I just received another e-mail from Angelfish. We need to respond quickly or two more people will die. They may be dead already."

"Remove the handcuffs, Pinto," said Austin. "I'll take him to the lieutenant."

"It'll be on your head, Rube," said Rogers. "The lieutenant will be pretty pissed off for putting up with his bullshit. She wants him in jail if he acts up."

"I'll take the responsibility, Rogers," said Austin. "You and Pinto are in the clear."

The handcuffs were removed, and Ben ran to the command center, Austin right behind him.

Ben showed Lela and Austin his cell phone display.

"Lurie, get us all of the forty-eight-year-old men and all the thirty-year-old women in the hospital right now," said Ben.

Lurie gasped. "My god," she said. "When will all this horror end?" Her fingers went to work on the computer keypad.

Ben looked at his iPhone's images from Billy's room. He saw two police officers in the room, one conversing with Amy. Billy was sleeping peacefully. A quick look at the vital sign trends reassured him that Billy was hanging in there and stable. Barely.

Which one will die? A forty-eight year-old married man with three kids or thirty year-old woman? thought Ben. *Who should I pick to die?* Ben closed his eyes. *I can't choose. How can I make this decision?* Ben picked up the mobile and reread the message. His right index finger was trembling. He felt his heart thumping hard deep inside his chest. *I've devoted my life to help and protect, not to make decisions as to which one should die. Or live.* He bit his lower lip. *I wonder if he has plans to kill them both regardless of my choice.*

"Here we go," said Lurie. "Nine forty-eight-year-old males and two thirty-year-old females." A touch of a button on her computer and the printer began. Ben took the list and read through it. Lela suddenly took it from him.

"What are you doing?" said Lela.

Ben dialed the number two then the send button.

"Let me help, Lela," said Ben. "Let me go up and check on these patients. You're too busy, and you don't have enough manpower."

"What's your plan?"

"It'll be much easier to check on two thirty-year-old women than nine forty-eight year-old men," said Ben. "I just e-mailed the bastard to tell him to kill the woman. I'll go check the two on the list." Lela handed the paper back to Ben, who ran out of the command center. He dialed Amy's cell phone. "Honey, there are four cops in there with you, right?"

"No, there are six. They're guarding the entrance to the whole unit. Nobody comes in or—"

"Let me speak with the one in charge." In a moment, a man's voice came on the line.

"This is Sergeant Bryant."

"Sergeant, I need your help to check on a couple of patients here in the hospital."

"The lieutenant would have my—"

"I'll give Detective Rose a call right now and have her call you in a second. Meet me in Room 402 as soon as you possibly can. And bring your guns."

"Where's Room 402 and the chart for that patient?" said Ben, out of breath.

"Who are you?" asked the security guard.

"Detective Ben Sinclair," he said showing his badge. "I have reasons to believe the patient in Room 402 is about to die, if she's not dead already. Have you seen anybody who doesn't belong here enter or exit that room?"

"I've been sitting here for over two hours," said the guard. "Nobody walked in or out of there except for the nurse. And—"

"I'm the nurse taking care of 402," said an older woman, standing up from behind a desk. "I've been in the room several times this shift. The last time was about fifteen minutes ago. The patient is sleeping. Nobody's been in or out besides me."

"What's she in for?" asked Ben.

"Broken pelvis, right femur, left humerus, sternum, and skull in a car accident two days ago. What's this all about?"

"There's a mass murderer in the hospital," said Ben. The nurse gasped, her hands to her chest. "The patient in Room 402 may be his next victim." Ben gestured for her to come with him and began to walk slowly and noiselessly toward the room, the nurse and security guard behind him a few feet. Ben pushed the door open gently and peered around in the poorly lit small area. He walked inside and saw no one except the sleeping woman, her leg in a white cast hung up by some contraption.

"Wake her up and take her vital signs," whispered Ben. He looked in the small closet behind him.

"Rosie," said the nurse touching the patient. "Wake up, hon,"

"Huh," the woman gulped. "What is it? What's wrong?"

"We're just checking up on you," said the nurse.

Ben poked the bathroom door open. It screeched as it swung in.

"Who are they?" asked the patient, pointing at Ben and the security guard, her voice shaky.

"The police," said the nurse, taking the woman's wrist. "Let me check your pulse." Ben cautiously took a step into the bathroom, looking side to side.

"Nobody," said Ben returning to the others. "Sorry for the intrusion, ma'am. Go back to sleep." He walked out into the hall. A police officer was just arriving. Breathless.

"This one's fine," he told the cop, then looked back at the nurse and security officer. "Watch her closely and make sure no stranger goes in her room. Or any other room, for that matter." Ben left the unit, looking at his computer list, then the uniformed officer. "Follow me to Room 676." Ben ran off with the cop behind him. Ben looked at his watch. It was two minutes to one. The two men entered the staircase and walked up two stairs at a time. When they reached the sixth floor, they entered a dark and silent corridor.

"Where's Room 676?" asked Ben, breathlessly. The cop and he looked in all directions.

"This way," said Officer Bryant. Both men started running down the hall.

At room 680, they both came to a halt. Bryant undid the strap around his revolver and placed his right hand around the holstered handgun. The two tiptoed by Room 679 and glanced quickly inside. Room 678 was next, the two now walking slowly, their backs to the wall, their eyes wide. The cop opened the door to Room 677 as the two passed by. It was empty.

"Here's 676," whispered Bryant. "Are you armed?" Ben shook his head. "I'll go first." The door was closed. Glock in hand, he gently pushed on the door. It creaked slightly as it opened. Ben remained right behind him, both walking on tiptoes. The room had a long anteroom before it opened up to the area containing the bed, which they could not see from their vantage point. All was dark. All was quiet. The only unrest Ben could appreciate was his own heart thumping ferociously inside his chest. His hands were sweaty, adrenalin gushing inside his veins. The door creaked again as they entered the anteroom. Ben held the door, preventing it from moving any further. Silencing it. The two squeezed in past the halfway-opened door and entered the chamber. All was silent. Both men tried to stifle their quickened breaths. Another step, a foot closer to the mysteries lying inside Room 676. Another pace. The room was in total darkness, minimal illumination trickling in from the outside hall. There was a closed door to the right. Ben spotted a window, all obscure beyond it by a dark, deep curtain of falling rain. The meager reflection from the windowpanes showed a bed, a person sleeping on it. The body under the covers moved slightly with a gentle whimper. Bryant looked back at Ben, who was right behind him. All eyes back on the dark room ahead. Another slow step toward the bed.

Suddenly, Ben's heart stopped. He heard footsteps right behind him, coming from the hall, and the now-familiar squeak of the door opening. Ben felt the air the door displaced rushing by his face. Two quick footsteps approached the cops as someone hurriedly entered the room. Ben and Bryant quickly turned to face the intruder. Bryant stepped in front of Ben, Glock now pointing at the figure's chest, trigger finger ready to squeeze.

33

Tim felt Amy's pain as he departed Billy's ICU room. He pushed the elevator's down button. He felt gloomy, his inability to solve the boy's predicament at the forefront of his mind. The elevator arrived, unoccupied. He entered it and pushed the down button. His thoughts switched from Billy to Derek, the twenty-year-old son he and his wife lost due to medical complications when he was convalescing from hip surgery following a football injury.

After a glorious senior year as the quarterback of his high school team, Derek had been coveted by several institutions but finally decided to attend Huntsman College several state lines away. Tim still remembered the game, replaying the incident over and over, in slow motion, in his mind. Though he tried to forget and put it all behind him, he had been unsuccessful at doing so for years. The tackle by the six-foot-something player of the opposing team as his helmet struck Derek's side repeated time after time in his memory. And there it was again. Tim heard the snap, the cheering crowd, the precise forward pass. The clash. The injury. The pain and agony. The surgery with promise of recovery and hope to walk again, though not on the gridiron. He would never play football, but there was much more to life than football. There was living. Then the slow recovery. Too slow. More pain. Then, the phone call: *Dr. Hughes, I'm afraid I have bad news. Your son took a turn for the worse. A massive pulmonary embolism.* The futile efforts at resuscitation. The tears. The funeral. The emptiness. The exhaustion. The divorce. And more emptiness.

Tim felt a tear escape and run down his cheek as the elevator door opened. He walked out of the elevator and headed down the hall, a sign indicating: *Research and Pathology Department.* He entered the pathology laboratory suite.

"Miranda, are you in here?" No answer. He heard a sound in the distance. A metal-on-metal scraping noise. Perhaps from the morgue. By the reefer.

The large laboratory contained six steel autopsy tables. Tim walked to the back of the large room toward a set of double doors. When he arrived there, he looked through the small window on one of the doors. There was a small rectangular area that appeared deserted. On the right of this anteroom, there was a large metal door that led to the huge refrigerator, where the bodies were stored awaiting autopsy or shipment elsewhere. To the left, another door, this one labeled *Closet* had been left slightly ajar. Tim had seen this door hundreds of times but always thought this closet to be an unimportant place and had never bothered to look in there.

"Miranda," he said. No answer. Tim went through the door and took a few steps toward the closet. It was then he noticed the air-conditioner vent to the left of the closet door had been tampered with, its metal register now on the floor beneath, leaving a small hole on the wall, about eight feet up.

Who's been messing with the vent? he thought.

He walked back to the refrigerator and peeked through the small window on the door. The inside of the refrigerator was pitch black. He opened the metal door and peered inside.

"Miranda." No answer. He closed the door aware how cold it was in the reefer.

He returned to the closet door and walked inside. There were brooms and mops and other assorted janitorial paraphernalia. In the back of this small space, there was another closed door, labeled *Air-Conditioning and Heating Units.* He opened it and entered a poorly illuminated small area. There was an enormous metal rectangular unit. A sign on it read: *General Comfort Air.* To the right of the air conditioner, Tim saw a large cylindrical tube which had been previously attached to a vent in the wall, but someone had disconnected the cylinder and pushed it aside. In the wall, there was now a large opening. Tim looked into the hole but saw only darkness. He massaged the back of his neck and returned to the pathology lab. He walked to a tabletop with multiple small bottles of chemicals and examined them, reading each label. He picked up one of them and pondered his next move. He placed the tiny container in his pocket.

Tim walked back to the broom closet and reentered the room beyond it. When he reached the big hole in the wall, he got on his knees and proceeded inside. A few feet after the opening, the passage divided. He strained to hear for distant sounds. None came. Tim turned to return to the closet when he heard a faraway thunderlike rumbling noise from the tunnel to his left. He entered the tunnel toward the thunder. After several yards, Tim realized there was some light in the distance. He crawled toward the light and soon reached the source of the dim illumination. It was an office. The grid had been removed and set aside, as it had at the other end. He peeked through the opening and into the unlit room. Not a sound or sign of life in there. He continued to crawl in the tunnel, passing by the opening into the office. Looking straight ahead into the tunnel, Tim saw only the endless black of total darkness. On his knees, he again strained to listen for distant sounds. He now heard falling rain and felt the mugginess of the early spring morn. Tim saw a sudden flash of light carried through the tunnel followed by the unambiguous clash of thunder. *This leads out to the parking lot,* he realized.

Tim looked at his cell phone and read the lighted display: *No signal.* He turned around slowly and made his way to the office he had just passed. His muscles were sore and his joints ached. He needed to stretch his legs, and the office would be a great place to stand for a minute. Several yards later, he emerged from the vent and into the room. He noticed a poster with respiratory-care equipment. The office was small with two windows looking out into the darkness of the night, an occasional lightning flash partly illuminating the room. A sign reminded the reader to wash one's hands after caring for a patient on a respirator, to avoid cross-contamination and spread of infections. A partially open closet revealed plastic tubes and oxygen hoses. Tim turned slowly toward the air-conditioning vent from which he emerged as he read some type of announcement on a blackboard. As Tim struggled to read the large letters and turn, there was a lightning strike right outside the window. The sudden illumination revealed the shadow of a tall man right behind him. Tim barely had time to gasp as he felt a sharp pain on his left temple caused by the blow from an object he barely saw coming.

When he regained consciousness, Tim was dazed and woozy, a giant-sized headache brewing. He noticed he was on the floor, the man's knee pressing down hard on his chest, making breathing a struggle. The room was dark. Tim tried desperately to get up, roll side to side, and claw at the man, but a strong grip to his neck choked him, paralyzing his further efforts to escape.

"What do you want with me," said Tim, his voice trembly and weak. When lightning again briefly squirted illumination into the room, Tim saw the man's neck and jaw towering over him. He noticed he was holding a syringe in his teeth. The man grabbed his shirt and yanked it up, revealing Tim's bare abdomen. The man shone a flashlight on the right upper quadrant of the belly and noticed the telltale scar of a cholecystectomy.

"Who are you?" Tim struggled to say.

"You got no gallbladder," said the man, his voice deep, his flashlight on Tim's face, blinding him. "I thought I read that on your medical records. I was hoping I was wrong. You're of no use to me." He recapped the syringe and placed it in his shirt pocket. "Maybe I'll let you live."

34

Only two and a half hours into his shift, and the urge to smoke was overpowering him.

"Josie," said Nathaniel, "I'm gonna sneak out for a smoke. Wanna come?"

"What if we get caught? I need this job," she said.

"We ain't gonna get caught. Meet me downstairs outside the cafeteria in five minutes."

"We'll get caught. I need this job," she said. "We can't go outside neither. The police have all the doors guarded. Can't get in or out. Ain't you heard?"

"Yeah, yeah, yeah. I heard. The whole hospital heard."

"I'll meet you at the cafeteria, but only for a cup of coffee."

"Five minutes. Don't make me wait, woman."

"Five minutes."

Josie had begun working at Heartland Regional eight months earlier. She had two young children to take care of alone, since her man left her almost a year ago. His departure was a welcomed change since he had become involved with the wrong crowd—drugs, alcohol, and gambling. She didn't want that kind of influence on her kids. Since coming to work at the hospital's laundry department, her life had improved considerably. As of late, she realized that Nathaniel was sweet on her. He was a good man and would provide a solid role model for her two youngsters. They lacked a father figure in their lives. If she played her cards right, maybe she and Nathaniel could make a life together.

Josie walked into the laundry room. Everything was progressing well. She assessed her machines. The next load to be ready would take at least thirty minutes, maybe more.

"Can I take my break now?" she yelled over the noisy machinery.

"Sure, Jo. I'll take mine after you get back. Gonna meet Nathaniel?" Amanda roared back from somewhere in the guts of the dryer room.

"You know it." Josie smiled as she closed the door behind her.

The cacophony diminished as she walked upstairs to the first floor, taking the back staircase. The halls in the rear portion of the hospital were devoid of any life at this time of the early morning. The cafeteria was located toward the front of the building, a more populated area. She would get the coffees ready, hers and Nathaniel's. A good woman will do that for her man, and she wanted Nathaniel to be her man.

Josie walked down the corridor. She didn't much care for these desolate passageways. The silence offered a sharp contrast to the eardrum-busting clamor of her workplace. Right here, right now, it was spooky. Creepy even.

A distant metallic sound behind her caused Josie to stop and turn her head. She looked down the corridor but saw not a soul. She looked back the way she was going, her hands shaking, her heart thundering. In the darkness, it was difficult to differentiate walls from ceiling or floor. It was like being trapped alone in a tube.

"Nathaniel, is that you?" she whispered. No sound returned. "Nathaniel," she repeated a little bit louder. Nothing. As she looked back in the direction leading to the cafeteria, far down two halls, she spied a passing shadow on a wall. "Nathaniel, is that you over there?" she said, her words trembling with fear. "You better not be trying to scare me." Silence. After a moment, Josie dared to take a few slow, cautious steps forward. She passed by a closed door, a sign overhead proclaiming *Respiratory Therapy*. A few more slow steps. She looked here and there.

"Boo!" said Nathaniel jumping in front of her from behind a door.

Josie shrieked, "I'm going to kill you." Her heart stopped for several beats. She punched his arm, "I'm going to kill you." Nathaniel ran away from her in the direction of the cafeteria, Josie in his wake. Every few feet, she slapped at his back. "You wait 'til I catch you, mister."

"You had it coming, girl," said Nathaniel. "You should have saw your face."

"I can't believe you did this to me," she yelled and punched him again.

"C'mon, girl. You must admit it was funny."

"Not for me, it ain't," said Josie. A few more steps, less hurriedly now. "Okay, it was a little bit funny." She slapped him again. "Jerk." Nathaniel put his arm around her, and the two walked toward the cafeteria. This part of the hall was well-illuminated. Several people were scattered about, some going in, others coming out, all in search of coffee, sodas, or snacks.

"I'm sorry, Josie. I couldn't help myself," he said.

"You scared the—"

Suddenly, they heard something. Something barely audible. A sound alternating between thumping and scratching. They both stopped.

"What was that?" said Nathaniel.

"I don't know," said Josie. "Listen, I hear it again." She turned to her right. "It's pounding, coming from that classroom over there."

"It's growing louder," he said, walking hurriedly toward the sound.

They arrived at a closed door about twenty yards from the cafeteria entrance. "Who's in there?" said Josie from right behind Nathaniel. He tried the door. It was locked. He pushed hard on the door to no avail.

"Let me out," a man said feebly from inside the room. More pounding, louder now. "We need help. Please get us out of here," said the man.

"The door's locked," said Nathaniel. "Can you unlock it from inside?"

They heard the man sob. A woman arrived.

"Who's in there?" she asked.

"Call security, Marsha," said Josie. "There's a man in there, probably hurt. There's a phone on the wall right down the hall a few feet." She nodded and left.

"We're getting help, sir. Just wait a few minutes," Nathaniel said. Other people were now approaching the conference room entrance.

"What happened?" said a woman in scrubs.

"Who's in there?" asked another.

"I don't know," said Nathaniel.

"Let us out," yelled the man pounding on the door.

"Stay calm in there. Help is on the way," someone said.

"Has anyone called security? asked a woman.

"There are policemen all over this hospital, except here. Where we need them," said a newly arrived man.

"Security is on their way," said Marsha, returning.

"We'll have the door opened soon. Are you hurt?" asked a woman in scrubs, her words slow and loud. Only sobs returned from the other side of the door.

"Are you hurt?" asked another woman, wearing a white lab coat. "This is Dr. Emily Julian from the emergency room. Is anyone hurt in there?"

"I'm hit on the head. My skull is bleeding," said the man in between sniffles. "But I think my friend is dead." More sniffles. "She's not breathing." More weeping.

"Call upstairs and get a couple of ER nurses and a couple of stretchers down here stat." Dr. Julian paced back and forth. "Where the hell is that security guard with a key? Somebody is dying in there. Come on!"

35

Bryant's index finger began to pull on the Glock's trigger, the barrel aimed right at the chest of the person entering Room 676.

"Who's in here?" said a woman wearing a nurse's uniform, turning on a light switch. Glock in hand, Bryant released his breath, quickly pointing the handgun to the floor.

"Goddamn it," said Bryant. "I almost shot you."

"Who the hell are you?" said Ben.

"Phyllis Corn," said the woman. "I'm the night shift nursing supervisor."

"What are you doing here?" asked Bryant.

"I heard footsteps coming down the hall. I wanted to see what was going on."

"That's a really a good way to get shot," said Ben.

"Not usually, it isn't," she said. "Not in a hospital."

"Well, it is today," said Bryant.

"Okay, let's all take a deep breath here," said Ben. "Phyllis, help us check out this patient here. After that, help us go through this list of male patients. We'll go much faster with your help."

"This is the last male patient on the list," said Ben. "Room 912."

"I'll find the chart," said Phyllis.

"Bryant, check the room," said Ben, sitting down at the nurse's station."

Bryant nodded. "I'm on it," he said, right hand on holstered Glock. He disappeared into the hospital room.

"What time is it?" said Ben.

"It's twenty past one," she said. Her eyes scanned the chart rack and she pulled one out. "Room 912." She placed the chart on the table in front of Ben. "Do you need me to translate?"

"Please."

"Jake Mahoney, age forty-eight, in with chest pains, enzymes normal, no heart attack. Positive stress test." Her eyes perused the chart for relevant information. Ben was reading along over her shoulder.

"Oh here we go—Father Jake Mahoney," he said. *You're probably not having an affair and most likely not the father of three children.*

"He's having a cardiac catheterization this morning," said Phyllis.

"This isn't our guy either, Phyllis."

A few moments later, Bryant returned to the nurse's station.

"The patient's fine in his room, watching TV," said Bryant. "He told me he couldn't sleep. He's not seen anybody in his room in hours. I checked his closet and bathroom, all clear."

"Well, that's all of them. None of the patients on the list were harmed," said Ben.

"I'm so sorry for startling you down on the sixth floor," said Phyllis.

"We've all been on the edge around here lately," said Bryant. "I guess hunting for a mass murderer can do that to you." He produced a small mobile device from his pocket, which was vibrating. "Walkie-talkie call," he said turning the volume knob on. The speaker came alive.

"Sergeant Bryant," squawked the device. "This is Lieutenant Lela Rose. Are you there? Over."

"This is Bryant. Yeah, Lieu, we're done. We checked all the patients, and they're all just fine. Over."

"Get back to your post in ICU," she said. "I want Sinclair in the command post pronto."

"I'm going to let you in on the investigation," said Lela. "But, Ben, if you as much as burp in my presence or fuck with me in any way—"

"I get it, you're in charge," said Ben. "Let's get to work."

She handed him his gun.

"I have a list of three suspects," said Lela sitting down. "The problem is, I don't have enough men to go look for all of them at the same time."

"Want me out on the street?" asked Ben.

"No fucking way," she said. "You are not to leave this hospital."

"Okay, what do you want me to do?"

"You know Randall Dragone. What's your gut telling you about him? What priority should I give finding him?"

"I doubt he's the killer," said Ben. "I could be wrong, but my gut says low priority. Who are the other two?"

"A research doctor from here, Brent Weiner. I'll have my people start with him. I like him the most for the murders, at least on paper." Lela picked up another folder. "I'll send another group out to the Marvin McClellan residence. He's the head of pathology techs here at the hospital. We'll look for Randall Dragone when we're done with the first two."

"Okay," said Ben. "All we can do for now is wait."

"I wish," said Lela. "I was just informed of a dead woman found in a conference room down by the cafeteria. She was injected in the neck. And yes, she was thirty years old. I'm going to interrogate the man who was with her when she was assaulted. I'm guessing he's forty-eight and the guy she was having an affair with." Lela got on her feet and walked to the door. "I'll call you when I need you."

Ben took the opportunity to check up on Billy. He fished out his smartphone and directed it to display his son's ICU room. There was a lot of commotion, with two nurses and Dr. Claude Messing at his bedside. He was conversing with Amy. Within seconds, more personnel arrived, then Dr. Jenner.

Ben's phone vibrated. "I was about to call you," said Amy.

"What's going on?" asked Ben.

"Billy had several more seizures, his blood pressure is dropping again and fast, and his oxygen saturation suddenly plummeted to the seventies. Please come quickly."

36

"What's your last name, Mike?" said Lela. She was sitting down at the table in front of him. Next to her sat Colby, his police uniform impeccably ironed despite the late hour. He occasionally took notes.

"England, like the country," he said, his words quivering, his hands shaking.

"Where do you work?"

"I'm an orderly in Med-Surg. Sixth floor, mostly. Sometimes eighth."

"Tell me everything that happened. Don't leave anything out, however unimportant it may seem to you."

"Me and Marie—" Mike paused to blow his nose.

"Miss Marie Traylor?"

"Yes, me and Marie went into the conference room to . . ." he looked down at his trembling hands, "to have a good time." He looked back at Lela.

"To have sex?" said Lela.

"Yes." He retrieved another tissue from the box and wiped his tears.

"Go on," Lela said.

"I locked the door," said Mike. "But the man must have had a key. Somehow he came into the room when we were . . ." Lela nodded. "He came into the room and hit me on the head with something hard." Mike felt the surgical dressing on his head held in place by a white cap of bandages. "I went out. When I came to, I noticed Marie was laying right next to me, but she wasn't moving. I tried to wake her up, but she didn't respond at all. First, I thought she was hit on the head too. I could feel a sore spot on my head, and I knew I was bleeding from it. I could feel the blood. When I went to check her head for bleeding, I saw that she wasn't breathing right." He removed another tissue from the box and blew his nose.

"What do you mean, not breathing right?"

"Her breaths were more like slow gasps. Very slow gasps. She was breathing like a dying person." Mike began to sob, tears streaming down his face. Lela placed her hand on his shoulder.

"Were the lights on?" she asked.

"No. The lights were out the whole time. There was a little bit of light from the moon outside the windows, but because of all the clouds, there was very little light."

"So then what did you do?"

"I dragged myself to the door. I was dizzy. I needed to throw up. I couldn't get up. I couldn't open the door." He looked up from his hands on his lap slowly and met Lela's gaze. "The ER doc said I had a concussion." Lela nodded. "I started to yell for help and bang on the door."

"Okay, I know that some people heard you and got security. The door was unlocked by security." Mike nodded. "I only have a few more questions for you, Mike."

"Okay," he agreed, his eyes back on his trembling hands resting on his lap.

"Did you recognize the man who attacked you?

"No."

"Did you see the man's face?"

"No."

"You've been saying it was a man who attacked you," said Lela. "How did you know it was a man? Why not a woman? Maybe your wife?"

"Wait," interjected Mike, his eyes again on Lela's. "I did see him. I saw his shadow. And his reflection. In the window. Yes, I saw him. I saw his reflection just before Marie screamed. Before he hit me on the head."

"Can you describe him?" said Lela.

"He's a big guy—six foot, maybe more. Strong muscles. And fast. He had a cap on his head. A baseball cap." Mike nodded, his eyes intermittently finding Lela's.

"Could you see what color clothing he was wearing? Any smells or birthmarks you might have noticed? Any tattoos?" asked Lela.

"What?" said Mike.

"Any tattoos, birthmarks?" she repeated.

"Smells?" he said, his tremulous hand gesturing her to stop. "There was an unusual smell. I remember a smell right before I was hit on the head." Mike's eyes squinted, and slowly he brought his right hand to his nose. He took a whiff. "Some weird type of smell."

"Can you think of where you might have smelled anything like it before? Like a bakery? A laundry room? A basement? A paint shop?"

"No, some weird smell," said Mike. "Maybe a little bit of a fishy smell. Like fish gone bad, but not really. It was faint." He grabbed the water bottle on the table near him and took a drink. "I've never smelled anything like that before. Never." Mike looked at his hands then back at Lela. "I'm sick to my stomach. I need to throw up," he said. Lela walked him to the door. Two policemen with MP-5 semiautomatic rifles stood right outside the door.

"This officer will go with you," said Lela, nodding to one of the two cops who followed the man away from the command center.

"Do you think he did it?" asked Colby. "He could have killed her and faked the head injury himself. The idea that he couldn't open the door, even if he did have a concussion."

"He's innocent," said Lela. "Innocent of murder. Guilty of bad judgment."

"How can you be sure?"

"He doesn't have what it takes to commit these murders," said Lela. "Besides, he's not smart enough. Or tall enough."

Mike returned to the command center. The two sentinels positioned themselves again by the door, their hands on the MP-5 rifles. Mike, a wad a tissues in his hands, once again sat down in front of Lela and Colby.

"Do you think you'd recognize that odor if you smelled it again?"

"I'll never ever forget that smell as long as I live." Mike blew his nose. He took another tissue and wiped his fallen tears.

"This man knew you were having an affair with Ms. Traylor. He knew your age and hers, and he knew where you were tonight. He also knew when you'd be there. Can you think of any explanation for all this? Who would know all these facts about you and Marie?"

"I don't know," said Mike. "I'm married. I'm not going around telling anybody about my affair with—" Mike looked at Lela who was staring deeply into his eyes.

"How about Marie?" said Lela. "Would she have told anybody? Her best friend?"

"I don't know. Maybe."

"Who's her best friend? Anyone here at the hospital?"

"Her best friend is Sarah," said Mike. "They're inseparable. They always tell each other everything."

"Sarah who?" asked Lela.

"Pickens. Sarah Pickens."

37

They had to put the tube down my throat. My breathing muscles finally got too weak to do the job. I remember I had to breathe so heavy before. It was as if I was running a marathon. Now that the tube is in my lungs, the machine provides the breaths for me. That's a strange sensation. The sleeping medications, now and again, wear off; and that allows me to become aware. My lungs fill with the push from the machine. Weird feeling. Then my lungs empty out. I can tell they are all very worried about me. Worried that I will die. I can tell my mom is struggling not to break down, but once in a while, she leaves the room for a few moments. When she returns, she sniffles a lot.

I am struggling to move my muscles. I'm willing my right arm to move, but it won't. I feel like my brain cells have become disconnected from my body. I can no longer control it. This is the most unusual feeling ever.

"How's the BP?" a woman asks.

"It's been stable," another answers. "Knock on wood."

They closed my eyelids shut. I wish they had left them open. I think I could say so much with my eyes. I want to tell Mom I'm okay. I'm not in pain. And I believe she, Dad, and all the others can save me. I'll be okay, Mom.

"Is it time for lorazapam?" a nurse says.

"Yeah," a woman says. "Go ahead and give one milligram IV push."

Lora-something something. That's the stuff that puts me out. It clouds my thinking and makes me go to la-la land. When I get it, I can't think any longer. I go out into a deep sleep. She's giving me the shot in my IV now. It won't be long now until I sleep. Until my thoughts slow down and reality fades. Then dreams appear. But the dreams sometimes become awful nightmares. I feel I'm about to have one.

"The blood pressure just dropped," Billy hears someone yell.

"Call Dr. Messing, stat," another woman screams. "And Dr. Mathis too."

I see five huge birds of prey flying toward me, their wings spread, their beaks wide open, their claws open ready to grab at me.

"BP's going down," says a woman. "Call a code. Get those doctors in here now."

*   *   *

When Ben arrived in ICU, he noticed several people going in and coming out of his son's room. He couldn't see Billy, just personnel draining out of the small cubicle.

"Oh my god," said Ben. "What's just happened?"

Ben was escorted to the waiting room where Amy was sitting alone. She was sobbing, her eyes reddened and swollen. The two embraced. Then Ben walked to the door, his eyes down the hall on the entrance into Billy's ICU room.

"BP in the sixties," a nurse yelled.

"What's the O2 sats now?" asked Natalie.

"Fifty-eight," said a therapist.

Drs. Messing and Mathis ran inside, their white coats disappearing into the crowd.

"Increase dopamine rate to the maximum," said Dr. Mathis. "We got to get that BP over ninety, or else we'll lose him."

"Get more saline bags," yelled a nurse. "We've run out in this room."

"Let's give a blood transfusion," said Dr. Messing. "I had ordered two units of red cells, and they're ready to administer."

"I agree. Let's give both units," said Natalie. "Hurry up, we don't have much time."

Ben bit his nails as he stood by the doorway into the waiting area.

"I can't wait anymore," Ben told Amy. "I have to see my son."

"Ben, wait," said Amy. "There's nothing . . ." Ben left Amy's side and rushed into Billy's room against the grain.

"BP is coming up," he heard Natalie say. "90 over 54."

Ben saw relief in everybody's faces.

"He's coming around," said Billy's respiratory therapist. "O2 sats improving again."

Billy lay on the bed, peaceful.

"He's stabilizing again, Ben," said Natalie. "Let's go give Amy the good news."

*   *   *

When Ben entered the command center, Lela was dismissing two police officers.

"Reinforce all exits in and out of the hospital and the research laboratory," she said. She gestured for Ben to sit and she did the same. Lurie was at her computer.

"Just like the e-mail said, a thirty-year-old female nurse was having sex with a forty-eight-year-old male," said Lela. "I found a needle mark on her neck, just like all the others."

"What about the gallbladder?" said Ben.

"Didn't take it. I don't know exactly why, but he doesn't seem to be interested in gallbladders any longer. Just the thrill of the kill now."

"And keep us busy and out of his way," said Ben.

"He may not have taken the gallbladder because of time," said Lela. "They were pretty close to the cafeteria, and people going by may have worried him about getting caught."

"We have another gallbladder full of whatever it fills up with to give David and Jack."

"One more thing about the interview," said Lela. "He recalls a faint, weird smell on the killer. I took him to the research lab where David is working, and he recognized the smell there. That ties the killer to the research lab once again."

"We already established that pretty damn well," said Ben. He got up.

"Sit your ass down. I'm not done with you yet," said Lela.

"I'll stand," said Ben.

"You made the incorrect assumption that the people in the e-mail were hospitalized patients. Had you not assumed that, we might have had a better chance to—"

"Goddamn it, Lela," said Ben. "If you knew any better, you should have said something then. It's too late now to sling shit in my face, isn't it?"

"Sit the fuck down, Detective," said Lela standing up. "I told you, I'm not fucking around with you. You want to work for me, do as I tell you." Her double-barrel gaze was on his. "Sit your ass down." He looked away for a second then looked back at her and sat down.

"We all made that assumption," said Ben.

"That's exactly my point here, Detective," said Lela sitting down. "We're all tired and stressed. Fatigue has set in hours ago and the killer is counting on that. We need to stay ahead of him and start thinking outside the proverbial box. We both fucked up. Let's not make the same mistake again."

The e-mail chime came out of Ben's pocket. He removed the cell phone and read the message. "Who should die next? Press one for a healthy eighty-seven year-old woman, or press two for a twenty-three-year-old man with cancer."

"This is getting old," said Lela. The cell phone in Ben's hand began vibrating, followed immediately by the familiar chime.

"You got to be kidding," said Ben. "There must have been a delay from the time he sent the e-mail to the time I received it. Reception here is very spotty."

"What's this message say?" said Lela.

Ben gave his cell phone to Lela. *You could have saved one of them, but you were too late. Again. They will both die.*

38

"Nurse, I think my grandson stopped breathing a few minutes ago," said Mrs. Rutherford, a tissue in her hand. She wiped at her tears again. "Will you please see if it's over? Brady has suffered for so long."

The nurse approached the bed. She pulled the covers down to waist level and examined Brady's chest for respiratory movements. She produced a stethoscope from her pocket and listened to his chest.

"Yes, Mrs. Rutherford, I'm afraid Brady's gone. I'm sorry," said the nurse, looking at her watch. "Time of death is two-oh-three in the morning." She bowed her head down and then looked back at the older woman. "Can I get you anything, Mrs. Rutherford?"

"No, I'm fine, thank you dear. In fact, I'm relieved. His battle with cancer and his suffering is over." She wiped more tears.

"I'm happy the family decided to make him a no code. Brady is now in a better place." She bowed her head again. "Would you like me to call anyone for you?"

"Give me a few minutes alone with my grandson. I'll call the rest of the family myself, soon. I'm glad it was my night to stay with him. But I wish we had more time. I was hoping his parents and sister would have one last chance to see him. Alive. It wasn't meant to—"

Two men entered the room wearing police blues, guns drawn. Behind them, Lela said, "I'm Detective Rose. We're investigating a—" She noticed the intense pallor on the face of the young man on the bed. "Did he just—"

The nurse nodded. "Yes, he was a DNR. Do not resuscitate. His death has been expected for the last several days. There's really nothing to investigate in here, Officers."

"Can I check him for needle marks?" Lela approached the bed and stopped. "He has an intravenous line, doesn't he?"

"Yes, for pain medication," said the nurse.

"Excuse me, Detective Rose, but what's this all about?" said the older woman, now standing.

"I'm sorry for your loss, ma'am. We have reasons to believe a serial killer is here in the hospital, killing patients," said Lela. "Has an unknown man been in this room recently?"

"No, I didn't see—" began the nurse.

"Yes," said the older lady at the same time. "A male nurse was in here about fifteen minutes ago and injected something in Brady's IV. He told me it was for pain. I did wonder why he needed to give any medicines for pain since Brady was sleeping comfortably at the time. Do you think that man ended my Brady's life sooner than . . ." she sighed deeply. "To end his suffering?"

"I think your grandson was murdered, ma'am," said Lela. "Can you describe this man?"

"He was tall, five-eleven, maybe six-foot tall—he was wearing a baseball cap. He had a funny odor to him. That's why I didn't drink the water."

"What water?"

"After he injected the medication into Brady's IV, I thanked him. Something came over me, and I started to cry. I tried my best not to wake up my Brady. I knew he needed his rest. The man poured me a glass of water. He seemed so nice. He seemed to be caring and polite." She wiped her tears with a tissue.

"But you didn't drink the water?" asked Lela.

"He insisted that I do. Very nicely, though. He said I must drink it to feel better."

"But you didn't?"

"I pretended I put it in my mouth but I didn't. I pretended to swallow. The young man had a weird odor to him. His clothes smelled funny, like a faint fishy odor. It was faint but I have a great sense of smell."

"Then what happened?"

"After I pretended to swallow, he left in a hurry. When he left, I went into the bathroom and rinsed out my mouth."

"By any chance are you eighty-seven years old, ma'am?" asked Lela.

"Why yes, I am. I turned eighty-seven three weeks ago. How did you know?"

39

The two-story house on Palomino Court was quiet, as was the whole neighborhood. A gentle breeze rustled the leaves, providing the only sounds. Two Danville police cars and one state police car arrived, their wheels screeching to a halt, lights and sirens off. The vehicles parked several yards away from the property line, and four officers got out. The men walked briskly to the front of the house with guns drawn. With a nod and a silent signal of the hand from Austin, two of the officers rushed to the back of the home. Austin and the other cop walked up the three steps to the front door.

"We're in position," faintly squawked the walkie-talkie attached to the officers' belts.

"Knocking on the door now." The detective rang the doorbell followed immediately by heavy fist-knocking on the door.

"Danville PD, we have a warrant to search this house. Open the door immediately!" yelled Austin loudly in between hard banging.

"Who is at the door at this time of night?" said a man from within.

"Dr. Brent Weiner. We have a warrant to search your house and car. Open up right now," Austin said. The door opened slowly.

"What's this all about, Officer?" asked the man.

"Anybody else in the house?" said the other cop. Austin held up a police badge.

"No, my wife and kids are away. I'm alone."

"Do you have any weapons on you or on the premises?" said Austin.

"No, sir. I don't own any guns," he said, his voice shaking, his eyes fixated on the handguns the two cops held, their barrels pointing at the floor.

"These are warrants to search your home and vehicles," declared the detective handing the documents to the doctor. He picked them up with trembling hands and began to read.

"I can't read this right now," he said. "I'm too nervous. What's this all about, Officer?"

"All downstairs rooms are clear," yelled out one of the cops. "He's the only one here."

"I got the car and garage," said Austin. "You two got the rest of the house. Rickets, you stay with the doctor." Austin entered the kitchen and took a quick look around. A clock on the wall read two twenty-three. He opened a door. Beyond it were two cars, three bicycles of different sizes, and a neatly arranged counter.

Thirty-eight miles to the north, another group of police officers were setting up to knock on another front door. A mailbox read, *The McClellan Family*. All four corners of the home were covered by at least one cop. The rain had begun to fall again.

The house, rustic, with an elegant, old-style wraparound porch, had been a home for several generations of McClellans. In the back of the property, there was a red barn and beyond that, a large pond.

"I've known the McClellans for years," said Powers, walking to the front of the house with Sergeant. "Hell, I went to school with Marvin."

"I've been to their summer fish-fry parties many a time," said Sergeant.

"I can't believe Marv would do anything like this," said Powers.

"Good people go bad," said Sergeant. "We have a job to do." The two were now in position.

"Open up right now!" yelled Powers as he knocked hard on the front door. Nothing. Sarge nodded, and Powers banged on the door once more. No answer.

"Take it down," said Sergeant. A large battering ram hit the front door squarely in the middle. After the third smash, the door splintered at the hinges and gave way. Four cops entered the darkened home, flashlights over handguns pointing in every direction.

"Clear," yelled one the cops inside the darkened home, exiting the dining room and kitchen area. Lightning momentarily brightened up the room.

"Clear," somebody else cried out, this one from the east side of the home. "Master bedroom and bathroom's clear."

"Upstairs is clear. Nobody in the house, Sarge," shouted one of the cops.

"Mulligan and Rhodes, stay here. Call for the crime lab unit. They need in here ASAP," said Sergeant. "The rest of you, come down to the barn with me."

Heartland Regional Medical Center was being pounded by the storm. The timing between the lightning flashes beautifully brightening up the overhead sky and thunderous rumbles that followed was almost instantaneous, indicating that the squall was right above the hospital. Another flash illuminated Lela's window. Her cell phone vibrated.

"Lieutenant, this is Oscar Gonzalez."

"Where are you, Gonzalez?" said Lela.

"I've been on cruiser patrol all shift, Lieutenant. There's something you need to know. I received the pictures of the three men you're looking for."

"Did you spot one of them?" asked Lela. She threw her shoulders back and her eyes brightened.

"I've been busy, as you can imagine being the only patrol car out here. But I just got a chance to review the mugs on my laptop. I made a traffic stop earlier in the shift."

*   *   *

The old Chevy Impala slowed down and pulled to the side of the road. Right behind, the police cruiser stopped a few feet away, red lights flashing.

"Get out of the car, sir," said Gonzalez, his right hand on the holstered Glock. "May I see your driver's license, registration, and proof of insurance?"

"What's the problem, Officer?"

"Your rear bumper is about to fall off," said Gonzalez. "Very loose. It could create a serious accident if it falls off while you're driving."

The man got out of his vehicle and produced three documents from his wallet. He handed them to the cop.

"I see what you mean," said the man looking at the back of his car. A dented bumper with many scratches, devoid of chrome in multiple areas, was in place on the left side but had fallen several inches on the right. The man shook it gently, the bumper moving freely, then falling a few more inches on that side. "This sucker could fall off any moment." He squatted down to closely examine the bumper. "I can assure you I'll get this fixed today. I have some rope in my trunk. I'll tie it down real good for now."

"I'll give you a hand with it," said Gonzalez. "I'll let you off if you promise to get it fixed permanently within twenty-four hours."

"That's very kind of you, Officer," the man said. "You don't have to help me."

"That's okay, I don't mind," said Gonzalez. "I'll be right back." The cop got into his police car and used the radio. As he did, he noticed the man opened up his trunk and used a blanket to cover its contents on the right side. He pulled out a rope from the left side of the trunk and quickly closed the lid. Gonzalez squinted his eyes and approached the man who was on his knees by the bumper.

"Unit Charlie-Nine," squawked his radio. "Motor vehicle accident with possible injuries intersection of Michigan and Fifth. Please respond. Unit Charlie-Nine."

"I got to go," said Gonzalez entering the police car.

"Thank you, Officer," said the man turning over his shoulder. "I'll get this fixed."

*   *   *

"When I looked at the pictures, that man looks to be Randall Dragone," said Gonzalez. "He had the right build and hair color. I just thought you should know."

"Yeah, thanks, Gonzalez." Lela thought for a second. "Did you look at his driver's license?"

"Yeah, I did. But I didn't run it through the computer or take down any info on it. It was so long ago. I just can't be sure."

"What was in the trunk of his car?" said Lela. "Did you see anything?"

"Sorry, Lieutenant. It did make me suspicious. But I didn't see anything."

"What time was it about?"

"I'd say around four, maybe five in the afternoon."

"Where was he headed, do you know?"

"Well, that's another thing, Lieu. This all happened as he was approaching the hospital campus. In fact, where we stopped to tie up the bumper was in one of the parking lots at Heartland."

40

Lela made a phone call to Colby and conveyed the information she discussed with Patrolman Gonzalez. "Alert all law-enforcers at Heartland that Randall Dragone may be inside this hospital. I want every officer to have a picture of Dragone in their hands, and I want a thorough search throughout the facility. No stone is to be left unturned."

Lela and Ben entered the command center. Mrs. Joy Rutherford was ready to be interviewed.

"I'm so sorry for everything you've been through this evening. And your loss, Mrs. Rutherford," said Lela.

"You believe the mass murderer I've been seeing on TV killed my grandson?" said Mrs. Rutherford.

"Yes," said Lela. "I also believe he tried to poison you, but you were smart not to swallow the water."

"We've analyzed a sample of the water he poured for you to drink," said Ben. "It was heavily concentrated with the same poison that killed your grandson and all the other victims. At that high concentration, you would have died quickly if you had ingested it."

Mrs. Rutherford's mouth remained opened. Silent. She took a deep breath.

"Detective, I wasn't smart not to have the water, just lucky." She looked down at her hands.

"Mrs. Rutherford, you're the only person alive, that we know of, to have seen this man," said Lela. "Will you tell us everything about this evening and your encounter with him? Everything. Don't leave anything out."

"Yes, I'll try," said Mrs. Rutherford.

*   *   *

"Brady, are you still hurting? It seems you've been in a lot of pain the whole day."

"The pain meds in my IV haven't been doing much, Grandma," said Brady. "But they are now. I'm beginning to feel comfortable. And very sleepy."

"You need your rest, Brady," said Grandma. "Try to get some sleep. I'm here right next to you."

Finally, Brady fell asleep. Grandma walked to the window and looked outside. The sun was peering through in between thick layers of clouds. There was a large parking lot to the left, a beautiful pond barely seen to the right. The ducks that normally swam in those waters had left hours ago. Droplets of rain here and again were gentle reminders of the imminent squall. Grandma looked back at Brady. His full, slow breaths portended the deep rest his cancer-ravaged body required. He was weak and exhausted, a peaceful smile almost forming on his face.

A tall man wearing a grayish-white baseball cap and light blue nurse's uniform came into the room. He had well-manicured brown hair and a beard. "I have more meds for Brady," he said.

"Brady's finally resting now," said Grandma. "His nurse just medicated him about half hour ago. I don't think it's . . ." The man walked briskly to Brady's side and injected a syringeful into his IV rapidly.

"He needs this medicine to rest," said the man. "This will allow him to rest much longer. Rest he sorely needs, huh?" Grandma nodded, bowed her head and again looked out the window into the underbelly of the approaching thunderstorm.

*   *   *

Sitting in front of Lela in the Command Center, Mrs. Rutherford broke down and began to cry.

"That's what the man meant," she sobbed. "Brady will rest much longer now, the rest he sorely needs." Lela offered a tissue, then, placed her hand on the woman's shoulder.

"This man knew Brady's age," said Lela. "That's easy to look up in the computer. But he also knew *your* age. Do you know how?"

"I told him when he brought us our dinners, earlier in the evening."

"He brought you and your grandson food?" asked Lela.

"Yes, that's how he knew my age," said Mrs. Rutherford. "He brought in our dinner trays earlier. He looked at Brady's armband. His age and birth date are written there in big numbers just under his name. Then he asked me if I was the one getting a birthday cake. I joked with him that I had plenty of birthdays for a lifetime." She forced a smile. "I told him my age."

"Ben," whispered Lela. "Have Colby and Lurie work on a picture array?"

"I'm on it." Ben began texting his request.

"Any name tags on the man, Mrs. Rutherford?"

"I don't think so," she said slowly. "No, I don't believe he had a nametag on him."

"Okay, what else? Any distinguishing features? Any scars, birthmarks, tattoos?"

"No, none of those."

"What else can you remember?" said the detective.

"Just the smell. He had an unusual smell."

Lela and Ben exchanged glances.

"What can you tell us about the smell?" said Ben.

"An odor I had never smelled before. It was faint. The best description I can give you is that it was fishy, but not really. Not really unpleasant, although for some reason it made me not drink the water he poured for me. I just think that food preparation and distribution should be done with the utmost cleanliness. Even the smallest of an unusual odor, and I'm wondering about the cooking process. My husband and I used to own and manage a diner here in town. For forty years, we served people. I have always had a sensitive nose. My Harold would always tell me my nose was special. He always—" she smiled. "I'm sorry, I digress." Her smile faded. "When the man left, after he dropped off the dinner trays, I was going to ask the other nurse for different food for my Brady and me, but he was so sick to his stomach—he didn't want to eat anyhow. And I had lost my appetite seeing him like that." Mrs. Rutherford wiped her tears with a tissue.

"Mrs. Rutherford, was the odor on the man or in the water? Or the food?"

"On him and the water. I didn't notice it on the food."

"Do you think you could identify the man or this odor if you saw or smelled it again?" asked Lela.

"Oh, yes. Without a doubt. I'll never forget that man or that smell as long as I live."

Lela placed her hand on the old woman's and said, "May I show you some pictures?" Lela gestured to Ben, who walked to the door receiving an envelope from Colby. Ben approached the table and sat down. He removed the pictures from the envelope and arranged them on the table in front of the old woman. "Take you your time, Mrs. Rutherford. Do you recognize any of these men here?"

She slowly scanned the pictures. There were eight photos of men with beards, arranged in two rows of four. Number two, four and five were pictures of Brent Weiner, Marvin McClellan and Randall Dragone.

"None of these men look familiar," said Mrs. Rutherford looking up from the pictures.

"Okay, now, if you don't mind, I'd like to take you to our research laboratory and see if you can smell the peculiar odor in there."

"Sure, anything I can do to help," said Mrs. Rutherford, forcing a smile.

Ben and Lela got up and walked the older woman slowly to the laboratory. They nodded to the four policemen guarding the entrance.

Mrs. Rutherford stared around the laboratory. They walked slowly to the back where David was busy looking through a microscope.

"Where's Jack?" said Ben.

"You scared the shi—" said David. "Sorry, I didn't realize you were here. Jack went over to the storage room to fetch a couple of reagents."

"This is Mrs. Rutherford," said Lela. "We just came to show her around a second. We'll leave you to your work." Ben and Mrs. Rutherford nodded. The three walked out of the lab.

"So, Mrs. Rutherford, did you smell anything in there?"

"Most definitely, I did. Whatever that gentleman in there was working on has the same faint odor I smelled upstairs on that man. But the man looking through the microscope in the lab wasn't the man who killed my grandson."

"Okay, Mrs. Rutherford. You have been most helpful," said Lela.

"You're welcome. Now, put the son of a bitch who took my Brady from me in jail until he rots," said Mrs. Rutherford.

"Johnston and Colby," Lela yelled. "Take Mrs. Rutherford up, back to her family. Get her info for the report and so that we can reach her later, if we need her." The uniformed cops nodded and accompanied the older lady out.

"I've been thinking, Lela," said Ben. "We need to do a massive evacuation of the hospital and get as many people out of here as we can. I think the shit's about to hit the fan."

"Ben, when I need your input, I'll ask for it," said Lela. "That would be the wrong thing to do for many reasons. Right now, Ben, I don't have time to explain it to you."

"Hear me out," said Ben. "We could start to move people out and—"

"And cause massive panic," said Lela. "We don't have the manpower to even begin—"

"We could move as many as—"

"No, goddamn it," yelled Lela. "I said no!" She walked to the window and looked outside. The rain was coming down hard, and an occasional lightning flash poured into the room. "Are we good on this?"

Ben nodded. "Okay, do it your way."

"Now we know the killer is definitely a lab worker working with tetrodotoxin," said Lela. "I wonder how long the odor would stay on a person after working with the poison?"

"I don't know," said Ben. "Probably not that long. It's pretty faint to begin with."

"So it's likely the killer is working on the poison right now."

"Miranda, David and Jack are the only ones we know who are working on the poison here. We can rule out Miranda, and Mrs. Rutherford ruled out David. Besides, he's too short to fit the description and profile."

"And he's been out of town during the murders," said Lela. "I checked on him. We can clear him as a suspect."

"Unless there is another lab in the hospital where the killer is at work right now, that leaves Jack, but he's in a wheelchair," said Ben. "Besides, he doesn't wear a beard. There must be others. Other research lab workers. I guess Randall Dragone and Marvin McClellan know their way around a laboratory. And they both wear beards."

"A beard is something you can buy at any store around Halloween, Ben. I myself have one at home. I go as Blackbeard the Pirate." She smirked. "The wheelchair. The wheelchair." She squinted her eyes. "Why is Jack in a wheelchair?"

41

David took a moment to consider the reaction of chemicals developing in front of him. He tapped the test tube and scrutinized its content. On the tabletop was a small beaker with several milliliters of a clear fluid.

"Is it soup yet?" said Jack, wheeling his chair nearer.

"I was beginning to worry about you. Where have you been?"

"I told you I was going to the bathroom and grab some reagents from the closet," said Jack. "Are you ready to see the end result of the mixture?"

"You need to get a bigger pee bag," said David. He poured the contents of the test tube into the beaker and swirled the mixture around. "This should be our antidote." David twirled the beaker again and looked at the contents at eye-level. "Jack, I've done most of the work while you constantly go to the bathroom," said David. "Now watch, since this is your lab, you'll get all the credit and glory."

"This isn't about glory, man," said Jack. "It's all about saving a young man's life. I used to think you were a brilliant researcher, David, but now I see you're an asshole like all the others. It's all about glory and fame."

"Yeah, yeah. Cry me a river, why don't you," said David picking up the beaker. A light blue discoloration appeared slowly out of nowhere. "The reaction has reached its climax." He placed a drop of the chemical on a slide and positioned it under the electron microscope.

Jack wheeled his chair toward the scope, "We may be making history."

"I wonder if this chemical has antiarrhythmic potential," said David. "It's a sodium channel blocker, like quinidine, procainamide, and lidocaine, well-known antiarrhythmic agents. Theoretically, it should be the perfect drug to treat patients with heart rhythm disorders. This stuff could be worth a lot of money."

"Oh, I was wrong," said Jack. "It's not just about fame and glory with you. It's also about money."

"Which one of those are you personally against?" said David. "Fame? Glory? Money?" David concentrated on his analysis, his eyes peering into the microscope. "I think we got an antidote. A definite reaction. Take a look."

David stepped aside and Jack took a turn examining the reaction through the microscope. Jack pushed off the table, his wheelchair rolling backward slowly. He had a smile on his face.

"I think *I got it*," said David. "This is *my* design. This is *my* invention. What did you really contribute, Jack? This will bring me fame, glory, and money. I may win the Nobel Prize for Science."

"You're pretty insensitive," said Jack. "We've worked together to—"

"Hey, boys," said Miranda, walking into the lab. "How's your progress?"

"There's a definite reaction," said David. "The tetrodotoxin molecule is completely involved by the new compound. I'm sure this will provide a blockade. Now let's figure out if the new drug is toxic by itself and what the dose ought to be for a person of Billy's size and age."

"I'll start the calculations," said Jack. He wheeled his chair to a computer screen, his head bowed. He began typing on the keyboard. "I want to do a computer simulation first, then try it on a couple of mice. Miranda, we need your help with dose calculation and analysis for safety."

"Sure, you got it," she said.

"I'm going to take a break while you run the simulation and calculations," said David. "Either of you want some coffee?"

"No, thanks," said Jack.

"None for me," said Miranda, looking through the microscope.

David entered the break room. He began making coffee. While the machine dripped, David found a Styrofoam cup. There was a stack of them in a drawer under the counter. There was also a container full of sweeteners and sugar. He took one and dumped its contents inside the cup. He opened the refrigerator under the countertop and looked inside. He poured cream into the waiting cup.

"This is the slowest coffee maker I've ever seen," he said, watching the *drip, drip, drip* of liquid into the pot. He peeked inside the vending machine standing in the corner of the room. Nothing in there spoke to him. Nothing he couldn't live without. An old newspaper was spread out on a table. He picked it up but nothing grabbed his attention. He massaged his tired neck muscles.

Rain tapped on the window, inviting him to look outdoors. It was pitch dark out. Suddenly, lightning sparked, illuminating the trees. Then a thunderous noise rumbled deep inside his chest. Utter darkness again covered the outside world. David saw his own reflection on the window glass. Another flicker of lightning. When the flash returned to dark, David suddenly became aware that there were now two figures reflecting back from the windowpane. He turned around. A tall, muscular man was standing right there, his big hands quickly approaching his collar. David felt his heart thump hard in his chest. He tried to speak, but the man's stranglehold on his neck from behind him choked him of air. David thrashed about in vain, reaching as far back as he could trying to grab any part of the man who stood behind him, both hands gripping his neck, stealing his life.

"You won't share the glory with the cripple, you don't deserve to live," said the man's raspy voice. "How's your gallbladder, doc?"

David tried to yell, but only muffled gurgles came out his mouth. Weakened by the struggle, David felt his strength dwindle down, his hopes of staying alive fading rapidly.

The man's powerful right hand continued to choke hold David, but his left hand grabbed something out of his shirt pocket. While David fought for his life, he spied the man's reflection on the window in front of him. He saw the silhouette of a syringe come toward him and felt the prick on his neck. The man let go of David's neck and quickly injected a syringeful of poison into his neck. As the thunder faded, the only sound left was that of a few gurgles of a man destined to die very soon.

42

Lela paced the floor. Her cell phone chimed.

"Sarge," she said. "What's going on over there?"

"The McClellan property seems deserted, but there's a lot to search for with only eight men, Lieu. Any more help coming from the fibbies or staters?"

"There are FBI and county and state police people on the way, but they won't be here for a while. Maybe another hour. Any evidence that McClellan may be the murderer?"

"Not yet, Lieu, but we still have a lot of work to do here. I'll keep you informed," he said.

"Who's going after the third person of interest?" asked Lela. "Randall Dragone?"

"Nobody yet. We don't have enough manpower to do all three searches. Austin Rube is supposed to go look for Dragone's whereabouts when he finishes with Dr. Weiner's."

"Okay, I'll call him. I want proof one of these three citizens is the mass murderer, and I want him in my jail ASAP. Sarge, call me with a report in thirty minutes." She hung up the phone.

"Ma'am," said Lurie from behind her.

"Please give me some good news," said Lela. "I really need it."

Lurie walked into the command center, Ben behind her. "I have something for you," she said. "I've been working on McClellan. He's supposed to be in Florida for the last week. I checked with the airline, but they report he never used his ticket. We checked with the resort in Florida, but he never checked in."

"He never left town," said Lela. "He's still here." She smirked. "He's been here all along."

43

Mom, Dad, I don't know if I should be a doctor or a police detective when I grow up. Can I be both? Both help people. Yeah, I want to be both.

Years passed and Billy was a middle-schooler. *I love science. I love to learn about the body and how it all works. I can help people feel better and save their lives when they're dying from some disease. Like Mom used to do.*

More years went by so quickly. Billy was fishing with his Dad. A few feet away, Mom had just finished packing up the picnic plates and plasticware. *I love you, Mom and Dad. This is so peaceful and quiet out here. I wish this moment could last forever.*

Billy could smell the intense odor of sickness. The air in the small ICU cubicle was flooded with stenches of chemicals, machines and bodies of people coming and going, all there to help promote his recovery, but all of them failing. *Mom, I don't feel so good,* he tried to yell out, but no words would come. *I'm weak and shaky on the inside. Something is very wrong. I feel I'm going to die real soon. Right now. I don't want to die. I want to get well and live. Mom, what's happening to me?* yelled Billy inwardly, but no outward sound would be heard. *Mom. Dad. I feel I'm slipping away. Don't let me die. Please, Mom and Dad. I don't want to die. I don't want to leave you.*

The monitors did not fluctuate significantly and, therefore, gave no clues of Billy's inner turmoil. The mood in the small ICU room was somber. Billy remained motionless except for the pushed air entering and leaving his lungs.

Amy fought back tears, although, right now, she wished, most of all, to be strong for her boy, his life rapidly slipping away. Each swoosh of the respirator pushing air into Billy's lungs cut deeper and deeper into her spirit. The frustration of the medical personnel, given their inability to save such a young life, was palpable and highly contagious. All efforts to reverse the course of the poison invading Billy's body had been futile. And time was running out. Amy looked up at the wall in Billy's room. A crucifix. A clock.

How much longer? thought Amy. *How much time do I have with Billy?* Amy looked from the crucifix to the clock. Then back to the crucifix.

At Billy's bedside was Natalie. She had been with Billy practically since he first arrived at Heartland, just a bit over twelve hours ago. Her long white coat was no longer wrinkleless. Her usual indomitable, determined, and intelligent demeanor had been replaced with exhaustion and defeat. She looked at Amy.

"Wish we could do so much more," she said. Amy nodded.

Billy Sinclair, a sixteen year-old with uncombed brown hair, lay unresponsive on the ICU bed, eyes taped shut, a tube secured in his mouth. *Swoosh.* Another breath by the mechanical ventilator, another few precious seconds of life. Overhead, the monitor registered the heart rhythm which was, at this time, stable. To the side, a series of numbers continued to tell the grim tale of Billy's deteriorating cardiorespiratory status. Blood pressure was 72 over 46, a very low reading, especially since strong intravenous medications were being administered, invigorating Billy's circulatory system to keep fighting. With every *drip, drip, drip* came several milligrams of "don't give up." Earlier, the heart rate had been running in the mid-to-high one-twenties but Billy's pulse had recently started to drop despite the aggressive medication regimen. Now at fifty-two beats per minute, the medical staff began to recognize this could well be a sign of bad things to come. And soon.

"Wish I could do more," repeated Natalie.

"I'm here with you, baby. Don't give up, Billy," whispered Amy. "You'll get better soon." Amy's blond hair was uncharacteristically disheveled. Her usually cheerful blue sparkly eyes were cheerless. She was beyond depleted, left bone-dry of any strength after all these hours of brutal physical and emotional struggle to keep her boy alive.

Natalie gestured for Amy to walk outside the room.

The two women reached the nurse's station. "Amy, you need a break," said Natalie. "You look so exhausted."

"When you're the mom of a dying child, there are no breaks. Not until Billy gets better."

"There's only so much you can do," said Natalie. "There's only so much anybody can do."

Amy began to cry, and Natalie came to her and hugged her. "I don't know how much more of this I can take," said Amy.

"You have to begin to prepare for the worst," said Natalie. "We may not be able to save Billy."

Amy nodded and wiped her tears.

The room abruptly came to life as the heart monitor's *bleep, bleep, bleep* suddenly slowed and deteriorated into a straight line. A loud alarm proclaimed the urgency of the situation. Medical personnel rushed into Billy's room. A nurse put the bed rails down and hopped on the bed kneeling right next to Billy.

"No pulse," she yelled. "I'm starting CPR."

"Call a code, ICU Room 3, stat," someone else yelled out to the secretary. "Call code blue."

A respiratory therapist unhooked Billy from the respirator and hooked up a bag onto the breathing tube and began manual ventilation. She squeezed the bag, pushing air into Billy's lungs.

"One, one-thousand, two, one-thousand, three, one-thousand . . ."

"Get the crash cart stat!"

44

Miranda's body was feeling the burden of physical overwork. But it was her brain power that was beginning to register critically low. She had done multiple autopsies in the last several hours, and it was all beginning to take a toll on her. Her head ached, her neck was stiffening up, and her leg muscles stung. Her critical reasoning was sluggish and getting worse by the minute.

"I'm sinking fast," she said to the microscope. She labeled the slide and made an entry in her logbook. "I need a power boost." Massaging her neck, she slowly made her way to her office. She grabbed her purse from her desk drawer and removed some cash.

"It's just me," she said to the guards.

"Go ahead, doc," said one of the unsmiling officers writing something on his clipboard.

"Do you ever smile, Officers?" said Miranda, strolling away. She walked down a few short, quiet, dark corridors and finally reached the break room. She noticed the coffeepot was on, the pot completely full. She picked up the Styrofoam cup with a small amount of milk on the bottom. Miranda looked about. A bright flash outside the window was followed by a loud thunder. She walked out the door and ran to the research laboratory. She opened the door and stood there for a moment. Nobody in sight. She scanned all the usual spots where the two researchers had typically settled to perform their work. No one. She began to worry. Eerie silence. Suddenly, she heard a door opening from behind her, startling her, stealing her breath away.

"What are you doing here?" said Jack, wheeling his chair nearer to her. "Not enough dead bodies for you in the morgue?" He was holding his cell phone up to his ear.

"Don't scare me like that, Jack," she said. "You almost gave me a heart attack."

"Sorry. Who let you out of your cage again?"

"Where's David?"

"I don't know. He went to get coffee a few minutes ago and hasn't returned." He propelled his wheelchair closer to Miranda, his mobile phone in his lap. "Hey, guess who I just saw out and about outside the—" Jack put up his index finger then pointed to his earpiece. "Detective Rose, this is Jack Stevenson in the research lab. I was just over in the chemical closet to get some stuff, and on my way back, I think I saw one of our pathology personnel. A man named Marvin McClellan. The funny part is, he's supposed to be on vacation. He was wearing a police uniform." He listened for a few moments. "Okay, I'll be here." He hung up.

"That's crazy. Marv's on vacation, isn't he?" said Miranda. "He went to Florida, deep-sea diving."

"Well, that's what I thought too."

Lela hurriedly walked into the lab.

"Jack, tell me exactly what you saw," Lela said. "And where?"

"Well, I know this guy pretty well. We share an office. Marv is the head tech on the pathology side, and I'm the same on the research side. He's supposed to be off on vacation in Florida. I was coming back to the lab when I saw him. He was holding a gun of sorts. I couldn't see it well. He and I locked eyes for a split second. I called out his name, but he turned around quickly and started walking fast, down a hall and away from me. It was really weird."

"It couldn't have been Marv," said Miranda.

"What did the uniform look like?" said Lela. "And where did you see him, exactly?"

"Just outside this door," said Jack, his thumb pointing behind him. "The uniform? The light was pretty dim there. It looked like the uniforms all the cops are wearing around here."

"Could you tell if it was a Danville PD officer?" said Lela. "County or state police?"

"I can't tell those apart even up close and with good lightning, Lela," said Jack. "I'm sorry."

Lela nodded and looked around the lab. "Where's David?"

"He went for coffee a while ago," said Jack. "He should be back by now. I'm starting to worry about him."

"I was just in the break room," said Miranda. "It looks like David made a pot of coffee but never poured himself a cup. He's nowhere to be found."

"I'll check it out," said Lela. "I'll worry about David and Marvin McClellan. You two get back to work. We have a teenager to save."

Lela picked up her cell phone and left the lab in a hurry. Jack and Miranda exchanged glances.

"How's the antidote coming along?" said Miranda.

"We should be done with all the theoretical calculations in another ten minutes. Fifteen at the most."

"I understand Billy's not doing so well," said Miranda. "They just called a code in his room. Ben's wife called him up there a few minutes ago, and it didn't sound good."

45

"It'll be a special pleasure to harvest your gallbladder for my growing collection, Dr. David Robertson," said the man. "And I can see that you're almost ready." He placed a few cashews in his mouth and began to chew them. "I need some tea. Where can you get a good cup of tea is this godforsaken place?"

David's eyes were wide open, his breath now very shallow. His skin had begun to take on a deep bluish, cyanotic hue.

"You want to know why?" asked the man looking into David's terrified gaze. "Your eyes tell me you want to know why." He chewed another cashew. "These are pretty good nuts, David. If you weren't paralyzed, I'd give you one to try. You know cashews are good for your heart? But in your present state, you'd just choke on them. And your heart will stop here in a few more minutes, anyhow." The man took a deep breath. "Well, I'll tell you why I did it. I would have thought you'd have it figured out by now, David. Maybe you're not as smart as I thought you were, huh? Well, David, I needed your NanoTech sequencer. I can do so much more with it than you could ever imagine." He chewed two more cashews. "You know these NanoTechs are so hard to come by. You can't just go to your neighborhood hardware store and walk out with one. Oh, no. By the way, thank you for bringing it by. I gotta tell you, David. When you were unpacking it and setting it all up, I came so close to telling you not to bother. I was only going to put it back in the carrying case so I can take it out of here." He popped another cashew in his mouth. "But I needed a crash course in how to operate it." He swallowed. "Are you still in there?"

He leaned over and inspected David's pupils. The dying man's breaths were more feeble now, the remaining pathetic manifestations of life.

"The antidote?" he continued, "I've had that all along. What, you think I'd be experimenting with tetrodotoxin without having the antidote? Are you freakin' nuts?" He laughed. "Nuts, get it? Cashew nuts?" More laughter. "No, I know exactly how to make it. I've taken it myself, you know just in case. You never know if you're tired and take a swig of poison instead of tea, you know what I'm talking about?"

He stopped laughing. "What, you never make mistakes? If you're so fucking perfect, why are you the one struggling to get another breath?"

He walked to a window. The rain pounded on the glass panes, occasional lightning and thunder punctuating the storm.

"By the way, do you remember me now? I think you do. That twinkle in your eye tells me you remember me now. Yeah! What was it, about a year ago?" He paused. "I can't believe you didn't pick it up. You and I interviewed for the same position. Of course, you got the job. I didn't. What a mistake, huh?" He tossed another cashew into his mouth and chewed. "You and I sat right next to each other waiting to see that bitch, Amy Sinclair. She denied me a position in her glorious National Research Laboratories," he said. "The great Dr. Amy Sinclair dared to say *no* to me! Look at me now. I've invented a wonderful cure for heart rhythm disorder that'll save millions of lives every year." Sorrow suddenly overpowered him. "Christine," he said as he pulled out her picture from his wallet and placed it in front of David's unmoving stare. "This is all about Christine. Christine died because of Amy Sinclair. She picked you instead of me. So you see why you and she have to die? And her son too. She has to feel the pain of loss, just like I had to." He took a deep breath. "I took the most dangerous poison, tetrodotoxin, invented its antidote by myself and without nanotechnology. I took the combination of the two and figured out how to modify the molecule just enough to transform it from a deadly poison to a wondrous, miracle cure. I tapped into its healing powers, and now I will have all the fame and glory." He smirked. "With the nanosequencer, I can mass produce the chemical and have it available for human trials within a year, maybe less. What have you and the great Dr. Amy Sinclair done lately, huh?" He got up and paced. "Nothing, that's what. You and all the pathetic researchers here and at the Bioresearch Institute." He clenched his teeth and fisted his hands. "They take anybody here. Even the crippled. They would hire a goddamn paralyzed cripple, but not the most ingenious, brilliant researcher of all time." He shook his head. "They ain't worth a shit. Not here, not in your lab. Not compared to me and to my ability." He sat down next to David's near-lifeless body. "Can you still hear me, David?" he looked into his eyes. "With your dying breath, I want you to hear this. I will be great. I will become the most famous researcher in the world. You, all you'll become is a gallbladder donor."

And with that, David took his last feeble breath.

46

Ben was immediately escorted to where Amy sat in the waiting room. They ran to each other and hugged, tears running down both their faces. Ben walked to the door. Amy followed him and stood right behind him. From the doorway, they could barely see the entryway into ICU-3.

"I want to go see Billy," said Ben, pacing. He started out toward ICU-3.

"Not now, Ben," said Amy, holding on to Ben's arm. "They're working to save him. You'll be in their way." Ben stopped and nodded.

At the door to the waiting area, they witnessed doctors, nurses, and techs rush in and out of the small room.

"The whole thing seems surreal," said Ben. "This can't possibly be happening to our Billy. To our son."

"It doesn't look too promising, Ben," said Amy. "They're doing CPR and following protocol. The longer time goes on without a response, the worse the chances are for Billy." The silence in the quiet waiting room where the couple stood was in sharp contrast to the escalating commotion and noise coming from Billy's room.

"One milligram of atropine and another of epinephrine," someone shouted above the commotion. Amy cringed at the medication orders; orders she herself had given so many times while working on so many dying patients during her training. Other people's sons. Other people's loved ones.

"Let's try some vasopressin," said Dr. Messing.

"This can't be happening to us," Amy cried. Ben wiped her eyes with a tissue and the two embraced again. "It can't be our Billy in there," she said in between sobs. "It just can't."

A few feet away, the intense fight was on: "One, one-thousand. Two, one-thousand. Three, one-thousand," said the nurse, doing chest compression.

"Push another milligram of epi," yelled Dr. Mathis, eyes fixed on the heart monitor. "Continue CPR to circulate this epi—we'll check the monitor without CPR in two minutes."

"One milligram of epi," said a nurse, handing a syringe to Dr. Mathis, who was standing at the side of the bed. She received the medication and injected it briskly into the intravenous line.

"One of epi was in two minutes ago. This was the third epinephrine," she shouted.

"Okay, hold CPR for a sec. Let's see what the monitor shows," said Dr. Messing. The compressions were ceased, all eyes on the monitor. The respiratory therapist at the head of the patient squeezed the bag forcing oxygen into Billy's lungs yet again. The chest rose slowly then back down. "Continue CPR," the physician said. "How many atropines have we given?"

"Two," answered the recording nurse. "Want more?"

"No, not yet," said Dr. Mathis.

After a minute of chest compressions, Dr. Messing suddenly said, "Stop CPR again. I thought I saw some heart activity." All eyes turned again to stare at the monitor. One blip. Then another. Then several more. The alarm, until now loudly proclaiming a straight line, began its *beep, beep, beep* synchronously with the heartbeat now at ninety-eight times a minute.

"Blood pressure is eighty-four systolic," Ben and Amy heard Natalie say, triumphantly.

"We bought ourselves a little bit more time. But we have to get that antidote right now," said Natalie.

47

The two officers patrolled the first floor corridor, adjacent to the pathology wing.

"Do you think we'll catch this son of a bitch?" asked Owen Kirchner.

"Of course, we will," said Pedro Morgani. "Lieutenant Rose always gets her man. We'll catch him."

"Speaking of catching a man, are you coming over on Saturday?" asked Owen.

"Yes, I'll be over as I promised. And on time, this time."

They took a few more steps, the only sound arising from their boots striking the tiled floor.

"Stop," Owen whispered. Both cops held their breaths and drew their Glocks. "Did you hear that?"

"No. What was it?"

"I heard a metallic noise coming from one of these offices," he said softly, pointing to a few doors on the right side of the hall. "Listen."

The sound repeated. Both officers looked intently at one of the doors.

"It sounds like metal rubbing on metal," said Owen.

"It's in there. The Respiratory Department office," said Pedro. "I heard it too, that time."

"Should we call for backup?"

"Nah. It may be nothing. Let's check it out first."

"Okay. After you."

Both men stood by the wooden door, guns drawn and ready. Owen grabbed the knob and whispered, "One, two, three." He threw open the door, and both men entered the office. The room was dark, the only light coming from the poorly lit hall and the cloud-covered nightfall outside the window. There was a blackboard on one wall in front of which there was a desk. Other walls were adorned by posters.

"Is anybody in here?" said Owen. "Show yourself. Now!"

"Danville PD," said Pedro. "If there's somebody in here show yourself now, or you may get shot."

There was no sound. There was no movement. The officers pointed their service weapons and flashlights to all corners of the room.

"There's nobody here," said Owen. "Relax, Pedro. You can put your Glock down. I'm feeling a little foolish." Both officers holstered their handguns.

"Why is this air-conditioning vent cover out of place?" said Pedro, his light pointing at the metal screen. Both men approached the opening. Pedro looked inside.

"Anybody in there?" he asked, the echo of his words returning severalfold. "It's dark in there."

"Should we go in there and look around?" asked Owen. "The tunnel is plenty big for a man to go through on his knees."

"Yes, doggie style."

"Pedro, be serious now," said Owen. "Where does it look like the vent is going?"

"It probably goes back into the research and pathology lab area this way," said Owen pointing to his right, "and to the parking lot this other way. I can feel a slight breeze."

"Call up the LT and let her know what we found. This may be nothing or may be something important. Ask her what she wants us to do next," said Pedro.

Owen turned away toward the window to get enough light to make the phone call. A tall man appeared from underneath the desk beside Pedro. Before he could react, a small needle entered the right side of his collar, the poison immediately saturating his neck muscles. The man twisted the cop's neck, fracturing his cervical spine.

"What the—" Pedro said as he fell to the ground with a thud.

Owen allowed his cell phone to drop on the ground and went for his Glock. But it was too late. He too was swiftly overpowered by the man who placed his powerful arm around the officer's neck, making it hard for him to breath. Or move. The needle entered his neck, but the plunger remained undisturbed.

"How old are you, officer? Tell me a little bit about yourself and your partner over here, and I promise I'll make it quick and painless."

.

48

"Your son is dying," said Dr. Armstrong.

"What can be done to buy us more time, doctor?" asked Ben. Amy held her husband's hands firmly.

"I need to insert an Impella device."

"What's that exactly?" said Ben.

"I'll insert a catheter into his groin artery and advance a long tube which will reach into his heart. The device is an external pump that'll help his ventricle push blood out to his organs."

"How long can you keep him alive with the Impella?" asked Amy.

"It'll buy us a few more hours, but not many," said Dr. Armstrong. "I can't really say with any degree of certainty."

Ben took a deep breath. His gaze connected with Amy's. Then he looked at the doctor. "Go ahead. Insert the Impella."

Ben's iPhone vibrated in his pocket.

The message read: *From now on, since you and the police are still loitering around my hospital, you no longer have a choice. It is not 1 or 2. It is 1 and 2 and 3. Number 1 is a decorated thirty-two-year-old policeman; number 2 is a twenty-seven-year-old rookie with a promising career. By the way, they're faggots, both of them. So no big loss! Don't ask, don't tell! Number 3 is one of the no-goddamn-good researchers. The three of them will die in ten minutes unless you leave my hospital and take all your pig friends with you.*

"Amy, I need to go," said Ben.

"Angelfish again?"

"Yes." He kissed Amy then walked toward the exit. He dialed Lela's phone.

"Lela, he struck again."

"What's the e-mail say this time?"

"Two police officers and one of the researchers. He said the three of them will die unless we leave the hospital in ten minutes. I'm forwarding the e-mail to your cell phone now."

Lela read the forwarded message and said, "Leave the hospital? He knows we won't do that."

"Lela," said Ben. "I have to go see David and Jack and tell them we're out of time. We have to give the antidote as is. There is no time to do any more checks."

"You go do what you have to do," said Lela. "But Ben, we can't find David. He may be the researcher."

"That goddamn son of a bitch," said Ben. "When I get my hands on that—"

"Ben," Lela said. "Be careful."

Phone back in his pocket, Ben walked briskly downstairs. He was cleared by the police sentinels and entered the research laboratory.

"Jack," he yelled. No one answered. He saw no one in the large area. He walked around looking down each of the aisles. "Where are you?"

Lela visited one of her shift commanders who was stationed at the hospital's main entrance.

"Sergeant Hines," she said, "A word."

He walked over to her. She disclosed the contents of the last e-mail from Angelfish. "I want you to stop over at all stations." She bit her lip. "Make sure the men stay in groups of at least three—never alone. The killer is in the hospital and most likely wearing police blues. You check the identification of any law enforcer you don't know. There will be a few policemen from neighboring towns and agents helping out from the FBI, state or county police. If you don't know them and you can't verify their ID, cuff them and lock them up."

"Yes, ma'am, I'm on it."

"This bastard is gunning for my officers now. He wants to make this personal," Lela said. "Get this information out to all the cops."

"I understand, Lieutenant."

"Find out who among us is thirty-two and twenty-seven."

"I'm on it," he said.

"Remember, this guy is armed and dangerous." She tapped his shoulder. "Take one officer with you for safety. Go!" she said. "I got to go find me a damn dead researcher. Oh, what a fucking glorious night this has turned out to be." Lela gritted her teeth. "Wait 'til I get my hands on you, you son of a bitch. You'll regret everything you've done."

Lela dialed on her cell phone.

"Ruby, anything yet?" she asked.

"I left one man behind at the Weiner house to stay with the criminologists. I don't think he's our man, Lieutenant."

"Ruby, the killer is here at the hospital, and he just threatened to kill two of our cops and one of the researchers. Get as many people back here as you can. You take one man and find out where Randall Dragone has been staying. He's still a strong possibility as a suspect. I need to know where's he's been living and what he's been up to over the last few days. Call me as soon as you have something."

Next, she called the officer in charge at the McClellan property.

"There's definitely no one here, in the house or barn. We did find some chemicals in the basement in small clear vials. I'll have these analyzed, but that'll take forever," he said.

"By the time we know what these chemicals are, this will be all over. Take a whiff at the vials and tell me if it has a faint fishy smell."

"Yes, this stuff has a weird smell to it. I wouldn't necessarily call it fishy, but an odor I've never experienced before. Why?"

"I'll explain later. Leave a man there and bring everybody else back to the hospital. McClellan is still a strong possibility, and I think he's here at the hospital. Call me when you arrive here. Find out where the extra FBI and state police manpower is. We need as many capable bodies and guns on our side and here as soon as possible. I'm getting another call," said Lela rerouting her phone to the new caller.

"Yes, Lurie."

"Jack was indeed injured three years ago in a car accident," she said. "He's been in the wheelchair ever since, paralyzed from the waist down. He sees a doctor here in town by the name of Courtney Steele. He sees her periodically for care. There doesn't seem to be a question as to whether he is a paraplegic."

"Can you be absolutely sure?" said Lela.

"I hacked into the doctor's computer system. I have Stevenson's demographic information including his picture, and it's the same person. He's a paraplegic. No question."

"Okay. That rules out Jack," said Lela. There was a piece of paper on the table in front of her. She crossed out Jack Stevenson. On the list remained Marvin McClellan and Randall Dragone. She circled both names and put her pen down. "Good work, Lurie. Let me talk to the officers guarding your station. Can you hand them your cell phone?"

"One second." Lela heard footsteps, a door opening and some distant conversation.

"Yeah, Lieutenant, what do you need?"

"Who's this, Preston?"

"Yes, ma'am."

"How old are you?"

"Ma'am?"

"What is your goddamn age?" yelled Lela.

"Twenty-eight, Lieu."

"How old is your partner?"

"Can I ask him and call you when he comes back?"

"When he comes back from where? Preston, where the fuck is your partner now?"

"He went to the john."

"Look, son. There's a killer here at this hospital. He may be dressed up as a cop, and he is most definitely armed and dangerous. He just told us he's going to kill a thirty-two-year-old and a twenty-seven-year-old cop." She massaged her temples.

"He told us that, Lieutenant?" he said.

"Yes, he sent an e-mail. I bet this son of a bitch killer is within a hundred feet of your goddamn ass right now. You get the woman and her computer and you go find your partner in the fucking bathroom. He may be dead already."

49

Officer Jeffrey Mulligan stood alone in the unlit McClellan home. He was commanded to stay behind and await the arrival of a handful of the criminologists.

Jeffrey looked out the bow window in the living room. The house was surrounded by almost pitch blackness. Thunderous clouds prevented the moon from providing any illumination.

*   *   *

"Hey Jeff, want to see a ghost?" said Dryden.

"Mom said there's no such thing as ghosts," said Jeff, placing his toy revolver in its holster. "Let's play cowboys and Indians."

"I'm pretty sure there's no such thing as cowboys and Indians," said Warren. "But believe you me, there are ghosts."

"We saw one at the old Strathmore mansion just last night," said Dryden. "Want to go see it or not?"

"Dad told us never to go in that property," said Jeff. "Did you guys forget?"

"Why do you think he doesn't want us in there?" said Warren. "Because it's haunted."

"Let's go, Warren," said Dryden. "I told you he's too young to hang out with us fifteen-year-olds. He's too much of a baby." The two boys turned around and began to walk away.

"I'm not a baby," said Jeff. "I'm ten. I'm almost a teenager."

"Yeah," said Warren. He looked back and nodded his head. "Almost. You can hang out with us when you're a teenager. See you later, squirt." The two boys continued to walk away.

"What's a ghost like?" said Jeff. He took his toy gun out of its holster and held its grip tight.

"We'll tell you when you're old enough," said Dryden. "It's getting late. We're going to see the ghost. See you later."

Jeff ran to his brothers. "Okay, I'll come," he said. "Is it scary?"

"Look, you want to be a cop when you grow up, right?" said Dryden.

"Like Grandpa, Dad, Mom?" said Warren.

"Like us," said Dryden.

"We're going to be cops too," said Warren. "It's a family thing. The Mulligans are a family of police officers. Dad says we have blue blood."

"If you're a real Mulligan, you'll wear the badge one day," said Dryden.

"Dad said we'll be the first twins ever on the force," said Warren.

"Anyway, the point is this," said Dryden, on his knees, looking into Jeff's eyes. "When you're a cop, you go into situations where you're afraid and scared. It's part of the gig."

"So yeah," said Dryden. "Seeing a ghost is a little scary. But it's worth it."

"Very worth it," said Warren. The twins looked at one another then back at Jeff.

"Are you coming or not?" said Dryden. "It's ten o'clock and plenty dark out."

"We have to be home before mom and dad's shift ends at eleven," said Warren. Slowly at first then faster, Jeff nodded his head. He placed his toy gun back in its holster and clinched his jaw. "Let's go. I'm in."

The Mulligan boys rode their bikes in the dark, monstrous shadows lurking at every corner. There was a full moon out, few clouds in the sky.

"The subdivision ends here," said Jeff. "Dad told me not to ride my bike out of the subdivision." Jeff stopped and straddled the bike.

"Okay, then. Go back home," said Dryden.

"No, wait up guys," said Jeff, pedaling faster to catch up.

They rode in silence. Jeff could feel his heart thumping and his palms became sweaty. Ten minutes later, they arrived. It was a huge property, a river running through it. A large, dark, dilapidated house was surrounded by a broken-down fence, about ten feet tall. There was a gate only partially attached at its hinges. Three bikes on their sides, the boys pushed the gate in, a screech announced their arrival. Jeff looked at Dryden, then Warren.

"Follow us," said Dryden. The older boys fished out their flashlights from their pockets and proceeded onto the cement stairs leading to the massive front door.

"You didn't bring a flashlight?" asked Warren. "It's nighttime, you dumbass. Didn't you think you'd need a flashlight?"

"I was hoping to play cowboys and Indians in the house," said Jeff.

"Walk behind him us," said Dryden. Two light beams cut through the poorly illuminated walkway.

Jeff tripped on a hole on one of the cement stairs and fell. Warren helped Jeff to his feet.

"Five more stairs and we'll be at the entrance to the house," said Dryden.

"Guys, I'm scared," said Jeff. "Can we go back?"

"I told you, he'd chicken out," said Warren. "He's just too—"

"No, he's not," said Dryden. "He's a Mulligan. He'll be fine."

Warren turned the knob of the large door and pushed it open. The boys looked inside the house. Warren ventured in first, the others following right behind him. Moonlight barely reached the foyer through the broken-down windows, cobwebs nearly unseen. Warren batted at them, creating an opening through which the boys passed. There was a large room to the right and another to the left.

Warren pointed to the right with his flashlight. "This was the dining room," said Warren. Jeff looked into the darkness.

"To the left was the living room," said Dryden, his flashlight pointing the way.

"This is where Mr. Strathmore was murdered," said Warren. "His ghost sometimes hangs out in there. Do you see it yet?"

Jeff swallowed hard, his heart thumping mightily. "Not yet."

"Jeff, you stay here by the window," said Dryden. "We'll go check in the kitchen. Sometimes the ghost hangs out in there."

"Can I go with you?" said Jeff, looking in the direction of the flashlight beam, pointing to the window. "I don't want to be alone." Jeff turned back toward his brothers. "Warren. Dryden. Where are you guys?" He continued to turn until he had completed a full circle. "Where did you go? I need some light." Jeff dared to take a step toward the window. "Guys." Another step. "This isn't funny. Come back here." Another step, then another. He was now near the window. He looked outside but all he saw was darkness. A scratching noise caused him to gasp. He looked up at the top of the window and noticed a tree branch scraping on the glass. "Dryden." He extended his arm, hoping it would touch the window. "Warren." It was then Jeff saw two dim red lights coming toward him, two evil eyes glowering at him from the darkness. Jeff screamed and began to cry. He rushed backward until his body hit the wall. He slid and sat on the wooden floor, his feet moving, pushing him further back into the wall. The eyeballs kept coming. Slowly. Deliberately. Jeff heard the creaking of the floorboards from the monster's steps.

"Dryden!" Jeff yelled. "Warren, help me!"

Another step, closer, more groans from underneath the carpet.

"The ghost is here," Jeff screamed. "Help me!"

Dryden and Warren began to laugh. They removed their flashlights from inside their shirts allowing bright beams to point at Jeff's face.

"You should see your face," said Warren. Jeff continued to cry.

"Look, he pissed in his pants," said Dryden, his flashlight beam pointing at Jeff's expanding crotch stain.

*   *   *

Looking out the window toward the backyard, Jeff saw a dark void in the distance, to the far left, which he imagined to be the large pond he knew existed on the McClellan property. He had heard of the famous McClellan fish fries held every summer, although he had never attended. Intrigued to see what the pond looked like, Jeff pulled out the powerful flashlight from his belt and directed its beam to that general vicinity. What he saw made Jeff gasp and drop the light onto the wooden floor, the loud thud adding to the eeriness of the situation. With tremulous hands, he recovered the flashlight and directed it down the backyard once again. The pond was only a basketball court distance away from the house. He stared, unsure of what to think, moving the light slightly, side to side. He beheld several pairs of eyes reflecting the light back, just like the two eyes he saw at the Strathmore mansion so many years ago. Except now, these were real moving eyes. Eyes down low, hiding from view. Spying.

"Mulligan here, sir," said Jeff into his cell phone, his voice shaky with nervous energy. "Sarge, I think I see people down by the pond. Three, maybe four. Maybe more."

"Okay, calm down, rookie. We'll turn around and be there in less than fifteen minutes. Stay in the house. Lock the doors."

Jeff walked around checking that all outside doors and windows were closed and locked. Thinking about his recent training at the police academy, Jeff struggled to remain calm, his insides anything but tranquil. He felt his blood on fire.

Jeff found a place in the living room from which he could keep an eye on the backyard. He had not been able to visualize anyone, other than the spying eyes. *If I saw them, they saw me.* His right hand, which was holding his service revolver, was shaking. *Do they know I'm alone? And scared shitless?* Disgusted by his inability to hold the weapon steady, he decided to place it back in its holster. *I'm liable to shoot myself.*

"God help me if these guys decide to barge into the house before Sarge gets here," he whispered to one. "If they only knew how scared I am right now, they would." He took a soothing deep breath. "This is normal, Jeff. This is your first time facing this type of situation alone." Another sigh. "If they could know I'm alone in here." He massaged his neck muscles, all along spying outside the window, assessing all quadrants of the pitch-dark outdoors for the location of the offenders. "Please get here, Sarge. I can't do this alone much longer."

50

Ben ran down to the research laboratory, hoping to fetch a hefty dose of the intravenous antidote. When he arrived, he noticed Jack was examining the contents of several test tubes.

"Here it is," Jack said, showing Ben a test tube labeled *antidote.* "I'm trying to boost its effects by concentrating it. We're doing the last of the tests. We should have an antidote for you in—"

"Billy just had a cardiac arrest," said Ben. "He pulled through but only barely. We ran out of time, Jack. We need to go with what we have now."

"God bless it," said Jack. He stared into the test tube. "What about this? I can give you half the material I have now, and you can test it out as is. You can at least test it out to see if it has any benefit at all. Miranda and I will continue to work on the other half of the specimen to see about its safety and to continue to concentrate it. But Ben, consider this. You may be giving Billy a drug or a dose that is toxic. We may be precipitating Billy's death with this untested antidote."

Ben nodded and bowed his head.

"Let me talk to Amy and Billy's doctors."

"I wish we could have a little bit more time, Ben. As much as I want to save Billy's life, I'd really hate to make things worse than they already are."

"Things can't get any worse, Jack. We've run out of time. I'll give you an answer in a few minutes."

51

The police car transporting the two officers arrived at the McClellan property. Sarge and Riley got out of the vehicle and ran to the front door, scanning in all directions. Jeff opened the door and the two men walked in. The rain was pouring heavily, spreading the haze, and making visibility poor.

"Am I glad you're here," said Jeff.

"Are they still out there?" asked Sarge.

"I haven't seen them since I called you."

"Show me where you saw the people."

"I think they're hiding down low, behind the bushes near the pond."

"There are a couple of spotlights on the roof of the house pointing to the backyard in the direction of the pond," said Riley. "I saw them earlier when I walked out to check the barn."

Sarge walked to the kitchen and looked out a window facing the back of the home. "This is how you turn them on," he said, pointing to a set of light switches labeled *outside spotlights*. "Riley and I will get into position. When I give you the signal, turn all these switches on then meet us outside."

"Anybody else coming to give us backup?" asked Jeff.

"No, son. We're it. Everybody is busy at the hospital looking for the killer. But I bet you a hundred to one, that the man is right here. Right on this property, right outside this wall."

"And it looks like he's got some buddies with him," said Jeff.

"There are all kinds of chemicals down in the basement, and I bet you they're trying to get to that stuff," said Sarge.

"Let's do this," said Riley, his hand around his Glock.

"We'll go out the north-side door," said Sarge.

"Okay," said Jeff, his hands on his service belt.

As Sarge and Riley left the kitchen, Jeff looked again outside the windows. All he could hear was the persistent raindrops beating hard against the wooden walk-out porch and window sills.

"Turn on the lights," said his walkie-talkie. "Not seeing anybody yet. It's all quiet out here."

Jeff threw the switches. Floodlights dumped brightness onto the backyard. He opened the kitchen door, donned his raincoat and hood, then walked out onto the porch. He drew his gun and held it with both hands. He looked in all directions. To his right, the beams of the other two policemen's flashlights pointed in the direction of the pond, which was only partially illuminated.

"See anything, Jeff?" said Riley.

"No, nothing." The rain was coming down even harder now.

"Anybody out there? By the pond? This is the Danville PD. If there's anyone here, show yourselves before you get shot," said Sarge, advancing toward the water, his gun drawn. Jeff and Riley converged and followed right behind.

The pond was pelted by the falling raindrops. A gentle breeze caused the cattails to sway to and fro. The cops looked in all directions. Not a soul in sight.

"Walk around the pond," Sarge whispered. "I'll stay here and keep an eye out." Jeff nodded and walked rightward, Riley began in the opposite direction. With each passing step, Jeff felt increasing anxiety. *Why did I sign up for this?* Another step. More forceful thumping in his chest. *Why am I so damn scared?* His face was now completely soaked, his eyelids drenched. The bright lights on the house no longer provided adequate illumination beyond this point, only pitch darkness now in his path. He turned on his flashlight. Another step. Jeff's ankle twisted slightly as his foot landed on an unsteady rock. He caught his balance and paused for a beat. Another step. It was then that Jeff's heart stopped. A definite rustling sound, a definite movement a few yards away. He pointed his flashlight and revolver to where he heard the noise and allowed his trigger finger to squeeze. Once, then again. Two shots rang out into the quiet of the rainy night.

52

"I work here," said the man. "I'm an orderly on the surgical floor. My name is Lionel Galloway."

"Where's your hospital ID?" said Sergeant Hines. "Why are you away from your unit?" Lionel unclipped his ID badge from his scrub pants and presented it to Hines. Two police officers held Lionel by his arms. Hines examined the ID. "What were you doing here, Lionel?"

"I'm on break. I was looking for a place to have a smoke."

"We informed all the nursing units not to let any personnel roam the hospital," said Hines. "Were you told not to leave your unit?"

"No, nobody told—"

"What's the extension for your supervisor? I'll call right now to verify your story," said Hines, his cell phone ready to make the call.

"Okay," said Lionel. "I was told not to leave the unit. But I'm on break, and I need a smoke, man."

"My orders are to apprehend anybody roaming around the nonpatient areas without proper authorization," said Hines.

"This is ridiculous," said Lionel. "I've worked here for twenty years and—"

"I'll cut you a break this time and not put you in my jail," said Hines. Then he turned to face one of the cops holding on to Lionel's arm. "Tomlinson, escort him to his unit and advise his supervisor—"

"What are you the Gestapo?" said Lionel. "This is my place of work, man. I can walk around anywhere I want to."

"Are you trying to convince me I should put you away?" said Hines. "It won't take much."

"You don't have the right or authority to do that, man." Lionel twisted his body and swung his arms trying to free himself from the cops' grasps. "You can't just walk in here and—"

"Okay, you've convinced me, Lionel," said Hines. "Take him away to the downstairs jail until the morning. If he gives you any more trouble, place him under arrest, read him his rights, and take him to the city jail instead." The two cops placed Lionel in handcuffs and pulled hard on his arm forcing him to walk away from Hines.

"I have to go back to work in fifteen minutes," yelled Lionel.

The cops walked off with their prisoner, his hands behind his back.

"I'm going to sue you, the police," said Lionel. "And the town. The mayor. I'm going . . ." His words trailed off as he and the cops disappeared from sight.

"We've decided to do a test injection with half the antidote material you have already," said Ben.

"I thought you'd say that," said Jack. "I've sterilized and prepared half the material and it's ready to administer." He handed Ben a syringe labeled *antidote-untested*. I'll keep my fingers crossed."

Ben grabbed the syringe and ran upstairs.

He entered ICU-3. At Billy's side was Amy, Natalie, and Drs. Messing and Mathis.

Billy's chest moved up and down with every *swoosh* of the respirator.

Standing next to Amy, Ben held out the syringe. Amy took the syringe from him, reading the label. She bit her lip.

Amy began to cry and collapsed. Ben grabbed her under the armpits, preventing her from falling to the floor. He grabbed the syringe from her and handed it to Natalie, who had rushed to help Amy. Another nurse arrived at Amy's side and placed a chair under her.

"Are we all in agreement?" whispered Natalie. Dr. Mathis nodded. Dr. Messing nodded. Ben nodded. Amy stared at the syringe. Unmoving. Tears streaming down her cheeks. Breathless, all eyes on her, anticipating.

Suddenly, Billy's heart rate dropped to the eighties then forties and finally twenties, causing the bedside alarms to go off. Then nothing. Straight line. Blood pressure and heart rate monitors now indicating a straight line.

"Call a code blue, stat!" yelled Natalie. "Start CPR."

"Dr. and Mr. Sinclair, we need you to wait outside again, please," said a nurse. The couple held one another and together they slowly walked out of the room.

"Give one milligram of epinephrine and another of atropine," said Dr. Mathis above the commotion in the room.

Ben looked back into the room at the same instant Natalie's gaze looked for his. Their eyes connected.

"Give the antidote," mouthed Ben.

Natalie looked at the antidote syringe then back at Ben. She nodded.

"I will," she mouthed back.

53

The shrapnel hit with a thud, followed by a yelp. Jeff's two bullets fatally struck their target, the target that had dared to move in the darkness surrounding the pond. Three, maybe four, canines darted out, ears and tails down, and disappeared into the darkness.

"Are you okay?" said Sarge, running toward Jeff.

"Hit a coyote. A few others ran away into those woods," said Jeff.

"Coyotes?"

"Yeah. I saw some movement in the shadows, behind the cattails."

"You did the right thing, rookie," Sarge said.

"No people here, Sarge," said Riley, as he approached. "What were the coyotes doing here? Something mighty important kept them around." He bent down by the fallen animal and shined his flashlight on it. One bullet smashed into its skull spilling out brain matter and blood onto the grass. A second bullet entered the chest, a pool of pulsating crimson still draining onto its fur.

"There's gotta be something special here," said Sarge, pointing his flashlight at the point where the water met the sand.

"I smell something foul," said Jeff.

"It smells like a dead body. One that's been here for a long time," said Riley.

"Help me look through these cattails by the water. The stench is coming from here," Sarge said.

Three flashlights probed the night. As the cops walked toward the water, the stench of putrid decay amplified.

"Here it is," said Jeff. "Dead body." He directed his flashlight beam several yards to the right.

"Looks human," said Sarge. A human torso bobbed with the sway of the pond water. "Help me get the body out onto the shore." The three men grabbed at a ripped shirt and pulled.

"The coyotes have been feasting on it," said Jeff.

"For a long, long while," said Riley.

"Here's another, Sarge," said Jeff. "Is that another one over there?" The three men struggled to beach the bodies.

"Any more death out here?" said Riley, his flashlight exploring.

Lela and two of her officers searched the research suite.

"Hines, any word on Dr. David Robertson or Dr. Tim Hughes?" she said.

"So far, there have been no traces of either," said Hines. "Neither is answering their cell phones."

"I'm sure they're both dead," said Lela. "I know I'm being pessimistic."

"No, Lieutenant. You're being realistic," said Hines. "We've searched through every door, every hall, every everything. And more than once. And nothing."

"What gets me is that the e-mail only mentioned one researcher. Why are two missing in action? And up to now, we've been able to find the bodies pretty easily. They're almost left in the open for us to find. Why is this different?"

"Can one of them be the killer?" said Hines.

"Everything's possible," said Lela. "But both these men are highly unlikely to be involved. I've cleared both David and Tim from the suspect pool."

"Maybe one of the researchers was the intended target mentioned on the e-mail and the other was collateral damage," said Hines.

"I agree. He may have walked in on the kill and had to be silenced," said Lela. "But why not change the e-mail to two instead of one researcher? And where are the bodies? There has to be some secret place in here somewhere. Find it!"

"Get those three bodies to the morgue right away and get them ID'd," said Lela into her cell phone. "Were they injected in the neck? Can you tell?"

"It's hard to tell for sure," said Sarge. "But I think so."

"What about the gallbladders?" said Lela.

"He took them," said Sarge. "They had the typical gash. Seems like they've been underwater for a while."

"How come they haven't been found before?" said Lela.

"A rope was tying all bodies together by the feet. I'm sure it was attached to some weight to keep the bodies immersed. The rope must have broke."

"Do you think one of the bodies is Marvin McClellan?" said Lela.

"I can't tell," said Sarge. "Between the water, the fish, and the coyotes, there's too much decomposition to get an ID."

"Hines," said Lela, "let Miranda know there are three bodies coming her way. We need an ID on them pronto as soon as they arrive."

"Yes, ma'am," said Hines. "So who do you think the killer is?"

"We know the murderer is from the research lab here. We've ruled out everybody but McClellan and Dragone. One of them has to be the killer. Maybe both."

"Wasn't there a third strong possibility?"

"Yeah, a Dr. Weiner but he's in our jail right now. He's been there since more people died here at the hospital so I don't think he's it. We thought about Jack Stevenson. But he couldn't have done it. He's been in a wheelchair, paralyzed from the waist down, for three years. It has to be one of the other two."

"Well, my bet is that Marv is not the doer," said Hines.

Another two police officers arrived, both armed with MP-5 semiautomatic machine guns.

"We've searched the whole hospital. Neither McClellan nor Dragone are anywhere to be found, Lieu. They just ain't here." He handed Lela the pictures of the suspects. "Nobody's seen them anywhere."

"Well, keep looking and show the picture to everybody again. McClellan or Dragone is here and one of them is the killer. Don't stop until you find them."

54

Ben and Amy were still pacing in the waiting room. The commotion in the ICU had just subsided, and they knew they would be visited by one of the medical professionals soon. The door opened and in walked Natalie and Dr. Messing.

"The good news," said Natalie, "is Billy responded, though barely, to the medications to restart his heart. The bad news is that the antidote didn't seem to do any good whatsoever."

"I imagine there's still some chance the antidote will work slowly and that it'll take more time to see a reversal of the paralysis," said Dr. Messing. "But . . ." he shook his head slightly.

"I'll keep my hopes up," said Amy. "This is all new pharmacology. We can't know if the usual rules apply. It may just take a little bit longer."

Natalie nodded. "We urge the scientist downstairs to keep working on the preparation to give us as potent an antidote as soon as possible."

"Can we see him?" said Ben.

"Yes, I'll take you to Billy," said Natalie.

"Do you still have the syringe of the antidote?" said Ben.

"Yes. It's at the bedside."

"I'd like to take it downstairs," said Ben. They arrived at Billy's side.

Natalie handed the syringe to Ben, who brought it to his eye level and examined it up close.

"What are you going to do with it?" said Amy. "It's an empty syringe." Natalie looked on.

"I'd like to have it analyzed. There's still a drop or two left in the syringe. Hopefully that's enough to test."

"Test it for what?" asked Amy.

"I don't know, sweetheart. I guess it's the cop in me wanting to investigate all possibilities."

"What possibilities?" said Amy. "Do you think someone downstairs is foul playing?"

"I'll let you know what I find." Ben departed ICU-3.

55

Ben walked into the pathology laboratory and looked for Miranda.

"Have you determined if the antidote is safe for administration?" he said.

"It is safe. I just texted Jack to tell him to start making big quantities of the stuff to give Billy."

"I need a huge favor. Do you have time now?" said Ben.

"Sure. I have everything ready for the arrival of three bodies found in the McClellan pond. I'll need to work on identifying them as soon as they arrive, but I have a few minutes until they get here. What's up?"

"Will you tell me the contents of this syringe? There's not much there. Is it enough?"

"It should be enough to get an idea," said Miranda." This type of testing is more up Jack's alley. It'll be better if he—"

"No, I'd like for you to do the testing. Can you?"

"Sure," she said, slowly. "Can I ask why you don't want Jack to do the analysis?"

"Let's just say I have my reasons," said Ben.

"Can we go to the research lab?"

"Do you have the equipment to do it here?"

"Depends on what it is. I can test for simple molecules here. It would be more complete in—" she looked at the syringe and back at Ben. She took the syringe in her hand and walked over to a counter. "Not much in here, but it'll be enough." She sat down on a bench. Ben watched as Miranda analyzed the mysterious few drops of liquid that had helped Billy not at all from his precarious predicament. She placed a tiny drop of liquid from the syringe onto a microscope slide and placed it under the lens. She looked through the scope.

"What do you see?" said Ben.

She removed the slide and mixed a drop of a chemical from the counter. She looked at Ben. Then back to the slide.

"What is that stuff?" asked Ben, again.

She added a drop from another reagent bottle then placed the slide back under the microscope.

On the opposite side of the pathology laboratory, there was a door leading to the morgue, a larger room with specialized tables for autopsies. Beyond this area, there was a foyer, an anteroom with a metal door leading into the large walk-in refrigerator where the dead bodies were kept.

In the dark, a man looked out a small window on the door into the pathology laboratory, spying in the direction of Ben and Miranda. He was barely able to hear their voices, and he was unable to understand what they were saying.

"There isn't much time," he whispered to no one.

He turned around to face the fridge. He opened its metal door and entered the cold environment, his breath materializing into the air.

"Come here, my beauties," he whispered to the departed. "Let me have your hidden treasures." Surgical gloves were already on his hands, his scalpel ready to perform its miracles. He unzipped the first bag. It was labeled *Marie Traylor*. Within a few seconds, he made the incision, and the liver, stomach, duodenum, and pancreas spilled out. He pushed the organs out of the way to uncover the gall duct. A swift slash later and he held Marie's cold gallbladder in his hot hand. "Beautiful. Lovely," he said. "You're full of the good stuff, aren't you?" He tied the duct in a knot and placed the excised sac inside a fluid-filled bucket. "Who's next?" He unfastened the zipper of the body bag labeled *Brady Rutherford* and picked up his scalpel. "Let's see if yours is as nice as hers, shall we?"

And the gallbladder retrievals continued, the visible breath from the dissector the only sign of life in the cold, poorly lit reefer.

56

Lela's cell phone vibrated.

"Dragone is nowhere to be found," said Austin. "When he got out of prison, he checked into the address you gave me as his last known. It's a boarding-home type facility for men recently released from jail, but they haven't heard from or seen him there for three days."

"I know the place, and I know the man in charge. Nice man by the name of St. Louis. He has a lot of insight into the dwellers there. Did you talk to him?"

"I did," said Austin. "He thinks good ole Randy was up to no good. He doesn't know what, but he thought something was definitely going on."

"Did you look at his room?" said Lela.

"He doesn't have a room anymore. Somebody else is sleeping in there. I snooped around but nothing there except a lot of garbage. I got the new renter out to another room and locked the apartment for now in case we need to come back in the morning."

"Okay, Ruby. Come on back to the hospital. Right now, I need you here. The killer is here, and I need all the manpower I can get." She hung up the phone. *Who are you, you son of a bitch? McClellan or Dragone? I'm going to find you, catch you and throw the fucking switch myself when you get the chair. I will catch you, make no mistake about that. And you will pay.*

On the other side of the building, in an adjacent wing, there were three officers on patrol. They walked down a corridor and passed by an office door labeled *Respiratory Therapy*. The door was shut, but underneath it, two of the cops noticed a beam of a flashlight that came and went. A definite bright streak had appeared momentarily.

"What the hell was that?" Reyes whispered.

"A flash of light under the doorway," said Oman. "I saw it too. Could it have been lightning from the storm?"

"No, it lasted too long then repeated on and off too quick for lightning," said Reyes. "There's somebody in there with a flashlight."

The three cops stood to the side of the door, their Heckler & Koch MP-5 submachineguns at the ready.

"We checked out this office about twenty minutes ago," said Ingram. "It was clear and locked then."

"It ain't clear now," said Reyes. "I'm telling you, there's somebody in there."

"I'm calling for backup," said Ingram. "Guard the door. Be right back."

As he began to turn to walk away, he stopped suddenly. A man in his early thirties dressed in green scrubs emerged from the office. He was wearing a gray baseball cap and had a couple of days' worth of facial hair. The three law enforcers' semiautomatic weapons converged on him.

"Danville PD. Stop right there," the cops yelled. "Get on your knees."

"Hands up in the air where I can see them," commanded Oman. "Lay down on the floor. Do it now."

With hands in the air, shaking, and a look of horror in his eyes, the man knelt down then sprawled on the tile.

"What's wrong, Officers," he whimpered. "Did I do something wrong?"

Reyes laid down his weapon on the floor, out of reach of the suspect, and placed his right knee on the man's back, pinning him down forcefully so he could cuff him. Ingram signaled for Oman to enter the office and look for anyone else in there. He did but was back in moments.

"Nobody else in there."

"What's your name?" said Reyes. "Where's your ID?"

"Randy, Sir. Randolph McIntyre," he said, his face now a few short inches from the tiled floor. Reyes frisked him, Ingram holding the submachine gun, its business end pointing at the floor.

"Do you have any weapons on you?" said Reyes. "Guns? Knives? Needles? Anything? I'll be very angry if I get stuck on anything you're carrying on you."

"No, sir. Nothing."

"Do you work here?" asked Reyes.

"Yes, sir, I do."

"Where's your hospital ID?"

"I forgot it at home."

"Have a driver's license?" asked Reyes. "Any picture ID?"

"My wallet's in my car."

"Okay, let's get up," said Reyes. Oman and Ingram grabbed the man under his armpits and pulled him to his feet, his wrists handcuffed behind his back.

"Why are you doing this to me? I didn't do anything wrong."

"We're going to take you downstairs," said Ingram. "We're looking for a mass murderer, and until we know for sure and check out your identification, we need to hold on to you. Understand?"

"Am I under arrest?"

"No," said Oman. "We just need to verify who you are."

"What were you doing in there?" said Reyes.

"I'm a respiratory therapist. I came to the office to check the work schedule for tomorrow. When I came out of the office, you guys were there."

"Why didn't you turn on the office lights?" asked Ingram.

"I couldn't find the switch. I figured I'd use my pocket flashlight quicker and easier and get back to work once I looked at the schedule on the bulletin board in there."

"Let's go downstairs and straighten this all out," said Reyes. They began walking to the stairway.

"Lieutenant," said Oman into his cell phone. "We're bringing down a man we found without ID in the Respiratory Department office on the first floor. He says his name is Randy McIntyre, and he was snooping around in there with a flashlight."

"McIntyre or Dragone?" Lela asked.

"He says McIntyre, but no way to verify that. He's got no ID on him. He says it's in his car."

"Check it out, Oman," said Lela. "Don't let him out of your sight until you can be a million percent sure."

"Yes, ma'am,"

"What does he say he was doing in the office?"

"He says he was checking out tomorrow's work schedule. We're coming down with him now, and we'll check him out. I'll call you when I have something."

"What does he look like?"

"He's about six-foot tall with a brown beard."

"Are you shitting me?" she said. "Is he wearing a cap?"

57

"Just water?" said Ben. "Plain water? Are you sure?"

"Well, water and sodium chloride," said Miranda.

"Water and salt. Are you sure it doesn't contain some of the antidote?"

"I'm not detecting anything other than saline water. I can't be one hundred percent sure, but I'm not picking up any complex molecules like the antidote," said Miranda. "What's this all about, Ben?"

"Let me see if I understand you perfectly," said Ben. "Your analysis isn't one hundred percent conclusive but highly unlikely to have anything other than water and salt."

"Right." Miranda bit her lower lip. "Ben, Jack gave you this as a sample of antidote to try on Billy, didn't he? Do you think he just wanted to give you hope while he continued his analysis? Get you off his back for a while longer?"

"If he did, it was a cruel joke," he said. "I don't think so. Miranda, you have some of the antidote too, right?"

"Yes, I tested it for safety. Do you want me to test my sample? I can test it against the sample you brought to me in the syringe. We can see—"

The noise of a door opening sprang from the back of the room.

"Doc, where do you want these bodies?" asked one of two men from the entryway. They were wearing jackets labeled *Coroner's Office*, and were accompanied by three cops bearing semiautomatic weapons.

"Ben," said Miranda. "These are the three bodies found on the McClellan property. Lela wants me to work on ID'ing these people as soon as possible. I have to wait on your stuff until I get the ID work up done."

"I can't believe this is happening," said Ben.

"Bring the bodies in here, and place them on these autopsy tables," said Miranda.

The men wheeled a stretcher in, a black body bag enveloping an obvious body. The stretcher was placed parallel to the table; and four men, one at each corner, transferred the body bag over.

"One down, two to go. We'll be right back with another one," said one of them. The men disappeared passed the door.

Miranda came to Ben and placed her hand on his shoulder. "Ben, my testing shows the agent Jack gave me to test is safe to administer. Of course, I assumed it was the real antidote. If I've been testing salty water, it would test out as being safe."

"Oh man, what's going on here?" said Ben. "I hope somebody's been working on the fucking antidote. My son's dying upstairs, and he'll be dead soon without it."

"Hang on, Ben," said Miranda. "I'll work on this for you first. The ID on the bodies can wait a few minutes." She walked toward her desk and examined her test tubes with the ongoing analyses. "I'll have an answer for you in a moment." She placed a drop of a preparation on a slide then viewed the results through the lens of her microscope. She focused her objective and examined it thoroughly.

While Miranda worked, Ben walked over to a window and peered outside. The storm seemed to have picked up steam again. The wind flogged the glass panes in bursts and splashed rain all over the window. Occasional lightning illuminated fantastically the outside world, momentarily sending flashes of light rushing into the lab.

"There's no cellular reaction here, and there is no sodium channel blockade at the cellular level. The chemical Jack gave me to test does not appear, at least preliminarily, to have anything other than water and salt."

During this exchange, the men placed the remaining two body bags on the tables in the autopsy counters. In moments, the coroners and their police escorts were gone.

"Do you think Jack is part of this conspiracy?" said Miranda. "Is he working with the murderer?"

"I don't know," Ben said. "I don't know."

"I've worked with Jack for a while now," said Miranda. "I can't believe he would be capable of any of this."

She looked into Ben's eyes. "What should we do now?"

"Take a quick peek at the bodies in those bags," said Ben. "See if McClellan is one of the dead bodies?"

"I may be able to identify him." They walked over to where the black thick plastic body bags were. Miranda handed an autopsy lab garb to Ben and donned hers. He put it on then the goggles, as she had. Both placed menthol camphor ointment under their noses. She unzipped the first bag. The stench was unbearable for Ben, who withdrew to several feet away. More accustomed to the scent of decomposing bodies, Miranda carried on.

"The first body is definitely female," she said, moving on to the second bag. "The second is a man." She made an inspection of the facial remains. "Hard to tell. Too much decomp." She moved on to the third inspecting all side of the face and head then zippered up all bags. She walked over to where Ben was looking out the window.

"Can't make a definitive ID, Ben," said Miranda. "It'll take me a while to come up with fingerprints." Ben nodded. "But, Ben, for what it's worth, McClellan had a birthmark on his right temple. I think I see it on the third cadaver who is about the right size and built as Marv is, but the decomp is so advanced, I just can't—"

"I have to find an antidote," said Ben. "I have to get it now and save my boy. Please call Lela and let her know everything."

"What are you going to do?" asked Miranda, but Ben was already out the door.

58

"Lela, I told you before," said Lurie, "Jack Stevenson is a patient of Dr. Courtney Steele's. I hacked into her office records and found him in her database. I was a little bothered at the time by how easy it was to find his medical records. These things are usually protected and hard to get at. So I've been thinking and doing more research. More digging. Several things bother me now about Jack. For one thing, the picture in our employee database is exactly the same as in Dr. Steele's. These are pictures we typically have a secretary take on the spot to add to the medical or employee online records. It's taken with a digital camera that is hooked up to the computer to make it easier for the secretaries to do. So why would the same exact photo of him appear on both databases? One explanation is that someone, presumably him, imported his picture over to her computer system."

"Go on. You got my attention."

"I asked one of the officers to go out and read Jack's vehicle plate number and vehicle identification number from his car. The license number is registered to Jack Stevenson, and it is a disabled plate. But the VIN comes back to a stolen van from Ohio last year. I'm thinking he just forged medical records and got himself the disabled plate numbers after he stole the vehicle. Jack's driver's license is a regular license with no mention of him being disabled."

"That son of a bitch," said Lela.

"I have more," said Lurie.

Lela's eyes opened even wider.

"The van with the disabled plates has not been driven that much. The mileage the officers reported to me now and the mileage reported when it was stolen, indicates that it only has about two thousand miles on it, over the last year. And it's eight hundred miles just from where it was stolen to here. So I think this van is just for show. He must have another vehicle in the parking lot. Presumably a normal one with normal controls, if he is, in fact, not disabled."

"I'm going to love putting that son of a bitch down," said Lela, "just like the dog he is."

"I have more."

"Give me everything."

"I had looked for people that had computer access into the hospital and research files of all the abducted and murdered victims."

"I don't remember Jack Stevenson having come up in your search."

"That's right. That bugged me too. He's the only one with absolutely no computer connection to any of the victims. His login information has never ever been used in connection with any of the victims. He's had computer access to many other patients, but none at all with the murder victims."

"Good work, Lurie," said Lela. She walked to the door out of the command center and spoke to one of the policeman guarding the entrance. "We have to find Jack Stevenson right now. He may very well be the bastard we've been looking for. I want him in cuffs pronto. Get his picture out to all the men and show it to Mike England and Joy Rutherford." She took a deep breath. "We also have to find his vehicle out in the parking lot. We need to look for a suspicious car that is probably hidden from view and close to the building. Get an emergency warrant to search his car, office and computer. I don't care who you have to wake up at a quarter to three in the morning." Lela closed the door and walked back to Lurie's side. "I'm going to have officers escort you to Jack's office. I want you to dig through his computer files and find me conclusive evidence that Jack Stevenson is the mass murderer."

Ben was exhausted to a degree he had never known. He so wanted to return to Billy's side and be with him and Amy, but he had to see this mess through and bring the antidote to Billy. He hoped the cure had been developed and manufactured in this hospital lab, this very day, but where was it now? There was no way David Robertson would let him down. But where was he? Jack appeared to have changed sides, from rescuer to number one on the list of potential villains. And where was *he* now? His cell phone rang.

"Lela," he said. "I think Jack Stevenson—"

"Ben, Jack Stevenson is—"

"Sounds like you and I came to the same realization," said Ben.

"You first," said Lela.

"Miranda and I have gathered loads of circumstantial evidence to put Jack on top of our list of possibilities for the mass murderer."

"Like what?"

"Well, he gave me a syringe full of antidote to try on Billy, which did nothing for him. Miranda's preliminary testing shows it was probably just water and salt. Not conclusive, but pretty damning. The dead bodies from McClellan's pond are here in the morgue. Miranda is working on definitive identification, but she thinks one of the cadavers is McClellan. There's a spot on one of the bodies that resembles a birthmark Marvin has on his temple. Same shape and place, but she can't say for sure due to severe decomposition."

"Lurie just came up with a whole bunch of observations too," said Lela. "Nothing one-hundred-percent solid, but the evidence against Jack is quickly becoming more than just pretty damning." Lela summarized Lurie's discoveries. "We're searching his computer and office now."

"Meanwhile, we have to find him. I need to get the antidote to Billy. I'm sure he knows where it is."

"Have you gotten any more e-mails from Angelfish?" said Lela. "It's almost three o'clock. We're due to—"

"Hang on, Lela," said Ben. "I just got an e-mail from Angelfish."

"What's it say?" said Lela.

Ben read, "The next two to pay the price for your persistence and unwillingness to vacate the premises are the researchers—the out-of-towner and the cripple."

"What do you think?" asked Lela.

"It may be a trick to get us off his track or . . ." Ben stopped in midsentence. "Miranda is running this way."

Lela could hear rapid footsteps toward Ben.

"Ben, Ben," Miranda said. "Come with me. Quick."

"Ben, what is it? What's she saying?" asked Lela. "What does she want?"

"You have to come right now," yelled Miranda.

"Where, Miranda? Where are we going?" said Ben.

"Where is she dragging you, Ben?" asked Lela. "Where is she taking you?"

"To the morgue," said Miranda. "The gallbladders are gone."

59

Miranda led Ben by the hand to the morgue's refrigerator. Lela arrived soon afterward.

"What is it?" asked Lela.

Miranda opened up the metal door into the fridge. She turned on the lights. "Somebody's been collecting gallbladders." Miranda pointed to the half-open body bags, the cadavers inside all showing a large wide open gash in the abdominal area.

"Someone not very tidy," said Lela. There were pieces of tissue and pools of congealed blood all over the tables and floor.

"Let's go to the research lab," said Ben. Lela nodded. She removed her sidearm from its holster. Ben grabbed his revolver too.

"Miranda, you stay here," said Lela. "It's not safe for you. Where can you go and hide for a little while?"

"Hide? Are you kidding?" she said. "I'm going with you."

"I'm not going to argue with you," said Lela. "You need to stay out of the way."

"Lock yourself in the refrigerator," said Ben. "I'll come get you as soon as I can."

Without waiting for a reply, the two cops rushed away, revolvers drawn.

Six law enforcers rushed into the research laboratory, six gun barrels looking for a target. Quickly and decisively, the law-enforcement team dominated the area. In a ready-to-shoot stance, the cops looked around. There was not a soul in sight. The officers searched every row of laboratory counters, then all the adjacent rooms and closets. No one. Carefully, the group approached the area where Jack had previously been working.

"Well, lookie here," said Lela. By his special work table, Jack's wheelchair was overturned on its side, one of the wheels still turning. There was a pool of blood near it. Moving away from the congealed crimson, there were drag marks for several yards.

"Clearly indicative of someone being yanked—pulled toward the exit," said Austin pointing to one of the exit doors. Smashed beakers and test tubes and glass bits were strewn on the floor.

"Or someone wanted us to think that," said Ben. Lela nodded, her peering eyes scanning.

The officers walked about slowly.

"An empty syringe with a needle still attached," said Austin, looking inside a wastebasket.

"Any surgical gloves in there?" said Lela.

"No, ma'am."

"Bag the syringe, but be careful don't stick yourself with the needle," she said. "See if you can find fingerprints on the syringe. If you do, run them pronto." Austin nodded.

"Did you stage this whole thing, Jack?" said Ben softy, Lela at his side.

"It would be hard to execute this whole thing so quickly and so well." Ben and Lela looked all around then back at one another. "Then again, this may be what it appears to be. I just don't know."

"Did you notice the aquarium?" said Ben.

"The what?" she asked.

"Look at the aquarium. It was full of beautiful angelfish before. These fish are full of tetrodotoxin. All the fish are gone now. The killer can now make more poison. Lots more!"

"That bastard," said Lela, looking behind her at the fishless clear water. Just underneath the tank, there was a small net and a large puddle. "He took the poisonous motherfucking fish with him."

"Lieutenant," someone shouted from behind her. "You know that gadget I brought in from the airport when I picked up Robertson? The nano machine?"

"Yeah," she said turning around.

"It was set up on this table. I helped put it there myself," he said, pointing to an empty space on the counter. "It came in a suitcase with the logo NanoTech. I put it underneath that table."

"It's all gone," said Ben.

"What the hell," said Lela.

"Lieutenant," said Austin. "You'll want to see this."

"What now?" said Lela.

"There are two sets of distinct fingerprints. They came back to Marvin McClellan and Randall Dragone. None of the prints match Jack's."

"I was so sure Jack was involved," said Ben. "I'm not so sure anymore."

"My head is spinning so fucking fast, I'm getting sick to my stomach," said Lela.

Miranda waited until the footsteps she heard right outside the refrigerator door ceased and counted to one hundred. Only then did she dare to peek out of the reefer's small window, the area outside the metal door blurred from condensation. She used her lab coat sleeve to wipe the glass and peered out again. She saw a tall man wearing a grayish cap place a handful of nuts into his mouth. His back was to her. He was skillfully attaching a small canister to the air-conditioning vent. She noticed for the first time the vent's register down on the floor at the man's feet. Her frantic heavy breathing fogged up the small window once again. She felt for the locking mechanism on the steel door for the fifth time, again reassuring herself that the bolting pin was still in place and that she was safe. Her hands trembled, her heart thumped fast. Quietly, she slid down the large metal door and sat on the floor shaking, not from the cold this time, but from terror she felt inside. She took a deep breath and looked at her cell phone. No bars. The display indicated *Searching for signal.* She got up on her feet again, wiped the glass, and peered into the anteroom. The man was gone.

Where did you go? What are you up to now? She looked at her mobile again. *No signal.* Slowly, she withdrew the locking pin. She glanced out the small window. No one. Miranda opened the metal hatch slowly and looked out again, ready to push on the cold steel door with all her might and lock herself back in, if need be. All remained quiet. She tiptoed out of the fridge, noticing all at once the much-warmer temperature of the foyer. Her breathing was accelerated, her eyes searching side to side. She walked to the air-conditioner vent and examined the small container. She took a whiff and noted a faint but unmistakable fishy odor. *Tetrodotoxin.* And just like that, she put it all together. She removed her cell phone from her pocket again, her hands shaking even more vigorously now. *No signal.* She held onto the phone, moving it all about, hoping for a sign of reception. Miranda desperately walked briskly in a circle, her eyes on her cell phone. *No signal.* She looked around but knew there was no landline nearby. She required cover and quick. Somewhere. Anywhere but the refrigerator, where she was about to freeze to death. The man could return at any point and if he did, she'd be a dead woman. Miranda felt frozen with panic. *Which way did he go? Which way should I go?* She needed to text or go to the research laboratory and alert Ben and Lela. Miranda prayed for the courage to run away from this forsaken place, but to do so, she'd risk being caught by the madman on the loose. *If I only knew which way you went,* Miranda thought, intense fear clouding up her judgment. *Wherever I go may be in the direction he went, and I may be running right into his clutches.* To stay put was not the answer either. Miranda knew the man was very likely to return soon. She began to tiptoe toward the morgue when she suddenly stopped, her breath on hold, her ears piqued. There was a distant noise. Footsteps maybe. After a second of hesitation, Miranda ran away from the closet, where the sound seemed to have come from and entered the morgue. Desperately, she looked at her cell phone and saw one-bar of signal, come and go. She crouched underneath one of the autopsy tables and began to type a text message to Ben and Lela. She typed as fast as she could, a challenging task given her trembling fingers: *Get out of research lab! Tetrodoxin in A/C ducts. Killer spotted by cadaver fridge.* She heard the sound of a door open and close coming from somewhere behind her. Miranda stilled her breathing and closed her eyes, her body too frozen with fear to move. Distant, slow footsteps entered the morgue and became louder. Much louder. Miranda examined her cell phone again. No signal. *No! No! No!* she thought. *I need a signal, or I'm dead. Please, God.* She moved her cell phone side to side, her gaze on the signal meter. *Searching for signal.* Miranda forcibly pushed the send button repeatedly, tears cascading down her cheeks. She moved the phone side to side, up and down. *No signal.* The footsteps stopped a few yards away, Miranda was too frightened to dare look back in that direction. Then the footsteps began again, creeping closer to her. Horrified, Miranda sat still in the fetal position, her breath stifled.

Outside, the storm was reemerging from its quiescence, now growing even stronger than earlier. Miranda appreciated the rain pounding on the outside walls, with occasional deep roaring of the thunder. She suddenly gasped, aware the footsteps were now only a few feet away. She noticed the shadow of a man approaching the autopsy table she was under. The figure stopped by the table, his feet right next to hers. The man carried a syringe with a clear fluid. Miranda's heart began pounding even harder when she noticed he was kneeling down to look at her.

60

Terri suddenly stopped writing. She looked up from her paperwork and bit her lower lip.

"Something's wrong," she said to no one. "Something's definitely wrong." She dialed Miranda's cell phone.

"Hi, this is Dr. Miranda Phillips. Sorry I can't take your call right now. Please—" She hung up her cell. She looked at her watch. *Three in the morning. Have to go down to the lab and complete the bench work on the antidote. There's no time to waste.*

She struggled to get up from bed and walked to the door. The two nurses were talking at the nurse's station.

"You have to watch out for Dr. Phillips, the patient in 731," said Ruthie. "She's in there working on some antidote or something. She says she's going to save a boy who's been poisoned."

"Is she delusional?" asked Stella.

"Maybe," said Ruthie. "I told Dr. Phillips I would be placing an orderly with her after my shift to make her get some sleep and not leave her room."

"Good," said Stella. "As the only RN tonight, I'm glad you got an orderly. I can't keep close tabs on her overnight. When will the orderly arrive?"

"In a few minutes," said Ruthie. "Let me tell you about all the patients."

Terri looked outside the door. The nurses were distracted. Terri pushed the empty wheelchair as she tiptoed into Room 733 and entered.

"Mrs. Houston," Terri whispered, as she approached the older woman's bed. "Are you sleeping?" No reply. "Wake up, Mrs. Houston. We're going to switch rooms. Come on. Get up. I'll help you. Come with me." She pulled the over-sedated patient onto the wheelchair. "I'm sorry they over-medicated you, Mrs. Houston. You're going to spend the rest of the night in my bed." Terri placed a blanked over the older woman and wheeled her onto the hall.

Terri picked up the papers full of chemical formulae, her evening's work, and shoved them into her side pocket. With difficulty, she positioned herself comfortably inside the chair and wheeled herself to the door. She opened it up slowly. No one in sight. She proceeded toward the elevator, looking in all directions at every turn.

She pressed the down button and waited in the silence of the early morning hour. The elevator arrived and she entered. The doors closed behind her.

The rain poured steadily. Visibility was poor, making it difficult for the three officers to locate the car.

"How does the lieutenant think we're gonna find the motherfucking car in this rain?" asked Pratt.

"Ain't it a bitch to be a rookie? We get all the shit jobs," said Woody, the rain hitting his hooded parka hard.

"To tell you the truth, I'm not even sure what it is we're looking for. What did she say exactly?" yelled Pratt over the loud rainfall and a burst of thunder. In the short distance, they witnessed the sky brighten up spectacularly for the split-second of the lightning strike. Then thunder again, then another flash and more thunder.

"Reardon, take those two rookies," Woody said imitating the Lieutenant's voice, "and go out into the parking lot and catch pneumonia. You do it, because my Mr. Johnson is bigger than your little Baby Johnson. And I'm in charge here." He pretended to scratch his genitalia.

"Be *alert*," imitated Reardon. "This world needs more *lerts*."

"Come on, we have to find a vehicle that doesn't belong," said Pratt. "Let's take the task seriously. This is no laughing matter."

In the pouring rain of the thunderstorm, the three cops continued their search. There was a particularly bright lightning strike overhead. Through the mist, they saw a large portion of the immense parking lot, rows or vehicles parked neatly.

"This part here is the research and pathology wing," said Woody, pointing.

"That loading ramp is where they load up the dead bodies," said Reardon. "I've been there before."

"Should we spread out?" said Woody.

"No, lieutenant said to stay together," said Pratt.

The three officers walked down an alley, vehicles parked on both sides of them.

"I wish I knew exactly what the hell I was looking for," said Reardon, his face lit up by a particularly bright lightning strike overhead.

Terri saw the brilliant spark outside a window facing the elevator door. A deep rumble followed. She emerged from the elevator and advanced noiselessly toward the wing of the research and pathology laboratory. She looked down the dimly illuminated hall and saw only darkness and emptiness. She proceeded down the corridor until she reached another hallway. She turned the corner and saw many policemen with guns about fifteen yards away. They were outside the entrance into the research lab.

To her right, there was a dark hall, a sign overhead indicating *Microbiology Laboratory*. She turned her wheelchair down this corridor and pushed forward. Her trembling hand grabbed the doorknob. With difficulty, she managed to enter the micro lab. She saw no one inside. She looked out a window and saw the rain as it whipped steadily on the windowsill. She saw another bright lightning flash followed by the resonance of a loud thunder. Then a second lightning strike. And again, the sky roared.

The three cops continued to search the parking lot adjacent to the research lab wing. A lightning flash illuminated the sky then a loud thunderbolt shook the earth underneath their feet. The rain was cold, and their clothing offered little protection.

"This parking lot is bigger than I thought," said Pratt. "We've been out here for God knows how long and—"

"What is that over there?" said Reardon.

"Where?" said Woody.

"Over there," said Reardon, pointing to a poorly lit corner of the building, about twenty-five yards away.

"It's a garbage container," said Pratt. The rain flogged the building hard, allowing for only minimal visibility.

"I think I just saw some movement over there," said Reardon. There was a rectangular void in the darkness. Lightning struck again allowing the cops to see that the void was a dumpster. Even with the brief illumination, it was impossible to see beyond this box.

"Movement?" said Pratt. "We're in the middle of a thunderstorm. It's raining like crazy and the winds—"

"Did you see that?" said Reardon. "Somebody's moving over there. And I think there's a car behind that dumpster."

"Let's check it out," said Woody.

61

"You scared the hell out of me!" said Miranda, when at last she could breathe. "I thought I was going to die. I thought you—" Her gaze was on the syringe Tim was holding until she noticed the severe burn. "What happened?" She gently touched his left forearm and examined the burn.

"Shhh. He's right beyond that closet door. In the air-conditioning unit room. He uses the air-conditioning and heating ducts to get around the hospital without being spotted," whispered Tim.

"What should we do? Should we try to escape?"

"Not right now," said Tim. "If we try to leave now, he'll hear us. He's got a gun." Tim winced in pain. "Let's wait a few minutes then let's hide in the refrigerator. It has a lock. We'll be safe in there."

Miranda nodded.

A few minutes went by. Tim and Miranda remained under the autopsy table. They could hear footsteps and clinking noises.

"He's rigging up an apparatus to deliver tetrodotoxin into the research lab through the A/C vent," said Miranda. "I tried to warn the cops, but I don't have a signal on my cell phone. Does yours?"

Tim shook his head. "I wish. I've been looking at the meter but no signal. Once in a while I get a bar but not for long."

"Same with my phone," whispered Miranda.

Tim got on his knees and peered over the tabletop. "He's back inside the closet. Follow me. Hurry, but don't make any noise." The two tiptoed into the fridge and locked the door. Miranda introduced the pin into the locking mechanism and slid down to the floor, her back against the cold steel door. Tim sat right next to her.

"Who is he?" she asked. "I haven't been able to see his face. Anybody we know?"

"Jack Stevenson," said Tim.

"What about the wheelchair?" said Miranda. "The man I saw was standing."

"He's faking paraplegia," said Tim. He sighed. "I can't believe I hired him. I didn't see any of this coming."

"His actions are not your fault, Tim," she said. "What happened to you? The cops have been looking for you."

"He tied me up in his secret passageway. That's where he keeps his disguise. He has a cap and a fake beard. I freed myself by pouring sulfuric acid on the ropes. The acid ate easily through the restraints but also through my flesh."

"You need to get attention to this wound and quickly. It's pretty extensive and deep."

Tim nodded. "He travels through the ventilation duct out to the parking lot without being seen. He took the NanoTech and the angelfish full of tetrodotoxin out there. I'm guessing he's got a getaway car."

"What's in the syringe?" said Miranda.

"The antidote. We have to give this to Billy as soon as possible. If only we could get cell phone coverage. Are there any landlines in the refrigerator?"

"No," Miranda said, looking at her cell phone. "Coverage is usually pretty bad in this part of the hospital. Now with the storm brewing right over us, I'm getting no signal at all."

"We'll keep looking for a signal," he said. "If the storm let's up a bit, we might get something."

"Tim," said Miranda, "why didn't he kill you like all the rest?"

"No gallbladder," he said, lifting up his untucked shirt, showing the cholecystectomy scar. "Besides, he was going to use me as bait."

Miranda bit her lip.

"He should be gone soon again with another trip to the parking lot. His trips are anywhere from about five to twenty minutes. When he's gone, we'll get out of here and go alert the cops." Tim looked at his burn than back at Miranda. "I hope he doesn't realize I've escaped. He'll start looking for me."

"You said he was going to use you as bait," she said.

"When all his stuff is in his car, he plans to put me in the lab and get as many law enforcers as he can to come to my aid. He also wants to get Amy down here." Tears began to sparkle up his eyes. "He's got a detonator that will release tetrodotoxin into the whole research suite. That bastard wants to kill as many people as he can before he escapes."

"Did you see David?" said Miranda.

"He killed him and took his gallbladder. I saw him drag the body into the ducts that lead out to the parking lot."

"Goddamn, Jack," said Miranda. "You son of a bitch bastard."

"If he releases the toxin, the number of casualties will be large. There are probably twenty or thirty cops in this wing of the hospital right now. More if he—" Miranda put her hand over Tim's mouth, silencing him. They heard a noise right outside the refrigerator, the sound of a door opening then closing. Miranda's terrified gaze met Tim's. They heard erratic footsteps, a man pacing back and forth.

"He's right outside," she mouthed. He nodded.

Jack was beginning to feel his body slow down from intense fatigue. He sat down in the dark closet.

*   *   *

"Coffee or tea?" An offering of goodwill. The *thank-you-for-being-here* question. The *I-am-so-honored-you-applied-for-this-job-because-you're-the-answer-to-our-prayers* question.

"Tea, please," he said. He was wearing a dark blue suit. "One sugar, please." He sat in an ornate chair, facing a well-dressed woman with blond hair and blue eyes. "What do you think of my proposal, Dr. Sinclair?"

"I think it may have some promise," she said, serving the tea to her guest. "But it is very expensive. I'm not sure we'll be interested in pursuing such an expensive research project. Your projected financial requirements to complete this project would be almost a third of our total budget for the next year. This is simply too expensive for us right now."

"I'm willing to raise some private money and work on grants," he said. "I wasn't planning on telling you this, Dr. Sinclair, but my wife's been diagnosed with Brugada syndrome."

"I'm so sorry to hear that. I certainly can understand the fervor of your search for a cure to that dreadful disorder."

"My mission in life is to discover an antiarrhythmic medication that can help her stay alive. Her and others like her. I can prevent life-threatening heart rhythms if only I have the right equipment. The right lab. So you see, I have a personal reason to do this research."

"I'm afraid we simply cannot afford your protocol," she said. "I'm sorry." She brushed her hair behind her ear. "Besides, I'm afraid you're not a good fit for us."

"Why?" he said. "Did you get that from that stupid MMPI measure you insisted I take? What did it tell you about my personality? That I was crazy? Well, I am. Crazy enough to come up with a miracle cure for heart patients with deadly heart rhythms."

"I'm sorry. I'm afraid that is my final answer."

"Dr. Sinclair, what do I have to do to convince you that you're making a big mistake not accepting me? Your institution is one of the few that has the equipment necessary to perform my work. You have nanotechnology here, which is imperative for me. I don't have other options, and my work is crucial. Crucial for me to save my Christine. I'm afraid she may have a cardiac arrest and die. I can't live without her, Dr. Sinclair. I must continue my research so that—"

*   *   *

Jack shook his head rapidly as if to clear off his thoughts. He was very tired. But his work was almost completed and soon, his dream would become reality. He needed to persevere and see his project to its conclusion.

"You're worried about the damn money, wait until you see what your rejection will cost you, Dr. Amy Sinclair," he said to no one else in the closet. "And now that I have the right equipment in my hands, my project will come alive, and the whole wide world will know how important my work is and how *stupid* you were for turning me down. Because of you, Christine died in my arms. You didn't let me save her. And for that, Dr. Amy Sinclair, you will pay. But first, you will get a taste of what it's like to lose someone you love. Just like I had to."

Jack walked back into the air-conditioning vent.

"Where are you, Tim?" he said.

"He's going to find out I've escaped," Tim whispered softly. "If he hasn't already."

"That also means he's ready to release tetrodotoxin into the A/C system," said Miranda. "We have to alert Ben and Lela."

At that point, the refrigerator door knob moved. Miranda and Tim gasped, their hearts thumping. The knob moved again, this time being pushed and pulled madly.

"Tim, are you in there?" yelled Jack. More futile attempts to unlock the door. "Well, guess what? There's a ventilation port right out here.

Hold your breath, old man. I'm sending you some air with a fishy odor."

Tim and Miranda's gaze met, desperation and terror in their eyes.

"If this door doesn't open up in ten seconds, you're getting tetrodotoxin to breathe. You decide which way you want to die."

They heard a metallic noise coming from the outside vent just over their heads.

"Ten, nine, eight," said Jack. "Seven, six." A pause. "Okay, it's your choice. Five, four."

62

Billy's blood pressure and oxygen saturation were nearly inconsistent with life now. He was receiving the most potent of medications and the Impella device was laboring in parallel with his failing heart. Nurses and doctors rushed in and out of the room.

"How about if I sit with you?" said Dolly, sitting down in a chair next to Amy's. "You look like you need someone to talk to."

"I feel so powerless," said Amy. The nurse nodded. "Billy's a good young man with a bright future ahead of him. This can't be happening."

Amy's cell phone chimed. It was an e-mail.

Hello, Dr. Amy Sinclair. I'm Dr. Steven Jackson. Remember me? Are you sorry yet you didn't hire me now? I have the antidote that'll save your son. I made it in ten minutes. All the pathetic researchers working on it haven't been able to do it in hours. But I will give it to you. You alone." Amy's hands trembled, her stomach revolting. She read on, *Come down to the research lab right now, if you want this stuff. Come alone and tell no one. If the cops, your husband, or anybody else show up, I'll destroy the cure that can save Billy.*

"What's the matter?" asked Dolly. "I didn't think you could look any sicker, but I was wrong."

"Dolly, I just felt the nastiest sickening feeling inside me," said Amy. "I need to go downstairs. Will you watch over my son?"

"Sure, I will. But Amy, you aren't in any shape to leave this unit. I'm not even sure you're capable of standing by yourself."

"I have to go. I must go now. Hopefully, I won't be gone long."

"Let me go with you," said Dolly.

"No. I must go alone."

"Let me call your husband." Dolly looked intently into Amy's eyes. "He'll help you."

"No!" yelled Amy, getting to her feet. "Please promise me you won't call Ben. Promise me you won't tell anyone I left here."

"You're scaring me, Amy. Please rethink this."

"Please Dolly. Promise me," said Amy, tears flowing down her cheeks.

"You need help, Amy," said Dolly. "Why can't you see that?"

"Please watch Billy." She took a deep breath. Trembling but full of resolve, Amy walked out the ICU door.

Lela walked into Jack's office. Lurie was sitting in front of his computer.

"I checked out Jack's desktop. I found a file that had login information including passwords for Dr. Brent Weiner, Marvin McClellan, and Randall Dragone. Also, he has the passwords for Dr. Tim Hughes and Dr. Miranda Phillips. He's been gathering computer information using other people's login to put the blame on them."

"Well, it didn't work," said Lela. "I got you now, Jack, you bastard."

"One more thing," said Lurie. "Jack's computer desktop had the picture of a beautiful woman. With the help of the FBI computer expert in Chicago, we ran her facial features through a specialized program that allows recognition of unknown faces."

"I'm familiar with it," said Lela. "Who's the woman?"

"His wife, Christine," said Lurie. "Christine Jackson. Jack's real name is Steven Jackson. His wife died two months ago. She had a cardiac arrest a little over a year ago and survived it, but developed significant brain damage. She remained in a coma until she died. The abductions started a little while after her death."

"The provocative incident," said Lela. "The domino that toppled everything off . . ." Her words were interrupted by a radio transmission.

"Lieutenant Rose, this is Reardon. We found a suspicious vehicle parked behind a dumpster out here in the parking lot. The car is parked by a large exhaust vent, big enough for a man to come in and out. The car is locked, but there is a large suitcase labeled NanoTech inside. There is a plastic bag full of what appears to be dead fish."

"Reardon, call the Sarge and get more men. Stand guard there, and don't let the guy leave. That's his getaway route and vehicle. Report to me if you spot him. Remember, this guy is armed and dangerous."

Tim and Miranda looked at one another.

"Two, one, zero," said Jack. "Okay, I'm releasing tetrodotoxin into the fridge's ventilation system right now! Here it goes."

"He doesn't know you're in here," whispered Tim. "I'm getting out. You hide. Go!" Without waiting for a discussion from her, Tim pulled Miranda up on her feet and pushed her deeper into the dark refrigerator. He opened up the metal door and stepped outside. He closed the metal door behind him.

"You came out too easy, doc. What were you up to in there?" said Jack.

"I don't want to die of tetrodotoxin exposure," said Tim, his voice tremulous and feeble. "It's a horrible death. What are you going to do with me?"

Jack produced a small revolver from his pocket and pointed it at Tim.

"I'll take my antidote back," said Jack, removing the syringe from Tim's shirt pocket. "I was wondering where this went." He placed the syringe in his own shirt pocket then punched Tim on the stomach. Tim crumpled to the floor, a wave of dizziness and nausea washing over him.

"That's for stealing from me. Get up!" he said. "Open the fridge door. I want to look in there." Jack pointed the gun at Tim and gestured for him to get up. Tim struggled to get on his feet. Jack pointed toward the reefer door. Tim opened it. "Where's the light switch?" Jack followed Tim into the refrigerator.

"I don't know," said Tim. "Maybe outside?"

"No, it's not out there. I already looked. It's inside. Move!" he commanded signaling with the handgun. Tim took two slow steps. Jack shoved him hard from behind, causing him to fall on his knees. Tim felt shooting pains from both his hands and knees and yelp in pain.

"Find the light switch. Now."

Tim got up unhurriedly and walked to where he knew the switch was not.

"Is it here?" he asked.

"No, here it is," said Jack. In moments, bright lights dumped illumination into the reefer. "What were you hiding in here?"

"Nothing."

"Yeah, right. You can't be trusted. I should just shoot you right now and avoid all the trouble, but I still need you for bait." As he spoke, Jack's eyes scanned the refrigerator back and forth, returning to Tim every few seconds, his revolver pointing at the doctor's chest. Jack looked in every body bag. Only cold corpses. There were six pull-out drawers. He opened the first and saw a dead body in it. He pushed it shut with a metallic thud. He opened the second. It was empty. The third, empty. The fourth, a dead old woman. He grabbed the handle to open up the fifth drawer. As Jack pulled back on the drawer, Miranda's fist punched him square in the face, causing him to take two steps back. The blow was weak and uncoordinated and did little harm.

"Hiding inside a drawer for dead bodies," said Jack. "Very clever but too predictable for a pathologist." He pointed the gun at her and pushed Tim toward the drawer. "Help her out." Tim winced as the pressure of the push was directly on his acid burn producing a deep pain that nearly made him lose consciousness.

Miranda stepped out. Jack pointed the revolver at both doctors and gestured for them to walk outside the refrigerator.

"Why are you doing this, Jack?" said Miranda, a terrified look on her face.

"It's for the greater good," Jack said. "I've invented a drug that'll save millions of people who suffer from deadly heartbeat disorders. If a few have to be sacrificed in the process, who am I to ignore the potential of my creation?"

"What are you going to do with us?" she asked.

"I think I'm going to take you with me. You'll be great insurance for me, in case we get stopped by the cops as we get the hell out of Dodge." The three reached the warmer area right outside the cold storage space. "I'll shoot you both if one of you tries to escape."

"Jack, let her go," said Tim. "Take me. You don't need her."

"What makes you think you know what I need or don't need?" said Jack.

The three headed into the morgue and walked toward the exit. As they reached the door, Jack motioned for the other two to stand aside. Still pointing the gun at them, he cracked open the door.

Jack noticed the beehive of movement outside the door, law enforcers converging in the research laboratory. He closed the door, and the three returned deeper into the pathology suite.

"There's plenty cops in Research," said Jack. "I won't need you as bait in there." He gestured for the two to walk back toward the refrigerator. Jack activated the electrical fanlike device, and immediately an aerosolized mist from the canister began spewing its poison into the air-conditioning duct.

"In a few minutes, the breathable air in the research lab will be filled with tetrodotoxin and all those miserable pigs in there will die," said Jack, a smirk on his face.

63

Alone in the microbiology laboratory, Terri looked at the papers where she had sketched out chemical reactions. She wrote down the essential steps, one-by-one, the recipe for a cure.

Terri's body was frail, her hands trembling with the burden of the passing years and the lung cancer that now threatened her existence.

She stood at the counter, mixing a drop of reagent into a test tube. Her leg gave way and she fell on her knee. She managed to keep the test tube upright, the dropper hitting the tile. She struggled to get up and placed the test tube in a rack. She sat down on her wheelchair and took deep breaths.

"I will not surrender," Terri said to no one. "I will work through my aching joints and feeble muscles. I will persist, one step at a time."

She took another deep breath and stood up. She took the test tube and looked at its content. She looked at her paperwork and picked up another reagent bottle.

"Is Billy all right?" said Ben answering on the first ring.

"Mr. Sinclair," said a woman. "It's Dolly in ICU. I'm Billy's nurse. I've been contemplating back and forth whether to let you know or not."

"Let me know what, Dolly?" said Ben. "Is it Billy? What's happened to him?"

"Well, Amy asked me not to tell you or anyone else."

"You're killing me, Dolly," said Ben. "Tell me what?"

"Amy got an e-mail from someone about ten minutes ago. Whatever it was, it made her extremely upset and nervous. She just left the unit."

Ben ran his fingers through his hair, massaging his achy scalp. "What did the e-mail say?"

"She wouldn't tell me," said Dolly. "She looked awful. She was pale. She looked like hell. But she wouldn't listen. She insisted on leaving here alone and that I not call you or anyone else. But I knew I needed to let you know."

"You did the right thing, Dolly," said Ben. "Where did she go? Any ideas?"

"I know she tried to take the elevator down, but the police officers didn't allow her to. They asked her all kinds of questions, but she lied to them. She said she needed to go to her car in the parking lot. He refused to let her into the elevator. After a few minutes of discussion, she gave up and returned to the waiting room and sat down. A little later, I saw her sneak pass the cops and get into the stairway. She's climbing down the stairs as we speak."

"Thanks for calling me," said Ben. "Let me know right away if anything changes with Billy or if Amy returns to the unit."

"I will."

"Dolly, one more favor. Will you have one of the police officers come down the elevator near the stairway and meet me down on the first floor?"

Ben placed his mobile in his pocket and ran toward the stairway on the ICU side of the hospital. From the research laboratory, he could be there in less than a couple of minutes. *Don't do this to me. Not now, Amy. Please God, let her still be in the stairway. Please.*

Amy had just opened the first floor door when Ben arrived.

"Amy," he yelled. "Amy, wait."

"No, Ben. Don't come near me," she cried. "He'll destroy the antidote if he sees us talking." She tried to run away from Ben. She took two steps, stumbled for another, then fell down to the floor. She was pale. Her lips and shirt had remnants of vomit still attached.

"Sweetheart," said Ben on his knees, embracing her. "Why did you leave the ICU? It isn't safe down here."

Amy cried, her agony flowing out in rivulets. "I have to do this alone, Ben. I have to save Billy. Let me go. Leave me be!"

Ben took the cell phone she clutched in her hand and read the message still on display. "Amy, this is a trap. Who exactly is Steven Jackson?"

"Ben, I feel sick to my stomach," she said.

"It's okay, Amy. I'm here with you, baby."

"Dr. Steven Jackson," Amy said, "is a research PhD I didn't hire about a year ago, or so. He flunked the MMPI."

"MMPI?"

"Minnesota Multiphasic Personality Inventory. It's a test that shows personality traits and disorders. I insist on new recruits taking the test before I hire them. Ben, I thought then and know now he's crazy. That's why I didn't hire him. I think he's doing all this to get even with me. With all of us. My family."

"Steven Jackson. Jack Stevenson," said Ben.

"He wants me to come alone," said Amy. "He'll give me the antidote right now. I have to go. Alone."

"It's a goddamn trap, Amy. He'd never give you the antidote. He wants to kill you."

There was a ding as the nearby elevator door opened. Out of the elevator emerged two policemen, one of them pushing a wheelchair, the other holding an AK-47 machine gun. Wordlessly, the men nodded to each other.

"I have to go by myself," cried Amy. "Trap or no trap, I have to try."

"No!" said Ben, his words calm. "Amy, go upstairs with these officers. Be with Billy. He needs you up there."

"I have to try." Amy shook her head vigorously, tears flowing down her checks.

"I'll get the antidote," said Ben looking straight and deeply into her eyes. "You go upstairs, I'll take care of this." They hugged for a long moment.

Ben and one of the cops helped Amy into the wheelchair. "I'll take care of this."

Ben kissed Amy on her forehead and watched the trio disappear into the elevator.

The air-conditioning outlets overhead in the research laboratory had been off since the end of summer. Today's forecast called for rain and thunderstorms with temperatures in the fifties. Suddenly, an imperceptible breeze emerged from the vents, a tiny limp strand of hair hooked to the slits now waving gently with the airstream.

About twenty law enforcers were going inch by inch, making sure no hiding place in the research suite was missed.

Ben's cell phone vibrated as he walked briskly back to the research laboratory.

"Billy's going downhill fast again," said Amy. "Can't get a BP, and his heart rate is dropping. The EKG shows the poison has invaded Billy's heart. We're losing him, Ben. We need that antidote stat."

"We're still trying to find Jack and the antidote," said Ben. His iPhone vibrated yet again, then the chime of an incoming text message. "Keep

Billy alive at all cost. We need a little bit more time. I'll be up . . ." Ben's words ceased as he read the message. "Gotta go!" He placed his phone in his pocket and began running. In seconds, he reached the research laboratory.

Lela was reading from her mobile phone.

"Everybody out of the lab," Ben yelled. "Out of the lab, now."

"Poison is being delivered through the A/C ducts," Lela yelled out. "Hold your breaths and leave the lab now. Right now. Let's go, let's go!" A mass exodus begun in a stampede-like fashion.

"Do you have any men in Pathology?" asked Ben, when he and Lela reached the hall outside the research lab. "We need to find Miranda!"

"There are two men guarding the door into Pathology," said Lela. "But they're outside the lab."

"Everybody's out, Lieu," said a cop, closing the research lab door.

"Get gas masks on now," said Lela. "I had them brought to the command center. Keep a few men and stay here by this door. Guard it with your life. Nobody goes in, got it?"

"Yes, Lieutenant."

"Let's go to the pathology suite," said Ben. "Hopefully Miranda's still locked in the refrigerator." Lela signaled for several men to follow them.

In the anteroom right outside the reefer, Jack opened up a cabinet and removed a handful of restraining belts. He threw them at Miranda's feet.

"Tie him up to that chair," he told her. "You're going to be wonderful bait after all. You'll buy Miranda and me more time to get out to the car," said Jack.

He pulled out a toolbox from the closet and opened it up on the floor. He squatted down, removed a plastic canister and a screwdriver, and set them on the floor. He looked at Miranda, who was on her knees in front of Tim's chair.

"Hurry up with that," he said. "I'm going to put my gun down. I'm betting I'm faster than either of you. If you try anything foolish, I'll shoot you both. Understood?" Tim and Miranda nodded.

Jack put the gun on the floor at his feet and dumped the contents of the vial into a plastic canister. He picked up the revolver and stuck it in his belt. He began to rig up a connection of the canister to the ventilation system to the morgue. This was installed seven feet high on the wall. Miranda worked slowly, taking her time with the belts, which she had now secured to the chair. Her gaze met Tim's.

Jack looked away from the two of them, using a screwdriver on the canister. It was then that Tim charged with both hands. Jack felt the impact of the blow and toppled over to the floor. With the speed and agility of a falling cat, Jack was already shooting even before his body hit the ground. A bullet pierced Tim's forehead, causing him to fall backward. Miranda screamed and rushed to Tim's side. Brain matter spattered all over the wall behind him and now on the floor underneath him. Blood spewed into a massive pool of crimson surrounding his mutilated, disfigured head. Miranda sobbed, tears flowing briskly down her cheeks. Jack grabbed her arm and lifted her up to her feet, as if she was a rag doll.

"Let's go," he demanded, his gun in his other hand. He walked a few feet toward the canister. As his hand almost touched the switch, a bullet hit the wall just above the tetrodotoxin container. It was Ben's shot, from ten yards away. Lela and other officers were at his side, all guns pointed at Jack's chest.

"Drop it, scumbag," yelled Lela. Jack yanked on Miranda's arm pulling her toward him, using her as a human shield.

"To kill me, your bullet will have to pass through her first," said Jack.

"Ben, he's got the antidote in his shirt pocket," Miranda yelled out. "Take a shot. Do it."

"This doesn't have to end this way, Jack," said Lela. "Let her go and give us the antidote. If you do that, I promise you the courts will give you leniency for it."

"None of that matters to me," said Jack.

"Put your gun down, and give me the antidote, Jack," said Ben, taking a short step forward. "All these cops want to empty their guns into you. Lela and I can make sure you are treated with respect. Put the gun down, and hand over the antidote. My son is dying upstairs. He's not responsible for anything that happened to you. Let us save him."

"His death is revenge on your precious wife for what she did to me. To my Christine."

"It's not Billy's fault, Jack. Let us save him, and I'll see to it that you get the help you need to think straight. With rehabilitation, you can go back to the way it was before."

"Yeah, right," said Jack. "Can you get my Christine back?"

"I would if I could," said Ben, taking another half step, now about four yards away. "But you can still live a normal, productive life once you've been rehabilitated from your mental illness."

"Do you think I'm stupid?"

"I think you're brilliant. You just need some help, and if you help me save my boy, I'll help you get better."

Jack removed the antidote-containing syringe from his shirt pocket and held it up with his left hand. His right arm was around Miranda's neck, the revolver in his hand pointing up under her jaw.

"I'm going to step toward you very slowly," said Ben. "Please let Miranda go. You don't need her anymore." Another step, a few more inches closer.

"Stop right there, Ben. If you come any closer, I will shoot her. I mean it!" Jack yelled.

"Okay," said Ben stopping. "Take it easy, and don't make matters any worse than they already are."

"So my options are: number one, give you the antidote and the good doctor here, save Billy, and go to some crazy house forever. Number two, kill Miranda and destroy the antidote and end up in prison for the rest of my life. Or do I get the needle with number two?"

"Yes, you get the needle with number two," said Lela. As all the police gun barrels pointed toward him, Jack smirked as he thought. With a quick motion, he dropped the revolver and removed the plunger from the syringe. As he tipped the syringe over and the clear liquid began to quickly empty out, Ben was already moving, yelling, and shooting.

"No!" Ben screamed as he squeezed the trigger. A bullet thumped as it entered Jack's chest, its entry hole still devoid of blood. Jack stood unmoving for a second. Ben jumped forward, pushing Miranda away from Jack. As Ben fell on Miranda, protecting her from harm, multiple shots rang out, from Lela's gun first, then from all other officers. Jack fell backward, riddled with holes, each now dripping bits of his life onto the tile. By the time he hit the floor, the mass murderer's life had already ended.

Lela ran to the body, securing the killer's handgun. Ben got up slowly then helped Miranda to her feet.

"Are you okay?" he asked her.

"I'm okay." Ben's attention quickly shifted to what was left of the syringe labeled *antidote*, its contents mixed in an expanding pool of blood.

"Can we salvage enough antidote?" he asked, his gaze on Miranda.

She slowly shook her head. "The antidote has a high volatility point. It has already evaporated," she whispered. "I'm sorry, Ben."

"Can you make more?" said Ben. "We found notes David left of the antidote manufacturing process."

"I can give it a try."

"Let's do it," said Ben.

"Wait," said Miranda. "The first step is we need to get a gallbladder full of material from someone who was poisoned with tetrodotoxin.

Earlier, Jack harvested the gallbladders from all of the poisoned bodies in the morgue. Where are they?"

"I know where they are," said Lela. She pulled out her walkie-talkie from her pocket. "Reardon, this is Lieutenant Rose, are you there?"

"Reardon here."

"The bad guy's down. There should be a container of sorts with a whole bunch of gallbladders in the car." Lela looked at Miranda.

Miranda spoke into the radio, "They look like light green sacs, and they're probably on ice."

Then Lela said, "Gain access into the car and bring the gallbladders in here pronto."

"Yes, Lieutenant." She put her mobile device in her pocket and looked into Ben's sad eyes.

"Lela, I shot him out of desperation. He chose to end my son's life instead of saving his own. I felt so much rage, I couldn't—"

"Don't blame yourself, Ben. He deserved to die," said Lela.

"Why did *you* shoot? And your men?" said Ben.

"I am Spartacus," said Lela with a forced smile. "You did exactly what I would have done had I been in your place. If you were the only shooter, there would be questions about conduct and other bullshit like that. Questions by people who work in offices with windows overlooking beautiful views. Out here in the real world, we take care of each other. I shot, which made my men shoot. There are bullets from all of us in that son of a bitch. We are all Spartacus. Who will they blame now?"

Ben bowed his head. "Thank you."

The cops scattered, walking around slowly, observing the scene. Lela noticed the canister rigged to the research lab air-conditioning vent.

"Is this tetrodotoxin?" she asked. Miranda nodded. She walked to it, donned some surgical gloves she found in a box on a nearby table, and unhooked the contraption. Ben and Miranda followed her. Lela held the container at eye level. Ben, Miranda, and Lela gave it a glance. She placed the canister on a nearby countertop.

"Run fresh air into this air-conditioner vent," Lela told one of the officers. He nodded.

It was then they heard a loud explosion, shaking the building. Two windows in a far corner of the pathology laboratory imploded, debris flooding the area, reagent bottles falling from the countertops.

"It came from right outside those windows," said Ben.

"Reardon, this is Rose, over," said Lela into the walkie-talkie. "Reardon, are you there," she repeated. No response. "Reardon, please respond." Nothing.

"Lieutenant Rose, this is Troy O'Hara," said a young man. "We opened up the car door, but there was an explosion. Three of us are hurt bad, Lieu. I think Reardon is dead," said the officer.

"I'll get you some help, Troy. Hang in there. How's the car and its contents?"

"The car is ablaze. Everything in it was destroyed." There was a second of silence. "Lieu, before the explosion, we found three dead bodies in the garbage container out here by the car. Two were our own, Ma'am. The two missing cops, Officers Owen Kirchner and Pedro Morgani. The third body matches Dr. David Robertson's picture. All bodies were cut with a big gash in the upper portion of the belly."

"Okay, son. I'll get you help right away." Lela put down her communicator. "Are you two okay in here?" she asked Ben and Miranda. Both nodded. Then Lela turned to the group of officers. "Let's get out there. Call EMS and the fire department." The law enforcers ran out, leaving Ben and Miranda alone.

"Miranda, I'm going to take the poison," said Ben, his gaze on hers. He grabbed the container with tetrodotoxin from the tabletop. "I want you to remove my gallbladder, make the antidote, and save my boy."

"What if we remove Billy's gallbladder?" asked Miranda.

"There's no time. He's too unstable," said Ben. "Please do this for me."

"I can't," said Miranda. "We'll find another way. We'll—"

"There is no time," said Ben, unscrewing the top off the container. "I'm going to inject the poison. Miranda, I want your promise that you'll carry this through. Take my gallbladder and make the antidote. Save my boy." He looked deep into Miranda's eyes. They both remained still. Unmoving. Silent.

"Ben, this is illegal, immoral, and unethical," said Miranda. "I can't just watch you kill yourself."

"Miranda, please. It's illegal and all those things, but it's also the only way I can save my son. We've been through a lot together in the last twelve hours. Please, let me save my son."

64

For the last half hour, the activity in Billy's room had increased. Nurses and techs drew blood for testing, adjusted the respirator settings on the ventilator, and monitored vitals and urine output. Suddenly, Billy's monitor showed the heartbeat slowing down into a straight line.

"Call a code," yelled a nurse. "We got straight line on the heart monitor and blood pressure. Get the crash cart. Stat."

"Code blue, ICU-3! Code blue, ICU room 3. Code blue," shouted multiple beepers.

"Start CPR. One milligram of epinephrine and one milligram of atropine stat," said Natalie.

"I'm sorry, Amy," said Dolly. "You have to leave now." She guided Amy to the waiting room. Amy had run out of tears and words long ago. "Do you want me to call your husband?"

Amy shook her head. "No."

"I'm sorry I have to leave you alone," said Dolly. "I need to—"

"Please don't let Billy die," whispered Amy. Suddenly, she was alone in the large waiting room.

In Billy's cubicle, the resuscitation team had little hope of being successful this time. There was no blood pressure despite aggressive CPR and multiple stimulatory intravenous medications.

"Why isn't the Impella device working?" asked Dr. Messing.

"Tetrodotoxin paralyzes the heart," answered Dr. Armstrong. "It makes the heart stiff, rocklike. While there's tetrodotoxin in the system, nothing's going to work. Not even the Impella."

"Hold compressions for a second. Let's see what the heart rhythm is without CPR," said Dr. Messing. The wavy line caused by chest compressions ceased as quickly as the rescuer stopped resuscitation.

"Straight line still," said Dr. Armstrong. "Continue CPR?"

"How long have we been at this?" asked Dr. Messing.

"Sixteen minutes," said Dolly.

"How many rounds of medications have we given?" said Dr. Messing.

"Four," replied Dolly.

"We usually use two. Three at most," said Dr. Messing. "Nothing's working that we've given intravenously."

"Want to try intracardiac?" said Dr. Armstrong.

"We haven't done that in decades. Do you think it'll work?" said Dr. Messing.

"We have nothing to lose and everything to gain," said Dr. Armstrong. "We're losing him as is. None of us has ever resuscitated a patient following tetrodotoxin poisoning, right? Billy is different than everybody else you and I have ever worked on, so why not try it?" Dr. Messing nodded.

"Greta," said Dr. Armstrong. "Give me one milligram of epinephrine on a long needle. I'm going to inject it directly through the chest and into the heart."

"We don't carry intracardiac needles any longer," Greta said.

"Get me a spinal needle. Hurry up." And she did.

Greta handed Dr. Armstrong a syringe with one milligram of a powerful cardiac stimulation medication attached to a six-inch needle.

"Here's the plan, team," said Dr. Armstrong. "When I say go, I want you to stop chest compressions. Greta will scrub Betadine on the chest for a few seconds, then I'll stick this long needle in between Billy's ribs and inject this stuff right into his heart."

"I'm ready," said Greta. "Say when."

"Go!" said Dr. Armstrong. Greta went to work scrubbing the chest area free of skin bacteria. All others took a step back. The doctor felt for the ribs on Billy's chest wall and advanced the long needle slowly into the skin. He pulled back on the plunger.

"Here it is," said Dr. Armstrong, as blood filled the syringe. "I'm in the heart."

"Hold the syringe still right there. I'll push the plunger in," said Dr. Messing, their eyes connecting. Within seconds, Billy's heart was being infused with adrenalin. The needle was withdrawn rapidly, all eyes on the monitor. Straight line. The steady tone of the bedside alarm proclaimed loudly that which all could see plainly. No heartbeat. Then, one wide blip appeared on the screen. A long period of straight line was again interrupted by another beat.

"It's an agonal rhythm," said Dr. Armstrong. "The rhythm of a dead heart."

"Should we quit?" Said Dr. Messing. "Is there any hope for this boy?"

Dr. Armstrong shook his head slowly and bowed his head. "No," he said, "there's no hope at all."

65

Step one, inject the dangerous poison into a human. Step two, let the subject die. Step three, wait ten minutes to remove the gallbladder. These steps have been provided by the killer already. Step four, empty the contents of the gallbladder into a beaker and add the contents of test tube labeled #1. Then mix in the contents of test tube labeled #2. Centrifuge for one minute, then add the contents of test tube #3. Centrifuge the mixture thoroughly for three minutes. The last step: administer Billy's lifesaving cure.

Terri put the paper down on the counter and took a deep breath. She walked to the window. The thunderstorm was beginning to move on, though an occasional flash of lightning still fleetingly illuminated the world outside the window.

Miranda felt caught up in an ethical whirlwind. *It would be noble to support Ben's fatherly decision to save his son's life, but to do so would mean to aid a man in committing suicide, a death Ben would eagerly welcome. But still, it would mean to take a healthy man's life. A life for a life. What if they both died? How will I feel then? After all, it may be too late for Billy regardless of what miracle cures we inject into his veins. Can I do this?*

"Please, Miranda. There are no alternatives. Please promise me, you will save my son." Ben's right hand trembled, the container of tetrodotoxin in his grasp.

"I don't think I can do it, Ben," Miranda said, her eyes moist.

"Miranda, you don't know Billy. He's a great boy. He's kind and funny. He's smart. He wants to be a doctor. He'll make a great doctor.

He'll save a lot of lives. He'll make a woman very happy and have a great family. He'll be the most wonderful dad. He has to have a chance at great things. And I can provide him the opportunity." Ben's eyes were sad, tears falling down his cheeks. Miranda remained silent.

"I'm not sure I can just watch you die," she said.

"I'm going to make this simple for you," said Ben. "I'm going to inject tetrodotoxin into my vein. You can choose to allow me to throw my life away for no good reason or use my gallbladder to save Billy's life. Your choice."

"Okay," said Miranda, her voice quivering. "I'll do it."

"Thank you," said Ben, grabbing the canister full of poison and a syringe from the tabletop.

He sucked the tetrodotoxin into the syringe. He placed a needle on the syringe and placed the instrument on the countertop. Miranda came to Ben and hugged him tight.

"You're a brave man, Detective Ben Sinclair," she whispered in his ear. "And a great dad."

"Thank you, Miranda," said Ben. He took a deep breath. "Thank you for helping me and my family."

Terri called Miranda's cell phone, but the call went straight to voicemail.

"Miranda, this is Mom. Please call me on my cell phone or at the microbiology lab, extension 3560, as soon as possible. I know how to make the antidote, and I wrote the steps down one by one. I have all the reagents ready to be mixed."

Earlier in the evening, she had felt a strong emotion, a feeling of doom, out of nowhere. Her motherly inner fibers had screamed at her, *Your child is in trouble. Go to her now.* Terri was a scientist. She certainly did not believe in mother's intuition. But why had her gut feeling shouted so at her earlier? *Something's wrong.*

She wheeled herself down the corridor leading to the research wing. Down the corridor, about twenty yards, she saw a large group of cops, her eyes fixated on their guns. As she approached, two cops walked rapidly toward her.

"Sorry, ma'am. No one in or out of this area," said one of them.

"I'm Dr. Terri Phillips. I need to talk to my daughter, Dr. Miranda Phillips, and her research lab assistant, Jack Stevenson. Or Dr. David Robertson. Or Dr. Tim Hughes. Can I get word to one of them, please?" she said.

"No, ma'am," said the officer. "I can't do that."

"Officer, I understand you're doing your job," Terri said. "But it's an emergency. It's extremely important that I communicate with Miranda, Jack, Tim, or David, as soon as possible."

"Sorry, ma'am. No one in or out. Those are my orders. And it's for your own protection as well. It's a war zone in there right now."

"My goodness. A war zone, you say?"

"Yes, ma'am."

"Is my daughter, Miranda, okay? And the others? Tim, Jack, and David?" she asked.

"Dr. Phillips," yelled Lurie from down the corridor. She was accompanied by an older police officer. Lurie ran to Terri. Her police escort followed her. The policeman nodded at the others, and the three men took a few steps back. The two women hugged.

"It's terrible in there," began Lurie. "Miranda is okay, now, but I know Jack had her—"

"Jack had her what, Lurie? What's going on?" said Terri.

"You haven't heard? Jack Stevenson was the mass murderer. He had Miranda held prisoner, as well as Dr. Hughes." Lurie wiped a tear. "Jack killed Dr. Hughes." Terri put her hand on her chest. "But Ben saved Miranda's life right before Jack was shot dead by the cops."

Terri stood, speechless, her hands now covering her mouth.

"Jack killed Dr. Robertson too," said Lurie.

Terri wiped her tears. "But you're sure Miranda is okay?" Lurie nodded. "What about Ben and Lela?"

"They're okay," said Lurie.

"What about the antidote to the poison? Did they give it to Billy yet? Is he doing better?"

"I don't know what has happened to the antidote," said Lurie.

"Officer, please tell me what you know," said Terri, looking straight at the older policeman.

"The killer destroyed the antidote before he was shot dead," said the cop. "Your daughter is trying to figure out how to remanufacture it from scratch."

"Will you help me get a message to her?" said Terri.

"My orders are to make sure Ms. Lurie gets home safely." This said, the police officer took Lurie by her arm and proceeded to the exit. "Sorry, we must leave now. I need to get back to work."

"Wait," said Terri. "What about the gallbladders of the poisoned victims? Do they have those?"

"No, they went up in flames when Jack Stevenson's car exploded," said the cop. "It exploded when the officers tried to open the door. I can't say any more."

"Lurie, I'm happy you're okay," said Terri. "You saved a lot of lives today." The old woman smiled.

"Goodbye, Dr. Phillips," said Lurie, as she and the cop disappeared from view around the corner.

"Will you please let me through?" said Terri. "I must see my daughter. Just for a few minutes."

"No, ma'am," said the guard. "Can't do that, ma'am. Sorry."

"Will you give her a message from me? I can write it down and—"

"No, ma'am," the cop repeated. "I must ask you to leave, right now. That way." He pointed back the way she had come.

"Will you have her call my cell?"

"That way, ma'am," he said.

"Please, Officer."

"Ma'am, go that way right now, or I'll be forced to place you under arrest and take you to jail."

Timidly, Terri wheeled her chair around and headed back to the microbiology lab. It was then she decided as to the next step she had to take. And there was a lot of work to do still. A lot of hard work.

Ben sat back in a recliner. Miranda kneeled down next to him. In so doing, she bumped her cell phone off its belt clip. She picked up the phone and glanced at its display. It read, *Searching for signal.* She placed the mobile on a tabletop, knelt back down, and kissed Ben on his cheek. She picked up her phone and held it at her side, her fists clenched.

"Goodbye, Ben." She stood up again and turned away, a new stream of tears spilling down her face. In front of her now, the window revealed the darkness of night blanketing the outside.

Ben removed his cell phone from his pocket and typed his last words. *I love you both more than life itself. It is willingly and with honor that I give my life to save yours, Will. I know you will do great things. Think of all the great times we've had together. We've had a great life and I regret nothing. Will, I'm sorry for not being able to see your life triumphs and all the accomplishments you will have. Amy, you are now representing both of us. I will live in your heart forever more. Take care of our son and our future grandkids, from both of us. Thank you for the great life you've given me for the last twenty years. Find new happiness, but always know I loved you and Will more than life itself.* He pushed the send button.

Ben folded his shirt back exposing his right upper arm. He positioned the tourniquet around his left bicep and guided the needle into a prominent vein. Easily and deliberately, he pushed the plunger in.

"Administered intravenously and in high concentration, tetrodotoxin will begin paralyzing the victims within seconds," he heard Miranda's words from earlier that day reverberate in his mind.

Once the poison was delivered completely, Ben forced his right hand to place the syringe back on the table and remove the tourniquet. This he accomplished with a bit of difficulty, muscle weakness already evident. Within a few more seconds, Ben felt complete loss of his muscle tone. His mind remained sharp. His tongue and lips seemed thick and heavy. He tried to lift up his right arm with all his might but the arm barely moved a few inches side to side. Then, all his muscles stopped responding to his brain commands completely. His mind willed his fingertips to move, even an inch. Nothing. His breathing suddenly became shallow and slow. Ben stared into the space in front of him, aware now he was powerless to move his gaze. Though he tried and tried, his eye muscle would not respond to his wishes. To his commands.

Slowly, Miranda turned and now watched Ben in silence. Tears fell down her cheeks, but she dared not wipe them. Ben too, felt a tear escape the side of his eyes and run down his face, then another. Then another. A few more seconds passed. His breathing became sonorous and raspy, then slow, shallow and wheezy. It was then that Detective Benjamin Sinclair took his last breath.

Miranda's fisted hands relaxed. Her cell phone fell loudly to the floor.

66

The monitor display over Billy's bed showed a straight line.

"We'll quit now," said Dr. Armstrong. Dolly reached up and pressed the power button on the heart monitor turning it off, quieting the ongoing loud alarm.

The respiratory therapist somberly unhooked the bag she was periodically squeezing forcing air into Billy's lungs. Natalie placed the sheet over Billy's face, his whole body now concealed.

"We all tried so hard," said Dolly.

"It's so difficult to see such a young life go," said Natalie.

Dr. Armstrong said, "I'm pronouncing William Sinclair dead at—"

"No, please don't give up," said Amy from the door.

"Amy, his heart isn't responding at all," said Natalie.

"Don't give up on my Billy," said Amy, sobbing.

"We have to. There's nothing else we can do," said Dr. Armstrong. Amy cried, her loud weeping now flooding the room.

"There's nothing else we can do," said Dr. Mathis. "We're so sorry."

Natalie came to Amy and put a hand on her shoulder. She bowed her head.

Suddenly, Dolly arrived with a brisk jog and glanced into the ICU cubicle. "I just got a call from research. They're rushing up the antidote to give Billy. They say to continue at all cost and not to quit." She smiled.

"Yes," said Natalie. "The miracle we've all been waiting for."

"You heard the lady," said Dr. Armstrong. "Resume CPR."

The respiratory therapist pulled back the sheet to waist level and rehooked her bag to the breathing tube. She initiated the periodic squeezes of the bag pushing oxygen into Billy's lungs. Dolly climbed up on the bed, kneeled next to Billy's chest and reinitiated chest compressions.

It was then that Amy's cell phone vibrated and chimed. Standing at the entryway into the cubicle, she fished the device from her purse and began to read the message. She gasped, her complexion becoming even paler. A few seconds later, Amy collapsed to the floor.

67

It was a beautiful sunny day. Saint Michael's Church was beginning to empty out now, but it had been standing room only, the last of a huge procession walking slowly to view the open casket in the front.

"There must have been thousands of people here to pay their respects," Lela whispered in Miranda's ear. "I don't think I've ever seen as many people in Danville, Illinois."

"There are all kinds of people here," said Miranda. "There are doctors, scientists, research people, patients, neighbors, friends, family, police, and the list goes on."

"Oh, look who just arrived," said Lela.

Miranda turned toward the back of the church. Amy Sinclair was walking slowly toward them against the grain of the exiting masses. Miranda's vision was blurred by the gathering tears.

Miranda, I'm in the microbiology lab, read the last e-mail dispatched by her mother. *I'm beginning the intravenous infusion of tetrodotoxin. Forgive me, Miranda, but this is what I feel I must do. I hope it's not too late for the boy. I want my end to have meaning and purpose. Come quickly. I love you very much. Miranda, you have been the best daughter a mother could possibly ever have.*

The three women hugged.

"Thanks for coming, Amy," said Miranda. "How are you feeling?"

"Better now. I wouldn't miss it for the world," said Amy. "I had to pay my respects to such a wonderful person. My family and I owe her so much. And you."

"She did what she felt she had to do it," said Miranda, "and now she's at peace."

Amy hugged her again. "Thank you from my family to yours."

"You're welcome."

"Two more people just arrived to pay their respects," said Lela, pointing to the main entrance door. Miranda and Amy turned. It was Ben and Billy, both being slowly wheeled into the church toward the coffin. A quick glance at the women was followed by a reverent nod. Green cylinders attached to the wheelchairs delivered oxygen via a clear tubing into their nostrils. The nurses slowly directed the wheelchairs down the center of the aisle and parked them by the coffin. Amy, Miranda, and Lela walked slowly toward them and stood right behind the wheelchairs. Amy put her hands on Ben and Billy's shoulders. Both men bowed their heads.

"Thank you, Terri," whispered Ben. "Thank you for your supreme sacrifice. Thank you for giving me my life back and my son." He looked over at the young man sitting in the wheelchair next to his. Their gazes met. Then Billy faced the coffin again.

"Thank you, Dr. Terri Phillips," said Billy breathlessly, in a raspy, tired voice.

Epilogue

"You know, besides my parents and my shrink, I haven't talked about this with anyone else in the whole wide world," he said. She looked at him, their eyes connecting.

"I feel special, Will," she said. "You are doing so much better from your posttraumatic stress syndrome. And I believe some part of that is the fact that you are now willing to share your feelings and thoughts with someone about what happened." She smiled. "I'm just honored that I am the one you chose to share with."

"Yeah, thank you for being there for me."

"I remember the day Dr. Gavin gave us a lecture on poison research and how to make them into cures," she said.

"I could smell the ICU odors, Lilly," he said. "The awful smell of my own charred skin when they repeatedly shocked my heart into rhythm."

"The sense of smell is very strong," she said. "But I can only imagine what you felt like."

"I don't remember feeling any physical pain," said Will. "But the smells will never go away."

"Maybe they will," said Lilly. "In time."

"Lilly, thank you for helping me heal." Will looked at his hands then back at her. "I couldn't have done it without you."

The two walked side by side, carrying their lunches. They sat by the lake underneath a large oak.

"Bologna and cheese," he said.

"Turkey and lettuce," she said.

"Yum!" said Will. Both smiled and took a sip from their water bottles.

"Will, tell me more about it," said Lilly. "I'm so fascinated by what you and your family endured that day."

"I could hear everything, but I was paralyzed," Will said. "A god-awful feeling. I could hear my mother cry and feel the agony and turmoil inside her." Lilly nodded. "All along, I prayed. Somehow, I knew, I just knew I was going to make it. I believed in my parents. I believe they would find a way to save me."

"Did they ever find out who the three bodies in the pond were?"

"Yeah, eventually they made a positive ID. They were Marvin McClellan, Randall Dragone, and a woman Marvin was dating at the time."

"So this," Lilly shook her head slightly, "*thing* is really going to become a miracle cure?"

"I don't know about that," said Will. "But there's a lot of ongoing interest and research, and hopefully, one day it'll be a medication you and I can prescribe to our patients with heart rhythm disorders."

"And it was discovered by a madman," said Lilly. She held his hands in hers. "It almost cost you your life, Will."

"He wasn't always a madman," Will said. "Dr. Steven Jackson was a brilliant researcher with a bright future ahead of him. He obtained his MD and PhD degrees from Northwestern and had a brilliant research mind. But when Christine had a cardiac arrest, his world was suddenly turned upside down. She was in a coma for a while, and that drove him nuts, day by day. He became obsessed with inventing a cure for deadly cardiac rhythms."

"This man had obvious genetic tendencies to psychopathology," said Lilly. "His wife was gluing him together. She was his anchor. When he lost her, he came unglued."

"Let me guess, you're doing your psych rotation this month, right?"

"You know I am." She tossed him a smile. He smiled back then took a bite of his sandwich.

"He definitely suffered from undiagnosed psychopathy. He had shown antisocial personality disorder traits ever since he was a child. He had tortured animals and been quite antisocial. But he learned to fake normal behavior. Christine somehow was able to normalize his life, and he thrived as a scientist. As a husband. When she died, he began to decompensate rapidly. He was fired from the research facility in Ohio where he was working and tried to get a job first with my mom in Indiana. When she turned him down, he decompensated even more, changed his name to Jack Stevenson, and applied in Illinois as a lab technician, at which he excelled."

"I can't help but feel some pity for him," Lilly said.

"I wish someone could have discovered what was tormenting him and intervened. He could have contributed a lot to science and research."

Both drank some water then bit into their sandwiches.

"What about soccer? Have you played since?"

"No, I haven't been able to exert myself," Will said. "I get short of breath pretty quickly now, but it's getting better and better."

"Maybe you can't play competitively, but I bet you'd be able to play recreationally. If not now, maybe soon. I play in a coed league. Do you want to give it a try?"

"I haven't thought about playing soccer in a long time. How about if I start by going to watch you play sometime?"

"I'd like that," said Lilly. "I'd like that very much."

OTHER BOOKS BY THIS AUTHOR:

- First Do No Harm

- Seconds From Revenge

Visit www.JanEiraBooks.com. Also available at www.amazon.com and others.

Books also available in all eFormats such as Kindle, iPad, iPhone, PDF, HTLM, Sony Reader, Nook, Adobe and Palm reading devices. Visit www.smashwords.com.

20422438R00142

Made in the USA
Lexington, KY
03 February 2013